NIGHTMARE IN TECHNICOLOR

He leaned round-shouldered out of the doorway, a brass poker glittering in his hand. He lunged toward me so close I could smell his breath. A dark drop flew from its hooked point and splattered the plaster wall like a splash of wet red paint. My eye stayed on it a millisecond too long. The poker seared the side of my head. It was a glancing blow, or I would have gone all the way out. As it was, the floor up-ended and rapped my knees and elbows and forehead.

I groped for my gun among jagged shards of light. The bright room beyond the doorway flashed with a hallucination's vividness. It was white and black and red. A girl lay on a white rug in front of a black fireplace. An inkblot of red spread around her.

Then the front end of the Sunset Limited hit the side of my head and knocked me off the rails into a deeper darkness.

THE
BARBAROUS COAST
ROSS MACDONALD

BANTAM BOOKS
TORONTO • NEW YORK • LONDON • SYDNEY • AUCKLAND

*This low-priced Bantam Book
has been completely reset in a type face
designed for easy reading, and was printed
from new plates. It contains the complete
text of the original hard-cover edition.*
NOT ONE WORD HAS BEEN OMITTED.

THE BARBAROUS COAST
*A Bantam Book / published by arrangement with
Alfred A. Knopf, Inc.*

PRINTING HISTORY
Alfred A. Knopf edition published June 1956
Condensation published in COSMOPOLITAN *under the title*
The Dying Animal
Bantam edition / June 1957

2nd printing ...... May 1966	5th printing ..... March 1976
3rd printing ...... June 1966	6th printing ...... June 1977
4th printing ..... April 1975	7th printing .. December 1979
8th printing .. August 1984	

ISBN 0-553-24268-7

Published simultaneously in the United States and Canada

*Bantam Books are published by Bantam Books, Inc. Its trade-
mark, consisting of the words "Bantam Books" and the por-
trayal of a rooster, is Registered in U.S. Patent and Trademark
Office and in other countries. Marca Registrada. Bantam
Books, Inc., 666 Fifth Avenue, New York, New York 10103.*

PRINTED IN THE UNITED STATES OF AMERICA

H   17 16 15 14 13 12 11 10 9 8

For

STANLEY TENNY

THE Channel Club lay on a shelf of rock overlooking the sea, toward the southern end of the beach called Malibu. Above its long brown buildings, terraced gardens climbed like a richly carpeted stairway to the highway. The grounds were surrounded by a high wire fence topped with three barbed strands and masked with oleanders.

I stopped in front of the gate and sounded my horn. A man wearing a blue uniform and an official-looking peaked cap came out of the stone gatehouse. His hair was black and bushy below the cap, sprinkled with gray like iron filings. In spite of his frayed ears and hammered-in nose, his head had the combination of softness and strength you see in old Indian faces. His skin was dark.

"I seen you coming," he said amiably. "You didden have to honk, it hurts the ears."

"Sorry."

"It's all right." He shuffled forward, his belly overhanging the belt that supported his holster, and leaned a confidential arm on the car door. "What's your business, mister?"

"Mr. Bassett called me. He didn't state his business. The name is Archer."

"Yah, sure, he is expecting you. You can drive right on down. He's in his office."

He turned to the reinforced wire gate, jangling his keyring. A man came out of the oleanders and ran past my car. He was a big young man in a blue suit, hatless, with flying pink hair. He ran almost noiselessly on his toes toward the opening gate.

The guard moved quickly for a man of his age. He whirled and got an arm around the young man's middle. The young man struggled in his grip, forcing the guard back against the gatepost. He said something guttural and inarticulate. His shoulder jerked, and he knocked the guard's cap off.

The guard leaned against the gatepost and fumbled for his gun. His eyes were small and dirty like the eyes of a potato.

Blood began to drip from the end of his nose and spotted his blue shirt where it curved out over his belly. His revolver came up in his hand. I got out of my car.

The young man stood where he was, his head turned sideways, halfway through the gate. His profile was like something chopped out of raw planking, with a glaring blue eye set in its corner. He said:

"I'm going to see Bassett. You can't stop me."

"A slug in the guts will stop you," the guard said in a reasonable way. "You move, I shoot. This is private property."

"Tell Bassett I want to see him."

"I already told him. He don't want to see you." The guard shuffled forward, his left shoulder leading, the gun riding steady in his right hand. "Now pick up my hat and hand it to me and git."

The young man stood still for a while. Then he stooped and picked up the cap and brushed at it ineffectually before he handed it back.

"I'm sorry. I didn't mean to hit you. I've nothing against you."

"I got something against you, boy." The guard snatched the cap out of his hands. "Now beat it before I knock your block off."

I touched the young man's shoulder, which was broad and packed with muscle. "You better do what he says."

He turned to me, running his hand along the side of his jaw. His jaw was heavy and pugnacious. In spite of this, his light eyebrows and uncertain mouth made his face seem formless. He sneered at me very youngly:

"Are you another one of Bassett's muscle boys?"

"I don't know Bassett."

"I heard you ask for him."

"I do know this. Run around calling people names and pushing in where you're not wanted, and you'll end up with a flat profile. Or worse."

He closed his right fist and looked from it to my face. I shifted my weight a little, ready to block and counter.

"Is that supposed to be a threat?" he said.

"It's a friendly warning. I don't know what's eating you. My advice is go away and forget it—"

"Not without seeing Bassett."

"And, for God's sake, keep your hands off old men."

"I apologized for that." But he flushed guiltily.

The guard came up behind him and poked him with the revolver. "Apology not accepted. I used to could handle two like you with one arm tied behind me. Now are you going to git or do I have to show you?"

"I'll go," the young man said over his shoulder. "Only, you can't keep me off the public highway. And sooner or later he has to come out."

"What's your beef with Bassett?" I said.

"I don't care to discuss it with a stranger. I'll discuss it with him." He looked at me for a long moment, biting his lower lip. "Would *you* tell him I've got to see him? That it's very important to me?"

"I guess I can tell him that. Who do I say the message is from?"

"George Wall. I'm from Toronto." He paused. "It's about my wife. Tell him I won't leave until he sees me."

"That's what you think," the guard said. "March now, take a walk."

George Wall retreated up the road, moving slowly to show his independence. He dragged his long morning shadow around a curve and out of sight. The guard put his gun away and wiped his bloody nose with the back of his hand. Then he licked his hand, as though he couldn't afford to waste the protein.

"The guy's a cycle-path what they call them," he said. "Mr. Bassett don't know him, even."

"Is he what Bassett wants to see me about?"

"Maybe, I dunno." His arms and shoulders moved in a sinuous shrug.

"How long has he been hanging around?"

"Ever since I come onto the gate. For all I know, he spent the night in the bushes. I ought to have him picked up, but Mr. Bassett says no. Mr. Bassett is too softhearted for his own good. Handle him yourself, he says, we don't want trouble with law."

"You handled him."

"You bet you. Time was, I could take on two like him, like I said." He flexed the muscle in his right arm and palpated it admiringly. He gave me a gentle smile. "I was a fighter one time—pretty good fighter. Tony Torres? You ever hear my name? The Fresno Gamecock?"

"I've heard it. You went six with Armstrong."

"Yes." He nodded solemnly. "I was an old man already, thirty-five, thirty-six. My legs was gone. He cut my legs off from under me or I could of lasted ten. I felt fine, only my legs. You know that? You saw the fight?"

"I heard it on the radio. I was a kid in school, I couldn't make the price."

3

"What do you know?" he said with dreamy pleasure. "You heard it on the radio."

I LEFT my car on the asphalt parking-lot in front of the main building. A Christmas tree painted brilliant red hung upside-down over the entrance. It was a flat-roofed structure of fieldstone and wood. Its Neutraesque low lines and simplicity of design kept me from seeing how big it was until I was inside. Through the inner glass door of the vestibule I could see the fifty-yard swimming-pool contained in its U-shaped wings. The ocean end opened on bright blue space.

The door was locked. The only human being in sight was a black boy bisected by narrow white trunks. He was sweeping the floor of the pool with a long-handled underwater vacuum. I tapped on the door with a coin.

After a while he heard me and came trotting. His dark, intelligent eyes surveying me through the glass seemed to divide the world into two groups: the rich, and the not so rich. I qualified for the second group, it seemed. He said when he opened the door:

"If you're selling, mister, the timing could be better. This is the off-season, anyway, and Mr. Bassett's in a rotten mood. He just got through chopping *me* out. It isn't my fault they threw the tropical fish in the swimming-pool."

"Who did?"

"The people last night. The chlorine water killed them, poor little beggars, so I got to suck them out."

"The people?"

"The tropical fish. They scooped 'em out of the aquarium and chunked 'em in the pool. People go out on a party and get drunk, they forget all the ordinary decencies of life. So Mr. Bassett takes it out on me."

"Don't hold it against him. My clients are always in a rotten mood when they call me in."

"You an undertaker or something?"

4

"Something."

"I just wondered." A white smile lit his face. "I got an aunt in the undertaking business. I can't see it myself. Too creepy. But she enjoys it."

"Good. Is Bassett the owner here?"

"Naw, just the manager. The way he talks, you'd think he owns it, but it belongs to the members."

I followed his wedge-shaped lifeguard's back along the gallery, through shifting green lights reflected from the pool. He knocked on a gray door with a MANAGER sign. A high voice answered the knock. It creaked along my spine like chalk on a damp blackboard:

"Who is it, please?"

"Archer," I said to the lifeguard.

"Mr. Archer to see you, sir."

"Very well. One moment."

The lifeguard winked at me and trotted away, his feet slapping the tiles. The lock snicked, and the door was opened slightly. A face appeared in the crack, just below the level of my own. Its eyes were pale and set too wide apart; they bulged a little like the eyes of a fish. The thin, spinsterly mouth emitted a sigh:

"I *am* glad to see you. Do come in."

He relocked the door behind me and waved me to a chair in front of his desk. The gesture was exaggerated by nerves. He sat down at the desk, opened a pigskin pouch, and began to stuff a big-pot briar with dark flakes of English tobacco. This and his Harris tweed jacket, his Oxford slacks, his thick-soled brown brogues, his Eastern-seaboard accent, were all of a piece. In spite of the neat dye job on his brown hair, and the unnatural youth which high color lent his face, I placed his age close to sixty.

I looked around the office. It was windowless, lit by hidden fluorescence and ventilated by an air-conditioning system. The furniture was dark and heavy. The walls were hung with photographs of yachts under full sail, divers in the air, tennis-players congratulating each other with forced smiles on their faces. There were several books on the desk, held upright between elephant bookends made of polished black stone.

Bassett applied a jet lighter to his pipe and laid down a blue smoke screen, through which he said:

"I understand, Mr. Archer, that you're a qualified bodyguard."

"I suppose I'm qualified. I don't often take on that kind of work."

"But I understood— Why not?"

5

"It means living at close quarters with some of the damnedest jerks. They usually want a bodyguard because they can't get anybody to talk to them. Or else they have delusions."

He smiled crookedly. "I can hardly take that as a compliment. Or perhaps I wasn't intended to?"

"You're in the market for a bodyguard?"

"I hardly know." He added carefully: "Until the situation shapes up more clearly, I really can't say what I need. Or why."

"Who gave you my name?"

"One of our members mentioned you to me some time ago. Joshua Severn, the television producer. You'll be interested to know that he considers you quite a fireball."

"Uh-huh." The trouble with flattery was that people expected to be paid for it in kind. "Why do you need a detective, Mr. Bassett?"

"I'll tell you. A certain young chap has threatened my—threatened my safety. You should have heard him on the telephone."

"You've talked to him?"

"Just for a minute, last night. I was in the midst of a party—our annual post-Christmas party—and he called from Los Angeles. He said he was going to come over here and assault me unless I gave him certain information. It jarred me frightfully."

"What kind of information?"

"Information which I simply don't possess. I believe he's outside now, lying in wait for me. The party didn't break up until very late and I spent the night here, what remained of it. This morning the gateman telephoned down that he had a young man there who wished to see me. I told him to keep the fellow out. Shortly after that, when I'd gathered my wits together, I telephoned you."

"And what do you want me to do, exactly?"

"Get rid of him. You must have ways and means. I don't want any violence, of course, unless it should prove to be absolutely necessary." His eyes gleamed palely between new strata of smoke. "It may be necessary. Do you have a gun?"

"In my car. It's not for hire."

"Of course not. You misinterpret my meaning, old boy. Perhaps I didn't express myself quite clearly. I yield to no man in my abhorrence of violence. I merely meant that you might have use for a pistol as an—ah—instrument of persuasion. Couldn't you simply escort him to the station, or the airfield, and put him aboard a plane?"

"No." I stood up.

6

He followed me to the door and took hold of my arm. I disliked the coziness, and shook him off.

"Look here, Archer, I'm not a wealthy man, but I do have some savings. I'm willing to pay you three hundred dollars to dispose of this fellow for me."

"Dispose of him?"

"Without violence, of course."

"Sorry, no sale."

"Five hundred dollars."

"It can't be done. What you want me to do is merely kidnapping under California law."

"Good *Lord*, I didn't mean *that*." He was genuinely shocked.

"Think about it. For a man in your position, you're pretty dim about law. Let the police take care of him, why don't you? You say he threatened you."

"Yes. As a matter of fact, he mentioned horse-whipping. But you can't go to the police with that sort of thing."

"Sure you can."

"Not I. It's so ridiculously old-fashioned. I'd be the laughingstock of the entire Southland. You don't seem to grasp the personal aspects, old boy. I'm manager and secretary of a very, very exclusive club. The finest people on the coast confide their children, their young daughters, to my trust. I have to be clear of any breath of scandal—Calpurnia, you know."

"Where does the scandal come in?"

Calpurnia took his pipe out of his mouth and blew a wobbly smoke-ring. "I'd hoped to avoid going into it. I certainly didn't expect to be cross-questioned on the subject. However, something has to be done, before the situation deteriorates irreparably."

His choice of words annoyed me, and I let the annoyance show. He gave me an appealing look, which fell with a thud between us:

"Can I trust you, *really* trust you?"

"So long as it's legal."

"Oh, heavens, it's legal. I am in a bit of a jam, though, through no fault of my own. It's not what I've done, but what people might think I've done. You see, there's a woman involved."

"George Wall's wife?"

His face came apart at the seams. He tried to put it together again around the fixed point of the pipe, which he jammed into his mouth. But he couldn't control the grimace tugging like hooks at the end of his lips.

"You know her? Does everybody know?"

"Everybody soon will if George Wall keeps hanging around. I ran into him on my way in—"

"Good God, he is on the grounds, then."

Bassett crossed the room in awkward flight. He opened a drawer of his desk and took out a medium-caliber automatic.

"Put that thing away," I said. "If you're worried about your reputation, gunfire can really blow it to hell. Wall was outside the gate, trying to get in. He didn't make it. He did give me a message for you: he won't leave until you see him. Over."

"Damn it, man, why didn't you say so? Here we've been wasting time."

"You have."

"All *right*. We won't quarrel. We've got to get him away from here before any members come."

He glanced at the chronometer strapped to his right wrist, and accidentally pointed the automatic at me.

"Put the gun down, Bassett. You're too upset to be handling a gun."

He laid it on the embossed blotter in front of him and gave me a shamefaced smile. "Sorry. I am a bit nervy. I'm not accustomed to these alarums and excursions."

"What's all the excitement about?"

"Young Wall seems to have some melodramatic notion that I stole his wife from him."

"Did you?"

"Don't be absurd. The girl is young enough to be my daughter." His eyes were wet with embarrassment. "My relations with her have always been perfectly proper."

"You do know her, then?"

"Of course. I've known her for years—much longer than George Wall has. She's been using the pool for diving practice ever since she was in her teens. She's not far out of her teens now, as a matter of fact. She can't be more than twenty-one or two."

"Who is she?"

"Hester Campbell, the diver. You may have heard of her. She came close to winning the national championship a couple of years ago. Then she dropped out of sight. Her family moved away from here and she gave up amateur competition. I had no idea that she was married, until she turned up here again."

"When was this?"

"Five or six months ago. *Six* months ago, in June. She seemed to have had quite a bad time of it. She'd toured with an aquacade for a while, lost her job and been stranded in

8

Toronto. Met this young Canadian sportswriter and married him in desperation. Apparently the marriage didn't work out. She left him after less than a year together, and came back here. She was on her uppers, and rather beaten, spiritually. Naturally I did what I could for her. I persuaded the board to let her use the pool for diving instruction, on a commission basis. She did rather well at that while the summer season lasted. And when she lost her pupils, I'm frank to say I helped her out financially for a bit." He spread his hands limply. "If that's a crime, then I'm a criminal."

"If that's all there is to it, I don't see what you're afraid of."

"You don't understand—you don't understand the position I'm in, the enmities and intrigues I have to contend with here. There's a faction among the membership who would like to see me discharged. If George Wall made it appear that I was using my place to procure young women—"

"How could he do that?"

"I mean if he brought court action, as he threatened to. An unprincipled lawyer could make some kind of case against me. The girl told me that she planned a divorce, and I suppose I wasn't thoroughly discreet. I was seen in her company more than once. As a matter of fact, I cooked several dinners for her." His color rose slightly. "Cooking is one of my hobby-horses. I realize now it wasn't wise to invite her into my home."

"He can't do anything with that. This isn't the Victorian age."

"It is in certain circles. You just don't grasp how precarious my position is. I'm afraid the accusation would be enough."

"Aren't you exaggerating?"

"I hope I am. I don't feel it."

"My advice to you is, level with Wall. Tell him the facts."

"I tried to, on the telephone last night. He refused to listen. The man's insane with jealousy. You'd think I had his wife hidden somewhere."

"You haven't, though?"

"Of course not. I haven't seen her since the early part of September. She left here suddenly without a good-by or a thank-you. She didn't even leave a forwarding address."

"Run off with a man?"

"It's more than likely," he said.

"Tell Wall that. In person."

"Oh, no. I couldn't possibly. The man's a raving maniac, he'd assault me."

Bassett ran tense fingers through his hair. It was soaked at the temples, and little rivulets ran down in front of his ears.

He took the folded handkerchief out of his jacket pocket and wiped his face with it. I began to feel a little sorry for him. Physical cowardice hurts like nothing else.

"I can handle him," I said. "Call the gate. If he's still up there, I'll go and bring him down."

"Here?"

"Unless you can think of a better place."

After a nervous moment, he said: "I suppose I have to see him. I can't leave him rampaging around in public. There are several members due for their morning dip at any moment."

His voice took on a religious coloring whenever he mentioned the members. They might have belonged to a higher race, supermen or avenging angels. And Bassett himself had a slipping toehold on the edge of the earthly paradise. Reluctantly, he picked up the intramural phone:

"Tony? Mr. Bassett. Is that young maniac still rampaging around? . . . Are you certain? Absolutely certain? . . . Well, fine. Let me know if he shows up again." He replaced the receiver.

"Gone?"

"It seems so." He inhaled deeply through his open mouth. "Torres says he took off on foot some time ago. I'd appreciate it, though, if you stayed around for a bit, just in case."

"All right. This trip is costing you twenty-five dollars, anyway."

He took the hint and paid me in cash from a drawer. Then he got an electric razor and a mirror out of another drawer. I sat and watched him shave his face and neck. He clipped the hairs in his nostrils with a tiny pair of scissors, and plucked a few hairs out of his eyebrows. It was the sort of occasion that made me hate the job of guarding bodies.

I looked over the books on the desk. There were a Dun and Bradstreet, a Southern California Blue Book, a motion-picture almanac for the previous year, and a thick volume bound in worn green cloth and entitled, surprisingly, *The Bassett Family*. I opened this to the title page, which stated that the book was an account of the genealogy and achievements of the descendants of William Bassett, who landed in Massachusetts in 1634; down to the outbreak of the World War in 1914. By Clarence Bassett.

"I don't suppose you'd be interested," Bassett said, "but it's quite an interesting story to a member of the family. My father wrote that book: he occupied his declining years with it. We really did have a native aristocracy in New England, you know—governors, professors, divines, men of affairs."

"I've heard rumors to that effect."

"Sorry, I don't mean to bore you," he said in a lighter tone, almost self-mocking. "Curiously enough, I'm the last of my branch of the family who bears the name of Bassett. It's the one sole reason I have for regretting my not having married. But then I've never been the philoprogenitive type."

Leaning forward toward the mirror, he began to squeeze a blackhead out of one of the twin grooves that ran from the base of his nose. I got up and roamed along the walls, examining the photographs. I was stopped by one of three divers, a man and two girls, taking off in unison from the high tower. Their bodies hung clear of the tower against a light summer sky, arched in identical swan dives, caught at the height of their parabolas before gravity took hold and snatched them back to earth.

"That's Hester on the left," Bassett said behind me.

Her body was like an arrow. Her bright hair was combed back by the wind from the oval blur of her face. The girl on the right was a dark brunette, equally striking in her full-breasted way. The man in the middle was dark, too, with curly black hair and muscles that looked hammered out of bronze.

"It's one of my favorite photographs," Bassett said. "It was taken a couple of years ago, when Hester was in training for the nationals."

"Taken here?"

"Yes. We let her use our tower for practicing, as I said."

"Who are her friends in the picture?"

"The boy used to be our lifeguard. The girl was a young friend of Hester's. She worked in the snack bar here, but Hester was grooming her for competitive diving."

"Is she still around?"

"I'm afraid not." His face lengthened. "Gabrielle was killed."

"In a diving accident?"

"Hardly. She was shot."

"Murdered?"

He nodded solemnly.

"Who did it to her?"

"The crime was never solved. I doubt that it ever will be now. It happened nearly two years ago, in March of last year."

"What did you say her name was?"

"Gabrielle. Gabrielle Torres."

"Any relation to Tony?"

"She was his daughter."

THERE was a heavy knock on the door. Bassett shied like a frightened horse.

"Who is it?"

The knock was repeated. I went to the door. Bassett neighed at me:

"Don't open it."

I turned the key in the lock and opened the door a few inches against my foot and shoulder. George Wall was outside. His face was greenish-gray in the reflected light. The torn white meat of his leg showed through a rip in his trousers. He breathed hard into my face:

"Is he in here?"

"How did you get in?"

"I came over the fence. Is Bassett in here?"

I looked at Bassett. He was crouched behind the desk, with only his white eyes showing, and his black gun. "Don't let him come in. Don't let him touch me."

"He's not going to touch you. Put that down."

"I will not. I'll defend myself if I have to."

I turned my back on his trigger-happy terror. "You heard him, Wall. He has a gun."

"I don't care what he has. I've got to talk to him. Is Hester here?"

"You're on the wrong track. He hasn't seen her for months."

"Naturally he says that."

"I'm saying it, too. She worked here during the summer, and left some time in September."

His puzzled blue look deepened. His tongue moved like a slow red snail across his upper lip. "Why wouldn't he see me before, if she's not with him?"

"You mentioned horsewhipping, remember? It wasn't exactly the approach diplomatic."

"I don't have time for diplomacy. I have to fly home tomorrow."

"Good."

His shoulder leaned into the opening. I felt his weight on the door. Bassett's voice rose an octave:

"Keep him away from me!"

Bassett was close behind me. I turned with my back against the door and wrenched the gun out of his hand and put it in my pocket. He was too angry and scared to say a word. I turned back to Wall, who was still pressing in but not with all his force. He looked confused. I spread one hand on his chest and pushed him upright and held him. His weight was stubborn and inert, like a stone statue's.

A short, broad-shouldered man came down the steps from the vestibule. He walked toward us fussily, almost goose-stepping, glancing out over the pool and at the sea beyond it as if they were his personal possessions. The wind ruffled his crest of silver hair. Self-importance and fat swelled under his beautifully tailored blue flannel jacket. He was paying no attention to the woman trailing along a few paces behind him.

"Good Lord," Bassett said in my ear, "it's Mr. and Mrs. Graff. We can't have a disturbance in front of Mr. Graff. Let Wall come in. Quickly, man!"

I let him in. Bassett was at the door, bowing and smiling, when the silver-haired man came up. He paused and chopped the air with his nose. His face was brown and burnished-looking.

"Bassett? You've got the extra help lined up for tonight? Orchestra? Food?

"Yes, Mr. Graff."

"About drinks. We'll use the regular bar bourbon, not my private stock. They're all barbarians, anyway—none of them knows the difference."

"Yes, Mr. Graff. Enjoy your swim."

"I always enjoy my swim."

The woman came up behind him, moving a little dazedly, as though the sunlight distressed her. Her black hair was pulled back severely from a broad, flat brow, to which her Greek nose was joined without indentation. Her face was pale and dead, except for the dark searchlights of her eyes, which seemed to contain all her energy and feeling. She was dressed in black jersey, without ornament, like a widow.

Bassett bade her good-morning. She answered with sudden animation that it was a lovely day for December. Her husband strode away toward the *cabañas*. She followed like a detached shadow. Bassett sighed with relief.

"Is he the Graff in Helio-Graff?" I said.

"Yes."

He edged past Wall to his desk, rested a haunch on one

13

corner, and fumbled with his pipe and tobacco pouch. His hands were shaking. Wall hadn't moved from the door. His face was red in patches, and I didn't like the glacial stare of his eyes. I kept my bulk between the two men, watching them in turn like a tennis referee.

Wall said throatily: "You can't lie out of it, you must know where she is. You paid for her dancing lessons."

"Dancing lessons? I?" Bassett's surprise sounded real.

"At the Anton School of Ballet. I spoke to Anton yesterday afternoon. He told me she took some dancing lessons from him, and paid for them with your check."

"So that's what she did with the money I lent her."

Wall's lip curled to one side. "You've got an answer for everything, haven't you? Why would you lend her money?"

"I like her."

"I bet you do. Where is she now?"

"Frankly, I don't know. She left here in September. I haven't set eyes on Miss Campbell since."

"The name is Mrs. Wall, Mrs. George Wall. She's my wife."

"I'm beginning to suspect that, old boy. But she used her maiden name when she was with us. She was planning to divorce you, I understood."

"Who talked her into that?"

Bassett gave him a long-suffering look. "If you want the truth, I tried to talk her out of it. I advised her to go back to Canada, to you. But she had other plans."

"What other plans?"

"She wanted a career," Bassett said with a trace of irony. "She was brought up in the Southland here, you know, and she had the movie fever in her blood. And of course her diving gave her a taste for the limelight. I honestly did my best to talk her out of it. But I'm afraid I made no impression on her. She was determined to find an outlet for her talent—I suppose that explains the dancing lessons."

"Does she have talent?" I said.

Wall answered: "She thinks she has."

"Come now," Bassett said with a weary smile. "Let's give the lady her due. She's a lovely child, and she could develop—"

"So you paid for her dancing lessons."

"I lent her money. I don't know how she spent it. She took off from here very suddenly, as I was telling Archer. One day she was living quietly in Malibu, working at her diving, making good contacts here. And the next day she'd dropped out of sight."

"What sort of contacts?" I said.

14

"A good many of our members are in the industry."

"Could she have gone off with one of them?"

Bassett frowned at the idea. "Certainly not to my knowledge. You understand, I made no attempt to trace her. If she chose to leave, I had no right to interefere."

"I have a right." Wall's voice was low and choked. "I think you're lying about it. You know where she is, and you're trying to put me off."

His lower lip and jaw stuck out, changing the shape of his face into something unformed and ugly. His shoulders leaned outward from the door. I watched his fists clench, white around the knuckles.

"Act your age," I said.

"I've got to find out where she is, what happened to her."

"Wait a minute, George." Bassett pointed his pipe like a token gun, a wisp of smoke at the stem.

"Don't call me George. My friends call me George."

"I'm not your enemy, old boy."

"And don't call me old boy."

"*Young boy,* then, if you wish. I was going to say, I'm sorry this ever came up between us. Truly sorry. I've done you no harm, believe me, and I wish you well."

"Why don't you help me, then? Tell me the truth: is Hester alive?"

Bassett looked at him in dismay.

I said: "What makes you think she isn't?"

"Because she was afraid. She was afraid of being killed."

"When was this?"

"The night before last. Christmas night. She phoned long-distance to the flat in Toronto. She was terribly upset, crying into the telephone."

"What about?"

"Someone had threatened to kill her, she didn't say who. She wanted to get out of California. She asked me if I was willing to take her back. I was, and I told her so. But before we could make any arrangements, the call was cut off. Suddenly she wasn't there, there was nobody there on the end of the line."

"Where was she calling from?"

"Anton's Ballet School on Sunset Boulevard. She had the charges reversed, so I was able to trace the call. I flew out here as soon as I could get away, and saw Anton yesterday. He didn't know about the telephone call, or he said he didn't. He'd been throwing some kind of a party for his students that night, and things were pretty confused."

"Your wife is still taking lessons from him?"

"I don't know. I believe so."

15

"He should have her address, then."

"He says not. The only address she gave him was the Channel Club here." He threw a suspicious look in Bassett's direction. "Are you certain she doesn't live here?"

"Don't be ridiculous. She never did. I invite you to check on that. She rented a cottage in Malibu—I'll look up the address for you. The landlady lives next door, I believe, and you can talk to her. She's Mrs. Sarah Lamb—an old friend and employee of mine. Just mention my name to her."

"So she can lie for you?" Wall said.

Bassett rose and moved toward him, tentatively. "Won't you listen to reason, old boy? I befriended your wife. It's rather hard, don't you think, that I should have to suffer for my good deeds. I can't spend the whole day arguing with you. I've an important party to prepare for tonight."

"That's no concern of mine."

"No, and your affairs are no concern of mine. But I do have a suggestion. Mr. Archer is a private detective. I'm willing to pay him, out of my own pocket, to help you find your wife. On condition that you stop badgering me. Now, is that a fair proposal or isn't it?"

"You're a detective?" Wall said.

I nodded.

He looked at me doubtfully. "If I could be sure this isn't a put-up job— Are you a friend of Bassett's?"

"Never saw him until this morning. Incidentally, I haven't been consulted about this deal."

"It's right down your alley, isn't it?" Bassett said smoothly. "What's your objection?"

I had none, except that there was trouble in the air and it was the end of a rough year and I was a little tired. I looked at George Wall's pink, rebellious head. He was a natural-born trouble-maker, dangerous to himself and probably to other people. Perhaps if I tagged along with him, I could head off the trouble he was looking for. I was a dreamer.

"How about it, Wall?"

"I'd like to have your help," he answered slowly. "I'd rather pay you myself, though."

"Absolutely not!" Bassett said. "You must let me do something—I'm interested in Hester's welfare, too."

"So I gather." Wall's voice was surly.

I said: "We'll toss for it. Heads Bassett pays, tails Wall."

I flipped a quarter and slapped it down on the desk. Tails. I was George Wall's boy. Or he was mine.

16

"He should have her address, then," _____ Carmel Club bar?" He threw a speculative look in Bassett's

xxxxxxxxxx _chapter_ 4

GRAFF was floating on his back in the pool when George Wall and I went outside. His brown belly swelled above its surface like the humpback of a Galápagos tortoise. Mrs. Graff, fully clothed, was sitting by herself in a sunny corner. Her black dress and black hair and black eyes seemed to annul the sunlight. Her face and body had the distinction that takes the place of beauty in people who have suffered long and hard.

She interested me, but I didn't interest her. She didn't even raise her eyes when we passed.

I led Wall out to my car. "You better duck down in the seat when we get up to the gate. Tony might take a pot shot at you."

"Not really?"

"He might. Some of these old fighters can get very upset very quickly, especially when you take a poke at them."

"I didn't mean to do that. It was a rotten thing to do."

"It wasn't smart. Twice this morning you nearly got yourself shot. Bassett was scared enough to do it, and Tony was mad enough. I don't know how it is in Canada, but you can't throw your weight around too much in these parts. A lot of harmless-looking souls have guns in their drawers."

His head sank lower. "I'm sorry."

He sounded more than ever like an adolescent who hadn't caught up with his growth. I liked him pretty well, in spite of that. He had the makings, if he lived long enough for them to jell.

"Don't apologize to me. The life you save may be your own."

"But I'm really sorry. The thought of Hester with that old sissy—I guess I lost my head."

"Find it again. And for God's sake, forget about Bassett. He's hardly what you'd call a wolf."

"He gave her money. He admitted it."

17

"The point is, he did admit it. Probably somebody else is paying her bills now."

He said in a low, growling voice: "Whoever it is, I'll kill him."

"No, you won't."

He sat in stubborn silence as we drove up to the gate. The gate was open. From the door of the gatehouse, Tony waved to me and made a face at Wall.

"Wait," George said. "I want to apologize to him."

"No. You stay in the car."

I made a left turn onto the coast highway. It followed the contour of the brown bluffs, then gradually descended toward the sea. The beach cottages began, passing like an endless and dilapidated freight train.

"I know how terrible I look to you," George blurted. "I'm not usually like this. I don't go around flexing my muscles and threatening people."

"That's good."

"Really," he said. "It's just—well, I've had a bad year."

He told me about his bad year. It started at the Canadian National Exhibition, in August of the previous year. He was a sportswriter on the Toronto *Star*, and he was assigned to cover the aquacade. Hester was one of the featured tower divers. He'd never cared much about diving—football was his sport—but there was something special about Hester, a shine about her, a kind of phosphorescence. He went back to see her on his own time, and took her out after the show.

The third night, she came out of a two-and-a-half too soon, struck the water flat, and was pulled out unconscious. They took her away before he could get to her. She didn't appear for her act the following night. He found her eventually in a hotel on lower Yonge Street. Both her eyes were black and bloodshot. She said she was through with diving. She'd lost her nerve.

She cried on his shoulder for some time. He didn't know what to do to comfort her.

It was his first experience with a woman, except for a couple of times that didn't count, in Montreal, with some of his football buddies. He asked her to marry him in the course of the night. She accepted his proposal in the morning. They were married three days later.

Perhaps he hadn't been as frank with Hester as he should have been. She'd assumed, from the way he spent money, that he had plenty of it. Maybe he'd let on that he was a fairly important figure in Toronto newspaper circles. He wasn't. He was a cub, just one year out of college, at fifty-five dollars a week.

Hester had a hard time adjusting to life in a two-room flat on Spadina Avenue. One trouble was her eyes, which were a long time clearing. For weeks she wouldn't leave the flat. She gave up grooming her hair, making up, even washing her face. She refused to cook for him. She said she'd lost her looks, lost her career, lost everything that made her life worth living.

"I'll never forget last winter," George Wall said.

There was such intensity in his voice, I turned to look at him. He didn't meet my eyes. With a dreaming expression on his face, he was staring past me at the blue Pacific. Winter sunlight crumpled like foil on its surface.

"It was a cold winter," he said. "The snow creaked under your feet and the hair froze in your nostrils. The frost grew thick on the windows. The oil furnace in the basement kept going out. Hester got quite chummy with the custodian of the building, a woman named Mrs. Bean who lived in the next flat. She started going to church with Mrs. Bean—some freakish little church that carried on in an old house on Bloor. I'd get home from work and hear them in the bedroom talking about redemption and reincarnation, stuff like that.

"One night after Mrs. Bean left, Hester told me that she was being punished for her sins. That was why she missed her dive and got stuck in Toronto with me. She said she had to purify herself so her next incarnation would be on a higher level. For about a month after that, I slept on the chesterfield. Jesus, it was cold.

"On Christmas Eve she woke me up in the middle of the night and announced that she was purified. Christ had appeared in her sleep and forgiven all her sins. I didn't take her seriously at first—how could I? I tried to kid her out of it, laugh it off. So she told me what she meant, about her sins."

He didn't go on.

"What did she mean?" I said.

"I'd just as soon not say."

His voice was choked. I looked at him out of the corner of my eyes. Blood burned in his half-averted cheek and reddened his ear.

"Anyway," he continued, "we had a kind of reconciliation. Hester dropped the phony-religious kick. Instead, she developed a sudden craze for dancing. Dance all night and sleep all day. I couldn't stand the pace. I had to go to work and drum up the old enthusiasm for basketball and hockey and other childish pastimes. She got into the habit of going out by herself, down into the Village."

"I thought you said you were living in Toronto."

"Toronto has its own Village. It's very much like the original in New York—on a smaller scale, of course. Hester got in with a gang of ballet buffs. She went overboard for dancing lessons, with a teacher by the name of Padraic Dane. She had her hair clipped short, and her ears pierced for earrings. She took to wearing white silk shirts and matador pants around the flat. She was always doing entrechats or whatever you call 'em. She'd ask me for things in French—not that she knew French—and when I didn't catch on, she'd give me the silent treatment.

"She'd sit and stare at me without blinking for fifteen or twenty minutes at a time. You'd think I was a piece of furniture that she was trying to think of a better place for. Or maybe by that time I didn't exist at all for her. You know?"

I knew. I'd had a wife and lost her in those silences. I didn't tell George Wall, though. He went on talking, pouring out the words as though they'd been frozen in him for a long time and finally been thawed by the California sun. He probably would have spilled his soul that day to an iron post or a wooden Indian.

"I know now what she was doing," he said. "She was getting her confidence back, in a crazy, unreal way, pulling herself together to make a break with me. The crowd she was playing with, Paddy Dane and his gang of pixies, were encouraging her to do it. I should have seen it coming.

"They put on some kind of a dance play late in the spring, in a little theater that used to be a church. Hester played the boy lead. I went to see it, couldn't make head nor tail of it. It was something about a split personality falling in love with itself. I heard them afterwards filling her up with nonsense about herself. They told her she was wasting herself in Toronto, married to a slob like me. She owed it to herself to go to New York, or back to Hollywood.

"We had a battle when she finally came home that night. I laid it on the line for her: she had to give up those people and their ideas. I told her she was going to drop her dancing lessons and her acting and stay home and wear ordinary women's clothes and look after the flat and cook a few decent meals."

He laughed unpleasantly. It sounded like broken edges rubbing together inside him.

"I'm a great master of feminine psychology," he said. "In the morning after I left for work she went to the bank and drew out the money I'd saved towards a house and got on a plane for Chicago. I found that out by inquiring at the airport. She didn't even leave me a note—I guess she was punishing me for *my* sins. I didn't know where she'd gone. I looked up some of her rum friends in the Village, but they didn't know, either. She dropped them just as flat as she dropped me.

"I don't know how I got through the next six months. We hadn't been married long, and we hadn't been close to each other, the way married people should be. But I was in love with her, I still am. I used to walk the streets half the night and every time I saw a girl with blond hair I'd get an electric shock. Whenever the telephone rang, I'd *know* that it was Hester. And then one night it was.

"It was Christmas night, the night before last. I was sitting in the flat by myself, trying not to think about her. I felt like a nervous breakdown getting ready to happen. Wherever I looked, I kept seeing her face on the wall. And then the telephone rang, and it was Hester. I told you what she said, that she was afraid of being killed and wanted to get out of California. You can imagine how I felt when she was cut off. I thought of calling the Los Angeles police, but there wasn't much to go on. So I had the call traced, and caught the first plane I could get out of Toronto."

"Why didn't you do that six months ago?"

"I didn't know where she was—she never wrote me."

"You must have had some idea."

"Yes, I thought she'd probably come back here. But I didn't have the heart to track her down. I wasn't making much sense there for a while. I pretty well convinced myself she was better off without me." He added after a silence: "Maybe she is, at that."

"All you can do is ask her. But first we have to find her."

✕✕✕✕✕✕✕✕✕ *chapter* 5

WE entered a dead-end street between the highway and the beach. The tires shuddered on the pitted asphalt. The cottages that lined the street were run-down and disreputable-looking, but the cars that stood in front of them were nearly all late models. When I turned off my engine, the

21

only sound I could hear was the rumble and gasp of the sea below the cottages. Above them a few gulls circled, tattletale gray.

The one that Hester had lived in was a board-and-batten box which had an unused look, like a discarded container. Its walls had been scoured bare and grained by blowing sands. The cottage beside it was larger and better kept, but it was losing its paint, too.

"This is practically a slum," George said. "I thought that Malibu was a famous resort."

"Part of it is. This is the other part."

We climbed the steps to Mrs. Lamb's back porch, and I knocked on the rusty screen door. A heavy-bodied old woman in a wrapper opened the inside door. She had a pleasantly ugly bulldog face and a hennaed head, brash orange in the sun. An anti-wrinkle patch between her eyebrows gave her an air of calm eccentricity.

"Mrs. Lamb?"

She nodded. She held a cup of coffee in her hand, and she was chewing.

"I understand you rent the cottage next door."

She swallowed whatever was in her mouth. I watched its passage down her withered throat. "I may as well tell you right off, I don't rent stag. Now if you're married, that's another matter." She paused expectantly and took a second swallow, leaving a red half-moon on the rim of the cup.

"I'm not married."

That was as far as I got.

"Too bad," she said. Her nasal Kansas voice hummed on like a wire in a rushing wind: "I'm all for marriage myself, went out with four men in my lifetime and married two of them. The first one lasted thirty-three years, I guess I made him happy. He didn't bother *me* with his Copenhagen snuff and his dirt around the house. It takes more than that to bother *me*. So when he died I married again, and that one wasn't so bad. Could have been better, could have been worse. It was kind of a relief, though, when *he* died. He didn't do a lick of work in seven years. Luckily I had the strength to support him."

Her sharp eyes, ringed with concentric wrinkles, flicked from me to George Wall and back again. "You're both nice-appearing young men, you ought to be able to find a girl willing to take a chance with you." She smiled fiercely, swirled her remaining coffee around in the cup, and drank it down.

"I had a wife," George Wall said heavily. "I'm looking for her now."

"You don't say. Why didn't you say so?"

"I've been trying to."

"Don't get mad. I like a little sociability, don't you? What's her name?"

"Hester."

Her eyes flattened. "Hester Campbell?"

"Hester Campbell Wall."

"Well, I'll be darned. I didn't know she was married. What happened, did she run away?"

He nodded solemnly. "Last June."

"What do you know? She's got less sense than I thought she had, running away from a nice young fellow like you." She inspected his face intently through the screen, clucking in decrescendo. " 'Course I never did give her credit for too much sense. She was always full of razzmatazz, ever since she was a kid."

"Have you known her long?" I said.

"You bet I have. Her and her sister and her mother both. She was a hoity-toity one, her mother, always putting on airs."

"Do you know where her mother is now?"

"Haven't seen her for years, or the sister either."

I looked at George Wall.

He shook his head. "I didn't even know she had a mother. She never talked about her family. I thought she was an orphan."

"She had one," the old woman said. "Her and her sister, Rina, they were both well supplied with a mother. Mrs. Campbell was bound to make something out of those girls if it killed them. I don't know how she afforded all those lessons she gave them—music lessons and dancing lessons and swimming lessons."

"No husband?"

"Not when I knew her. She was clerking in the liquor store during the war, which is how we became acquainted, through my second. Mrs. Campbell was always bragging about her girls, but she didn't really have their welfare at heart. She was what they call a movie-mother, I guess, trying to get her little girls to support her."

"Does she still live here?"

"Not to my knowledge. She dropped out of sight years ago. Which didn't break my heart."

"And you don't know where Hester is, either?"

"I haven't laid eyes on the girl since September. She moved out, and that was that. We have some turnover in Malibu, I can tell you."

"Where did she move to?" George said.

"That's what I'd like to know." Her gaze shifted to me: "Are you a relative, too?"

"No, I'm a private detective."

She showed no surprise. "All right, I'll talk to you, then. Come inside and have a cup of coffee. Your friend can wait outside."

Wall didn't argue; he merely looked disgruntled. Mrs. Lamb unhooked her screen door, and I followed her into the tiny white kitchen. The red plaid of the tablecloth was repeated in the curtains over the sink. Coffee was bubbling on an electric plate.

Mrs. Lamb poured some of it for me in a cup which didn't match hers, and then some more for herself. She sat at the table, motioned to me to sit opposite.

"I couldn't exist without coffee. I developed the habit when I ran the snack bar. Twenty-five cups a day, silly old woman." But she sounded very tolerant of herself. "I do believe if I cut myself I'd bleed coffee. Mr. Finney—he's my adviser at the Spiritualist Church—says I should switch to tea, but I say no. Mr. Finney, I told him, the day I have to give up my favorite vice, I'd just as soon lay down and fold my hands around a lily and pass on into another life."

"Good for you," I said. "You were going to tell me something about Hester."

"Yes, I was. I hated to say it right out in front of the husband. I had to evict her."

"What for?"

"Carrying on," she said vaguely. "The girl's a fool about men. Doesn't he know that?"

"It seems to be at the back of his mind. Any particular men?"

"One particular man."

"Not Clarence Bassett?"

"Mr. Bassett? Heavens, no. I've known Mr. Bassett going on ten years—I ran the snack bar at the club until my legs give out—and you can take my word for it, he ain't the carrying-on *type*. Mr. Bassett was more like a father to her. I guess he did his best to keep her out of trouble, but his best wasn't good enough. Mine, either."

"What kind of trouble did she get into?"

"Man trouble, like I said. Nothing that you could put your finger on, maybe, but I could see she was heading for disaster. One of the men she brought here to her house was a regular gangster type. I *told* Hester if she was going to have bums like him visiting her, spending the night, she'd have to find another house to do it in. I felt I had a right to speak out, knowing her from childhood and all. But she took it the wrong way, said she would look after her affairs and I could look after mine. I told her what she did on my property *was* my affair. She said, all right, if that's the way you feel about it she'd get out, said I was an interfering old bag. Which maybe I am, at that, but I don't take talk like that from any flibberty-gibbet who plays around with gunmen."

She paused for breath. An ancient refrigerator throbbed emotionally in the corner of the kitchen. I took a sip of my coffee and looked out the window which overlooked the street. George Wall was sitting in the front seat of my car with a rejected expression on his face. I turned back to Mrs. Lamb:

"Who was he, do you know?"

"I never did learn his name. Hester wouldn't tell me his name. When I took the matter up with her, she said he was her boyfriend's manager."

"Her boyfriend?"

"The Torres boy. Lance Torres, he calls himself. He was a fairly decent boy at one time, least he put up a nice front when he had his lifeguard job."

"Was he a lifeguard at the club?"

"Used to be, for a couple of summers. His Uncle Tony got him the job. But lifeguard was too slow for Lance, he had to be a big shot. I heard he was a boxer for a while and then he got into some trouble, I think they put him in jail for it last year."

"What kind of trouble?"

"I don't know, there's too many good people in the world to make it worth my while to keep track of bums. You could of knocked me over with a brick when Lance turned up here with his gunman friend, sucking around Hester. I thought he had more self-respect."

"How do you know he was a gunman?"

"I saw him shooting, that's how. I woke up one morning and heard this popping noise down on the beach. It sounded like gunfire. It was. This fellow was out there shooting at beer bottles with a nasty black gun he had. That was the day I said to myself, either she stops messing around with bums or good-by Hester."

"Who was he?"

"I never did learn his name. That nasty snub-nosed gun and the way he handled it was all I needed to know about him. Hester said he was Lance's manager."

"What did he look like?"

"Looked like death to me. Those glassy brown eyes he had, and kind of a flattened-out face, fishbelly color. But I talked right up to him, told him he ought to be ashamed of himself shooting up bottles where people could cut themselves. He didn't even look at me, just stuck another clip in his gun and went on shooting at the bottles. He'd probably just as soon been shooting at me, least that was how he acted."

Remembered anger heightened her color. "I don't like being brushed off like that—it ain't *human*. And I'm touchy about shooting, specially since a friend of mine was shot last year. Right on this very beach, a few miles south of where you're sitting."

"You don't mean Gabrielle Torres?"

"I should say I do. You heard about Gabrielle, eh?"

"A little. So she was a friend of yours."

"Sure, she was. Some people would have a prejudice, her being part Mex, but I say if a person is good enough to work with you, a person is good enough to be your friend." Her monolithic bosom rose and fell under the flowered-cotton wrapper.

"Nobody knows who shot her, I hear."

"Somebody knows. The one that did it."

"Do you have any ideas, Mrs. Lamb?"

Her face was as still as stone for a long moment. She shook her head finally.

"Her cousin Lance, maybe, or his manager?"

"I wouldn't put it past them. But what reason could they have?"

"You've thought about it, then."

"How could I help it, with them going in and out of the cottage next door, shooting off guns on the beach? I told Hester the day she left, she should learn a lesson from what happened to her friend."

"But she went off with them anyway?"

"I guess she did. I didn't see her leave. I don't know where she went, or who with. That day I made a point of going to visit my married daughter in San Berdoo."

xxxxxxxxxx *chapter* 6

I RELAYED as little as possible of this to George Wall, who showed signs of developing into a nuisance. On the way to Los Angeles, I turned into the drive of the Channel Club. He gave a wild look around, as though I was taking him into an ambush.

"Why are we coming back here?"

"I want to talk to the guard. He may be able to give me a lead to your wife. If not, I'll try Anton."

"I don't see the point of that. I talked to Anton yesterday, I told you all he said."

"I may be able to squeeze out some more. I know Anton, did a piece of work for him once."

"You think he was holding out on me?"

"Could be. He hates to give anything away, including information. Now you sit here and see that nobody swipes the hubcaps. I want to get Tony talking, and you have bad associations for him."

"What's the use of my being here at all?" he said sulkily. "I might as well go back to the hotel and get some sleep."

"That's an idea, too."

I left him in the car out of sight of the gate, and walked down the curving drive between thick rows of oleanders. Tony heard me coming. He shuffled out of the gatehouse, gold gleaming in the crannies of his smile.

"What happened to your loco friend? You lose him?"

"No such luck. You have a nephew, Tony."

"Got a lot of nephews." He spread his arms. "Five-six nephews."

"The one that calls himself Lance."

He grunted. Nothing changed in his face, except that he wasn't smiling any more. "What about him?"

"Can you tell me his legal name?"

"Manuel," he said. "Manuel Purificación Torres. The name my brother give him wasn't good enough for him. He had to go and change it."

"Where is he living now, do you know?"

"No, sir, I don't know. I don't have nothing to do with that one no more. He was close to me like a son one time. No more." He wagged his head from side to side, slowly. The motion shook a question loose: "Is Manuel in trouble again?"

"I couldn't say for sure. Who's his manager, Tony?"

"He don't got no manager. They don't let him fight no more. I was his manager couple years ago, trained him and managed him both. Brought him along slow and easy, gave him a left and taught him the combinations. Kept him living clean, right in my own house: up at six in the morning, skip-the-rope, light and heavy bag, run five miles on the beach. Legs like iron, beautiful. So he had to ruinate it."

"How?"

"Same old story," Tony said. "I seen it too many times. He wins a couple-three fights, two four-rounders and a six-rounder in San Diego. Right away he's a bigshot, he *thinks* he's a bigshot. Uncle Tony, poor old Uncle Tony, he's too dumb in the head to tell him his business. Uncle Tony don't know from nothing, says lay off muscadoodle, lay off dames and reefers, sell your noisy, stinky motorcycle before you break your neck, you got a future. Only he wants it now. The whole world, right now."

"Then something come up between us. He done something I don't like, I don't like it at all. I says, you been wanting out from me, now you can get out. We didden have no contract, nothing between us any more, I guess. He clumb on his motorcycle and tooted away, back to Los Angeles. There he was, a Main Street bum, and he wasn't twenty-one years old yet.

"My sister Desideria blamed me, I should go after him on my hands and knees." Tony shook his head. "No, I says, Desideria, I been around a long time. So have you, only you're a woman and don't see things. A boy gets ants in his pants, you can't hire no exterminator for that. Let him do it the hard way, we can't live his life.

"So one of these crooks he wants to be like—this crook sees Manny working out in the gym. He asks him for a contract and Manny gives it to him. He wins some fights and throws some, makes some dirty money, spends it on dirty things. They caught him with some caps in his car last year, and put him in jail. When he gets out, he's suspended, no more fights—back where he started in the starvation army."

Tony spat dry. "Long ago, I tried to tell him, my father, his grandfather, was *bracero*. Manny's father and me, we was born in a chickenhouse in Fresno, nowhere, from nothing. We got two strikes on us already, I says, we got to keep our nose clean. But would he listen to me? No, he got to stick his neck under the chopper."

"How much time did he serve?"

"I guess he was in all last year. I dunno for sure. I got troubles of my own then."

His shoulders moved as if they felt the entire weight of the sky. I wanted to ask him about his daughter's death, but the grief in his face tied my tongue. The scars around his eyes, sharp and deep in the sun, had been left there by crueller things than fists. I asked a different question:

"Do you know the name of the man that held his contract?"

"Stern, his last name is."

"Carl Stern?"

"Yeah." Squinting at my face, he saw the effect of the name on me. "You know him?"

"I've seen him in nightclubs, and heard some stories about him. If ten per cent of them are true, he's a dangerous character. Is your nephew still with him, Tony?"

"I dunno. I bet you he is in trouble. I think you know it, only you won't tell me."

"What makes you think that?"

"Because I seen him last week. He was all dressed up like a movie star and driving one of those sporty cars." He made a low sweeping motion with his hands. "Where would he get the money? He don't work, and he can't fight no more."

"Why didn't you ask him?"

"Don't make me laugh, ask him. He wooden say hello to his Uncle Tony. He is too busy riding around with blondes in speedy cars."

"He was with a blonde girl?"

"Sure."

"Anybody you know?"

"Sure. She used to work here last summer. Hester Campbell, her name is. I thought she had more brains, to run around with my nephew Manny."

"How long has she been running with him?"

"I wooden know. I got no crystal ball."

"Where did you see them?"

"Venice Speedway."

"Wasn't the Campbell girl a friend of your daughter's?"

His face set hard and dark. "Maybe. What is this all about, mister? First you ask for my nephew, now it's my daughter."

"I just heard about your daughter this morning. She was a friend of the Campbell girl, and I'm interested in the Campbell girl."

"I'm not, and I don't know nothing. It's no use asking me. What do I know?" His mood had swung heavily downward. He made an idiot face. "I'm a punchy bum. My brains don't think straight. My daughter is dead. My nephew is a crooked *pachuco*. People come and punch me in the nose."

ANTON'S windows overlooked the boulevard from the second floor of a stucco building in West Hollywood. The building was fairly new, but it had been painted and scraped and repainted in blotches of color, pink and white and blue, to make it look like something from the left bank of the Seine. You entered it through a court which contained several small arty shops and had a terrazzo fountain in the center. A concrete nymph stood with her feet in its shallow water, covering her pudenda with one hand and beckoning with the other.

I climbed the outside stairs to the second-floor balcony. Through an open door, I saw a half-dozen girls in leotards stretching their ligaments on barres along the wall. A woman with flat breasts and massive haunches called out orders in a drill-sergeant's voice:

"*Grand battement, s'il vous plaît. Non, non,* grand *battement.*"

I walked on to the end of the balcony, trailed by the salt-sweet odor of young sweat. Anton was in his office, short and wide behind the desk in a gabardine suit the color of lemon ice cream. His face was sunlamp brown. He rose very lightly, to demonstrate his agelessness. The hand he extended had rings on two of the fingers, a seal ring and a diamond to go with the diamond in his foulard tie. His grip was like a bull lobster's.

"Mr. Archer."

Anton had been in Hollywood longer than I had, but he still pronounced my name "Meester Arshair." The accent was probably part of his business front. I liked him in spite of it.

"I'm surprised you remember my name."

"I think of you with gratitude," he said. "Frequently."

"What wife are you on now?"

"Please, you are very vulgar." He raised his hands in a fastidious gesture, and while he was at it, examined his man-

30

icure. "Number five. We are very happy. You are not needed."

"Yet."

"But you didn't come to discuss my marital problems. Why do you come?"

"Missing girl."

"Hester Campbell again?"

"Uh-huh."

"Are you employed by that big *naïf* of a husband?"

"You're psychic."

"He is a fool. Any man of his age and weight who runs after a woman in this city is a fool. Why doesn't he stand still, and they'll come swarming?"

"He's only interested in the one. Now what about her?"

"What about her?" he repeated, offering his hands palms up to show how clean they were. "She has had some ballet lessons from me, three or four months of lessons. The young ladies come and go. I am not responsible for their private lives."

"What do you know about her private life?"

"Nothing. I wish to know nothing. My friend Paddy Dane in Toronto did me no favor when he sent her here. There is a young lady very much on the make. I could see trouble in her."

"If you could see all that, why turn her husband loose on Clarence Bassett?"

"His shoulders rose. "*I* turned him loose on Bassett? I merely answered his questions."

"You made him believe that she was living with Bassett. Bassett hasn't seen her for nearly four months."

"What would I know about that?"

"Don't kid me, Anton. Did you know Bassett before this?"

"*Pas trop*. He would not remember, probably."

He moved to the window and cranked the louvers wider. The sound of traffic rose from the Boulevard. Under it, his voice was sibilant:

"But I do not forget. Five years ago, I applied for membership in the Channel Club. They refused me, with no reason given. I heard through my sponsor that Bassett never presented my name to the membership committee. He wanted no dancing-masters in his club."

"So you thought you'd make trouble for him."

"Perhaps." He looked at me over his shoulder, his eye bright and empty as a bird's. "Did I succeed?"

"I stopped it before it happened. But you could have triggered a murder."

"Nonsense." He turned and came toward me, stepping with

31

feline softness on the carpet. "The husband is a nothing, a hysterical boy. There is no danger in him."

"I wonder. He's big and strong, and crazy about his wife."

"Is he rich?"

"Hardly."

"Then tell him to forget her. I have seen many like her, in love with themselves. They think they aspire to an art, acting or dancing or music. But all they really aspire to is money and clothes. A man comes along who can give them these things, and there is the end of aspiration." His hands went through the motions of liberating a bird and throwing it a good-by kiss.

"Did one come along for Hester?"

"Possibly. She seemed remarkably prosperous at my Christmas party. She had a new mink stole. I complimented her on it, and she informed me that she was under personal contract to a movie producer."

"Which one?"

"She did not say, and it does not matter. She was lying. It was a little fantasy for my benefit."

"How do you know?"

"I know women."

I was ready to believe him. The wall behind his desk was papered with inscribed photographs of young women.

"Besides," he said, "no producer in his right mind would give that girl a contract. There is something lacking in her —essential talent, feeling. She became cynical so young, and she makes no attempt to hide it."

"How did she act the other night?"

"I did not observe her for very long. I had over a hundred guests."

"She made a telephone call from here. Did you know?"

"Not until yesterday. The husband told me she was frightened of something. Perhaps she drank too much. There was nothing at my party to frighten anyone—a lot of nice young people amusing themselves."

"Who was she with?"

"A boy, a good-looking boy." He snapped his fingers. "She introduced him to me, but I forget his name."

"Lance Torres?"

His eyelids crinkled. "Possibly. He was quite dark, Spanish-looking. A very well-built boy—one of those new young types with the *apache* air. Perhaps Miss Seeley can identify him for you. I saw them talking together." He pushed his right cuff back and looked at his wristwatch. "Miss Seeley is out for coffee, but she should be back very soon."

32

"While we're waiting, you could give me Hester's address. Her real address."

"Why should I make things easy for you?" Anton said with his edged smile. "I don't like the fellow you are working for. He is too aggressive. Also, I am old and he is young. Also my father was a streetcar conductor in Montreal. Why should I help an Anglo from Toronto?"

"So you won't let him find his wife?"

"Oh, you can have the address. I simply wished to express my emotions on the subject. She lives at the Windsor Hotel in Santa Monica."

"You know it by heart, eh?"

"I happen to remember. I had a request for her address from another detective last week."

"Police detective?"

"Private. He claimed to be a lawyer with money for her, a bequest, but his story was very clumsy and I am not stupid." He glanced at his wristwatch again. "If you'll excuse me, now, I have to dress for a class. You can wait here for Miss Seeley if you wish."

Before I could ask him any more questions, he went out through an inner door and closed it behind him. I sat down at his desk and looked up the Windsor Hotel in the telephone directory. The desk clerk told me that Miss Hester Campbell didn't stay there any more. She'd moved out two weeks ago, leaving no forwarding address.

I was masticating this fact when Miss Seeley came in. I remembered her from the period when Anton divorced his third wife, with my assistance. She was a little older, a little thinner. Her tailored pinstriped suit emphasized the boniness of her figure. But she still wore hopeful white ruffles at her wrists and throat.

"Why, Mr. Archer." The implications of my presence struck her. "We're not having wife trouble again?"

"Wife trouble, yes, but nothing to do with the boss. He says you may be able to give me some information."

"My telephone number, by any chance?" Her smile was warm and easygoing behind her lipstick mask.

"That I could do with, too."

"You flatter me. Go right ahead. I can stand a smattering of flattering for a change. You don't meet many eligible males in this business."

We exchanged some further pleasantries, and I asked her if she remembered seeing Hester at the party. She remembered.

"And her escort?"

She nodded. "Dreamy. A real cute thing. That is, if you like the Latin type. I don't go for the Latin type myself, but we got along just fine. Until he showed his true colors."

"You talked to him?"

"For a while. He was kind of shy with all the people, so I took him under my wing. He told me about his career and all. He's an actor. Helio-Graff Studios have him under long-term contract."

"What's his name?"

"Lance Leonard. It's kind of a cute name, don't you think? He told me he chose it himself."

"He didn't tell you his real name?"

"No."

"And he's under contract to Helio-Graff?"

"That's what he said. He's certainly got the looks for it. *And* the artistic temperament."

"You mean he made a pass at you?"

"Oh, no. Not that I'd permit it. He's stuck on Hester anyway, I could see that. They were at the bar after, drinking out of the same glass, just as close as close." Her voice was wistful. She added by way of consolation to herself: "But then he showed his true colors."

"How did he do that?"

"It was awful," she said with relish. "Hester came in here to put in a telephone call. I let her have the key. It must have been to another man, because he followed her in and made a scene. These Latins are so emotional."

"You were here?"

"I heard him yelling at her. I had things to do in my own office, and I couldn't *help* overhearing. He called her some awful names: b-i-t-c-h and other words I won't repeat." She tried to blush, and failed.

"Did he threaten her in any way?"

"You bet he did. He said she wouldn't last a week unless she played along with the operation. She was in it deeper than anybody, and she wasn't going to ruin his big chance." Miss Seeley was a fairly decent woman, but she couldn't quite restrain the glee fluttering at the corners of her mouth.

"Did he say what the operation was?"

"Not that I heard."

"Or threaten to kill her?"

"He didn't say that *he* was going to do anything to her. What he said——" She looked up at the ceiling and tapped her chin. "He said if she didn't stay in line, he'd get this friend of his after her. Somebody called Carl."

"Carl Stern?"

"Maybe. He didn't mention the last name. He just kept saying that Carl would fix her wagon."

"What happened after that?"

"Nothing. They came out and left together. She looked pretty subdued, I mean it."

THERE was an outdoor telephone booth in the court, and I immured myself with the local directories. Lance Leonard wasn't in them. Neither was Lance Torres, or Hester Campbell, or Carl Stern. I made a telephone call to Peter Colton, who had recently retired as senior investigator in the D.A.'s office.

Carl Stern, he told me, had also retired recently. That is, he'd moved to Vegas and gone legit, if you could call Vegas legit. Stern had invested his money in a big new hotel-and-casino which was under construction. Personally Colton hoped he'd lose his dirty gold-plated shirt.

"Where did the gold come from, Peter?"

"Various sources. He was a Syndicate boy. When Siegel broke with the Syndicate and died of it, Stern was one of the heirs. He made his heavy money out of the wire service. When the Crime Commission broke that up, he financed a narcotics ring for a while."

"So you put him away, no doubt."

"You know the situation as well as I do, Lew." Colton sounded angry and apologetic at the same time. "Our operation is essentially a prosecuting agency. We work with what the cops bring into us. Carl Stern was using cops for bodyguards. The politicians that hire and fire the cops went on fishing trips with him to Acapulco."

"Is that how he wangled himself a gambling license in Nevada?"

"He didn't get a license in Nevada. With his reputation, they couldn't give him one. He had to get himself a front."

"Do you know who his front man would be?"

35

"Simon Graff," Colton said. "You must have heard of him. They're going to call their place Simon Graff's Casbah."

That stopped me for a minute. "I thought Helio-Graff was making money."

"Maybe Graff saw his chance to make some more money. I'd tell you what I think of that, but it wouldn't be good for my blood pressure." He went ahead and told me anyway, in a voice that was choked with passion: "They've got no decency, they've got no sense of public responsibility—these goddam lousy big Hollywood names that go to Vegas and decoy for thieves and pander for mobsters and front for murderers."

"Is Stern a murderer?"

"Ten times over," Colton said. "You want his record in detail?"

"Not just now. Thanks, Peter. Take it easy."

I knew a man at Helio-Graff, a writer named Sammy Swift. The studio switchboard put me on to his secretary, and she called Sammy to the phone.

"Lew? How's the Sherlock kick?"

"It keeps me in beer and skittles. By the way, what are skittles? You're a writer, you're supposed to know these things."

"I let the research department know them for me. Division of labor. Will you cut it short now, boy? Any other time. I'm fighting script, and the mimeographers are hounding me." His voice was hurried, in time with a rapid metronome clicking inside his head.

"What's the big project?"

"I'm flying to Italy with a production unit next week. Graff's doing a personal on the Carthage story."

"The Carthage story?"

"*Salambô*, the Flaubert historical. Where you been?"

"In geography class. Carthage is in Africa."

"It was, not any more. The Man is building it in Italy."

"I hear he's doing some building in Vegas, too."

"The Casbah, you mean? Yeah."

"Isn't it kind of unusual for a big independent producer to put his money in a slot-machine shop?"

"Everything the Man does is unusual. And moderate your language, Lew."

"You bugged?"

"Don't be silly," he said uncertainly. "Now, what's your problem? If you think you're broke, I'm broker, ask my broker."

"No problem. I want to get in touch with a new actor you have. Lance Leonard?"

36

"Yeah, I've seen him around. Why?"

I improvised. "A friend of mine, newspaperman from the east, wants an interview."

"About the Carthage story?"

"Why, is Leonard in it?"

"Minor role, his first. Don't you read the columns?"

"Not when I can help it. I'm illiterate."

"So are the columns. So's Leonard, but don't let your friend print that. The kid should do all right as a North African barbarian. He's got prettier muscles than Brando, used to be a fighter."

"How did he get into pictures?"

"The Man discovered him personally."

"And where does he board his pretty muscles?"

"Coldwater Canyon, I think. My secretary can get you the address. Don't let on you got it from me, though. The kid is afraid of the press. But he can use the publicity." Sammy caught his breath. He liked to talk. He liked anything that interrupted his work. "I hope this isn't one of your fast ones, Lew."

"You know better than that. I lost my fast one years ago. I'm down to my slider."

"So are we all, boy. With bursitis yet. See you."

I got the address in Coldwater Canyon, and went out to the street. The sun shimmered on the car roof. George Wall was slumped in the front seat with his head thrown back. His face was flushed and wet. His eyes were closed. The interior was oven-hot.

The starting engine woke him. He sat up, rubbing his eyes. "Where are we going?"

"Not we. I'll drop you off at your hotel. Which one?"

"But I don't want to be dropped off." He took hold of my right arm. "You found out where she is, haven't you? You don't want me to see her."

I didn't answer. He tugged at my arm, causing the car to swerve. "That's the idea, isn't it?"

I pushed him away, into the far corner of the seat. "For God's sake, George, relax. Take a sedative when you get back to the hotel. Now, where is it?"

"I'm not going back to the hotel. You can't force me."

"All right, all right. If you promise to stay in the car. I have a lead that may pan out and it may not. It won't for sure, if you come barging in."

"I won't. I promise." After a while he said: "You don't understand how I feel. I dreamed of Hester just now when I was asleep. I tried to talk to her. She wouldn't answer, and then I saw she was dead. I touched her. She was as cold as snow—"

"Tell it to your head-shrinker," I said unpleasantly. His self-pity was getting on my nerves.

He withdrew into hurt silence, which lasted all the way to the Canyon. Lance Leonard lived near the summit, in a raw new redwood house suspended on cantilevers over a steep drop. I parked above the house and looked around. Leonard had no close neighbors, though several other houses dotted the further slopes. The hills fell away from the ridge in folds like heavy drapery trailing in the horizontal sea.

I nailed George in place with one of my masterful looks, and went down the slanting asphalt drive to the house. The trees in the front yard, lemons and avocados, were recently planted: I could see the yellow burlap around their roots. The garage contained a dusty gray Jaguar two-door and a light racing motorcycle. I pressed the button beside the front door, and heard chimes in the house softly dividing the silence.

A young man opened the door. He was combing his hair with a sequined comb. His hair was black, curly on top and straight at the sides. The height of the doorstep brought his head level with mine. His face was darkly handsome, if you overlooked the spoiled mouth and slightly muddy eyes. He had on blue nylon pajamas, and his brown feet were bare. He was the central diver in Bassett's photograph.

"Mr. Torres?"

"Leonard," he corrected me. Having arranged the curls low on his forehead to his satisfaction, he dropped the comb in his pajama pocket. He smiled with conscious charm. "Got a new name to go with my new career. What's the mission, cap?"

"I'd like to see Mrs. Wall."

"Never heard of her. You got the wrong address."

"Her maiden name was Campbell. Hester Campbell."

He stiffened. "Hester? She ain't married—isn't married."

"She's married. Didn't she tell you?"

He glanced over his shoulder into the house, and back at me. His movements were lizard-quick. He took hold of the knob and started to shut the door. "Never heard of her. Sorry."

"Who does the comb belong to? Or do you merely adore bright things?"

He paused in indecision, long enough for me to get my foot in the door. I could see past him through the house to the sliding glass wall at the rear of the living-space, and through it the outside terrace which overhung the canyon. A

38

girl was lying on a metal chaise in the sun. Her back was brown and long, with a breathtaking narrow waist from which the white hip arched up. Her hair was like ruffled silver feathers.

Leonard stepped outside, forcing me back onto the flagstone walk, and shut the front door behind him. "Drag 'em back into their sockets, cousin. No free shows today. And get this, I don't know any Hester what's-her-name."

"You did a minute ago."

"Maybe I heard the name once. I hear a lot of names. What's yours, for instance?"

"Archer."

"What's your business?"

"I'm a detective."

His mouth went ugly. and his eyes blank. He'd come up fast out of a place where cops were hated and feared: the hatred was still in him like a chronic disease. "What you want with me, cop?"

"Not you. Hester."

"Is she in a jam?"

"She probably is if she's shacked up with you."

"Naw, naw. She gave me the brush-off, frankly." He brushed his nylon flanks illustratively. "I haven't seen the chick for a long time."

"Have you tried looking on your terrace?"

His hands paused and tightened on his hips. He leaned forward from the waist, his mouth working like a red bivalve: "You keep calling me a liar. I got a public position to keep up, so I stand here and take it like a little gentleman. But you better get off my property or I'll clobber you, cop or no cop."

"That would go good in the columns. The whole set-up would."

"What set-up? What do you mean?"

"You tell me."

He squinted anxiously up toward the road where my car was parked. George's face hung at the window like an ominous pink moon.

"Who's your sidekick?"

"Her husband."

Leonard's eyes blurred with thought. "What is this, a shakedown? Let's see your buzzer."

"No buzzer. I'm a private detective."

"Dig him," he said to an imaginary confidant on his left. At the same time, his right shoulder dropped. The hooked arm swinging from it drove a fist into my middle below the rib-cage. It came too fast to block. I sat down on the flagstones and discovered that I couldn't get up right away. My head was cool and clear, like an aquarium, but the bright ideas and noble intentions that swam around in it had no useful connection with my legs.

Leonard stood with his fists ready, waiting for me to get up. His hair had fallen forward over his eyes, blue-black and shining like steel shavings. His bare feet danced a little on the stone. I reached for them and clutched air. Leonard smiled down at me, dancing:

"Come on, get up. I can use a workout."

"You'll get it, sucker-puncher," I said between difficult breaths.

"Not from you, old man."

The door opened behind him, and featherhead looked out. She wore dark harlequin glasses whose sequined rims matched the comb. Oil glistened on her face. A terrycloth towel held under her armpits clung to the bulbs and narrows of her body.

"What's the trouble, hon?"

"No trouble. Get inside."

"Who is this character? Did you hit him?"

"What do you think?"

"I think you're crazy, taking the chances you take."

"*Me* take chances? Who shot off her mouth on the telephone? You *brought* the bastard here."

"All right, so I wanted out. So I changed my mind."

"Shut it off." He threatened her with a movement of his shoulders. "I said inside."

Running footsteps clattered on the driveway. George Wall called out: "Hester! I'm here!"

What I could see of her face didn't change expression. Leonard spread a hand on her terrycloth breast and pushed her in and shut the door on her. He turned as George charged in on him, met him with a stiff left to the face. George stopped dead. Leonard waited, his face smooth and intent like a man's listening to music.

I got my legs under me and stood up and watched them fight. George had been wanting a fight: he had the advantage of height and weight and reach: I didn't interfere. It was like watching a man get caught in a machine. Leonard stepped inside of a looping swing, rested his chin on the big man's chest, and hammered his stomach. His elbows worked like pistons in oiled grooves close to his body. When he stepped back, George doubled over. He went to his knees and got up again, very pale.

The instant his hands left the flagstone, Leonard brought up his right hand into George's face, his back uncoiling behind it. George walked backward onto the tender new lawn. He looked at the sky in a disappointed way, as if it had

40

dropped something on him. Then he shook his head and started back toward Leonard. He tripped on a garden hose and almost fell.

I stepped between them, facing Leonard. "He's had it. Knock it off, eh?"

George shouldered me aside. I grabbed his arms.

"Let me at the little runt," he said through bloody lips.

"You don't want to get hurt, boy."

"Worry about him."

He was stronger than I was. He broke loose and spun me away. Threw another wild one which split the back of his suit coat and accomplished nothing else. Leonard inclined his head two or three inches from the vertical and watched the fist go by. George staggered off balance. Leonard hit him between the eyes with his right hand, hit him again with his left as he went down. George's head made a dull noise on the flagstone. He lay still.

Leonard polished the knuckles of his right fist with his left hand, as though it were a bronze object of art.

"You shouldn't use it on amateurs."

He answered reasonably: "I don't unless I have to. Only sometimes I get damn browned off, big slobs thinkin' they can push me around. I been pushed around plenty, I don't have to take it no more." He balanced himself on one foot and touched George's outflung arm with the tip of his big toe. "Maybe you better take him to a doctor."

"Maybe I better."

"I hit him pretty hard."

He showed me the knuckles of his right hand. They were swelling and turning blue. Otherwise, the fight had done him good. He was cheerful and relaxed, and he pranced a little when he moved, like a stallion. Featherhead was watching him from the window. She had on a linen dress now. She saw me looking at her, and moved back out of sight.

Leonard turned on the hose and ran cold water over George's head. George opened his eyes and tried to sit up. Leonard turned off the hose.

"He'll be all right. They don't come out of it that fast when they're bad hurt. Anyway, I hit him in self-defense, you're a witness to that. If there's any beef about it, you can take it up with Leroy Frost at Helio."

"Leroy Frost is your fixer, eh?"

He gave me a faintly anxious smile. "You know Leroy?"

"A little."

"Maybe we won't bother him about it, eh? Leroy, he's got a lot of troubles. How much you make in a day?"

"Fifty when I'm working."

"Okay, how's about I slip you fifty and you take care of the carcass?" He turned on all his neon charm. "Incidently, I should apologize. I kind of lost my head there for a minute. I shouldn't ought to of took the sucker punch on you. You can pay me back some time."

"Maybe I will at that."

"Sure you will, and I'll let you. How's the breadbasket, cap?"

"Feels like a broken tennis racquet."

"But no hard feelings, eh?"

"No hard feelings."

"Swell, swell."

He offered me his hand. I set myself on my heels and hit him in the jaw. It wasn't the smartest thing in the world to do. My legs were middle-aging, and still wobbly. If I missed the nerve, he could run circles around me and cut me to ribbons with his left alone. But the connection was good.

I left him lying. The front door was unlocked, and I went in. The girl wasn't in the living-room or on the terrace. Her terrycloth towel was crumpled on the bedroom floor. A sun-hat woven of plaited straw lay on the floor beside it. The leather band inside the hat was stamped with the legend: "Handmade in Mexico for the Taos Shop."

A motor coughed and roared behind the wall. I found the side door which opened from the utility room into the garage. She was at the wheel of the Jaguar, looking at me with her mouth wide open. She locked the door on her side before I got hold of the handle. Then it was torn from my fist.

The Jaguar screeched in the turnaround, laying down black spoor, and leaped up the driveway to the road. I let it go. I couldn't leave George with Leonard.

They were sitting up in front of the house, exchanging dim looks of hatred across the flagstone walk. George was bleeding from the mouth. The flesh around one of his eyes was changing color. Leonard was unmarked, but I saw when he got to his feet that there was a change in him.

He had a hangdog air, a little furtive, as if I'd jarred him back into his past. He kept running his fingers over his nose and mouth.

"Don't worry," I said, "you're still gorgeous."

"Funny boy. You think it's funny? I kill you, it wasn't for this." He displayed his swollen right hand.

"You offered me a sucker punch, remember. Now we're even. Where did she go?"

"*You* can go to hell."

"What's her address?"

42

"Go to hell."

"You might as well give me her address. I got her license number. I can trace her."

"Go right ahead." He gave me a superior look, which probably meant that the Jaguar was his.

"What did she change her mind about? Why did she want out?"

"I can't read minds. I dunno nothin' about her. I service plenty of women, see? They ask me for it, I give 'em a bang sometimes. Does that mean I'm responsible?"

I reached for him. He backed away, his face sallow and pinched. "Keep your hands off me. And drag your butt off of my property. I'm warning you, I got a loaded shotgun in the house."

He went as far as the door, and turned to watch us. George was on his hands and knees now. I got one of his arms draped over my shoulders and heaved him up to his feet. He walked like a man trying to balance himself on a spring mattress.

When I turned for a last look at the house, Leonard was on the doorstep, combing his hair.

xxxxxxxxx *chapter* 9

I DROVE down the long grade to Beverly Hills, slowly, because I was feeling accident-prone. There were days when you could put your finger on the point of stress and everything fell into rational patterns around you. And there were the other days.

George bothered me. He sat hunched over with his head in his hands, groaning from time to time. He had a fine instinct, even better than mine, for pushing his face in at the wrong door and getting it bloodied. He needed a keeper: I seemed to be elected.

I took him to my own doctor, a G.P. named Wolfson who had his office on Santa Monica Boulevard. Wolfson laid him out on a padded metal table in a cubicle, went over his face and skull with thick, deft fingers, flashed a small light in his eyes, and performed other rituals.

"How did it happen?"

"He fell down and hit his head on a flagstone walk."

"Who pushed him? You?"

"A mutual friend. We won't go into that. Is he all right?"

"Might be a slight concussion. You ever hurt your head before?"

"Playing football, I have," George said.

"Hurt it bad?"

"I suppose so. I've blacked out a couple of times."

"I don't like it," Wolfson said to me. "You ought to take him to the hospital. He should spend a couple of days in bed, at least."

"No!" George sat up, forcing the doctor backward. His eyes rolled heavily in their swollen sockets. "A couple of days is all I've got. I have to see her."

Wolfson raised his eyebrows. "See who?"

"His wife. She left him."

"So what? It happens every day. It happened to you. He's still got to go to bed."

George swung his legs off the table and stood up shakily. His face was the color of newly poured cement. "I refuse to go to the hospital."

"You're making a serious decision," Wolfson said coldly. He was a fat doctor who loved only medicine and music.

"I can put him to bed at my house. Will that do?"

Wolfson looked at me dubiously. "Could you keep him down?"

"I think so."

"Very well," George stated solemnly, "I accept the compromise."

Wolfson shrugged. "If that's the best we can do. I'll give him a shot to relax him, and I'll want to see him later."

"You know where I live," I said.

In a two-bedroom stucco cottage on a fifty-foot lot off Olympic. For a while the second bedroom hadn't been used. Then for a while it had been. When it was vacated finally, I sold the bed to a secondhand-furniture dealer and converted the room into a study. Which for some reason I hated to use.

I put George in my bed. My cleaning woman had been there that morning, and the sheets were fresh. Hanging his torn clothes on a chair, I asked myself what I thought I was doing and why. I looked across the hall at the door of the bedless bedroom where nobody slept any more. An onion taste of grief rose at the back of my throat. It seemed very important to me that George should get together with his wife and take her away from Los Angeles. And live happily ever after.

His head rolled on the pillow. He was part way out by now, under the influence of paraldehyde and Leonard's sedative fists:

"Listen to me, Archer. You're a good friend to me."

"Am I?"

"The only friend I have within two thousand miles. You've got to find her for me."

"I did find her. What good did it do?"

"I know, I shouldn't have come tearing down to the house like that. I frightened her. I always do the wrong thing. Christ, I wouldn't hurt a hair of her head. You've got to tell her that for me. Promise you will."

"All right. Now go to sleep."

But there was something else he had to say: "At least she's alive, isn't she?"

"If she's a corpse, she's a lively one."

"Who are these people she's mixed up with? Who was the little twerp in the pajamas?"

"Boy named Torres. He used to be a boxer, if that's any comfort to you."

"Is he the one who threatened her?"

"Apparently."

George raised himself on his elbows. "I've heard that name Torres. Hester used to have a friend named Gabrielle Torres."

"She told you about Gabrielle, did she?"

"Yes. She told me that night she—confessed her sins to me." His gaze moved dully around the room and settled in a corner, fixed on something invisible. His dry lips moved, trying to name the thing he saw:

"Her friend was shot and killed, in the spring of last year. Hester left California right after."

"Why would she do that?"

"I don't know. She seemed to blame herself for the other girl's death. And she was afraid of being called as a witness, if the case ever came to trial."

"It never did."

He was silent, his eyes on the thing in the empty corner. "What else did she tell you, George?"

"About the men she'd slept with, from the time that she was hardly in her teens."

"That Hester had slept with?"

"Yes. It bothered me more than the other, even. I don't know what that makes me."

Human, I thought.

George closed his eyes. I turned the venetian blinds down and went into the other room to telephone. The call was to CHP headquarters, where a friend of mine named Mercero worked as a dispatcher. Fortunately he was on the daytime shift. No, he wasn't busy but he could be any minute, accidents always came in pairs and triples to foul him up. He'd try to give me a quick report on the Jaguar's license number.

I sat beside the telephone and lit a cigarette and tried to have a brilliant intuition, like all the detectives in books and some in real life. The only one that occurred to me was that the Jaguar belonged to Lance Leonard and would simply lead me around in a circle.

Cigarette smoke rumbling in my stomach reminded me that I was hungry. I went out to the kitchen and made myself a ham-and-cheese sandwich on rye and opened a bottle of beer. My cleaning woman had left a note on the kitchen table:

> Dear Mr. Archer, Arrived nine left twelve noon, I need the money for today will drive by and pick it up this aft, please leave $3.75 in mailbox if your out. Yours truly, Beatrice M. Jackson.
> P.S.—There is mouse dirt in the cooler, you buy a trap Ill set it out, mouse dirt is not sanitary.
>   Yours truly, Beatrice M. Jackson.

I sealed four dollars in an envelope, wrote her name across the face, and took it out to the front porch. A pair of house wrens chitchatting under the eaves made several snide references to me. The mailbox was full of mail: four early bills, two requests for money from charitable organizations, a multigraphed letter from my Congressman which stated that he was alert to the threat, a brochure describing a book on the Secrets of Connubial Bliss marked down to $2.98 and sold only to doctors, clergymen, social-service workers, and other interested parties; and a New Year's card from a girl who had passed out on me at a pre-Christmas party. This was signed "Mona" and carried a lyric message:

> True friendship is a happy thing
> Which makes both men and angels sing.
> As the year begins, and another ends,
> Resolved: that we shall still be friends.

I sat down at the hall table with my beer and tried to draft an answer. It was hard. Mona passed out at parties because she had lost a husband in Korea and a small son at Children's Hospital. I began to remember that I had no son, either. A man got lonely in the stucco wilderness, pushing forty with no chick, no child. Mona was pretty enough, and bright enough, and all she wanted was another child. What was I waiting for? A well-heeled virgin with her name in the Blue Book?

I decided to call Mona. The telephone rang under my hand. "Mercero?" I said.

But it was Bassett's voice, breathy in my ear: "I tried to get you earlier."

"I've been here for the last half-hour."

"Does that mean you've found her, or given up?"

"Found her and lost her again." I explained how, to the accompaniment of oh's and ah's and tut-tut's from the other end of the line. "This hasn't been one of my days so far. My biggest mistake was taking Wall along."

"I hope he's not badly hurt?" There was a vein of malice in Bassett's solicitude.

"He's a hardhead, he'll survive."

"Why do you suppose she ran away from him this time?"

"Simple panic, maybe. Maybe not. There seems to be more to this than a lost-wife case. Gabrielle Torres keeps cropping up."

"It's odd you should mention her. I've been thinking about her off and on all morning—ever since you commented on her picture."

"So have I. There are three of them in the picture: Gabrielle and Hester and Lance. Gabrielle was murdered, the murderer hasn't been caught. The other two were very close to her. Lance was her cousin. Hester was her best friend."

"You're not suggesting that Lance, or Hester—?" His voice was hushed, but buzzing with implications.

"I'm only speculating. I don't think Hester killed her friend. I do think she knows something about the murder that nobody else knows."

"Did she say so?"

"Not to me. To her husband. It's all pretty vague. Except that nearly two years later she turns up in Coldwater Canyon. She's suddenly prosperous, and so is her little friend with the big fists."

"It does give one to think, doesn't it?" He tittered nervously. "What do *you* have in mind?"

"Blackmail is most obvious, and I never rule out the obvious. Lance spread the word that he's under contract at Helio-Graff, and it seems to be legit. The question is, how did he latch on to a contract with a big independent? He's a good-looking boy, but it takes more than that these days. You knew him when he was a lifeguard at the Club?"

"Naturally. Frankly, I wouldn't have hired him if his uncle hadn't been extremely persistent. We generally use college boys in the summer."

"Did he have acting ambitions?"

"Not to my knowledge. He was training to be a pugilist." Bassett's voice was contemptuous.

"He's an actor now. It could be he's an untutored genius—stranger things have happened—but I doubt it. On top of that, Hester claims to have a contract, too."

"With Helio-Graff?"

"I don't know. I intend to find out."

"You'll probably find it's with Helio-Graff." His voice had become sharper and more definite. "I've hesitated to tell you this, though it's what I called you about. In my position, one acquires the habit of silence. However, I was talking to a certain person this morning, and Hester's name came up. So did the name of Simon Graff. They were seen together in rather compromising circumstances."

"Where?"

"In a hotel in Santa Monica—the Windsor, I believe."

"It fits. She used to live there. When was this?"

"A few weeks ago. My informant saw them coming out of a room on one of the upper floors. At least, Mr. Graff came out. Hester only came as far as the door."

"Who is your informant?"

"I couldn't possibly tell you that, old man. It was one of our members."

"So is Simon Graff."

"Don't think I'm not aware of it. Mr. Graff is the most powerful single member of the Club."

"Aren't you sticking your neck out, telling me this?"

"Yes. I am. I hope my confidence in you—in your discretion—hasn't been misplaced."

"Relax. I'm a clam. But what about your switchboard?"

"I'm on the switchboard myself," he said.

"Is Graff still out there?"

"No. He left hours ago."

"Where can I find him?"

"I have no idea. He's having a party here tonight, but you mustn't approach him. You're not on any account to approach him."

"All right." But I made a mental reservation. "This secret informant of yours—it wouldn't be Mrs. Graff?"

"Of course not." His voice was fading. Either he was lying, or the decision to tell me about the Windsor Hotel episode had drained his energy. "You mustn't even consider such a thought."

48

"All right," I said, considering it.

I called the Highway Patrol number and got Mercero:

"Sorry, Lew, no can do. Three accidents since you called, and I've been hopping." He hung up on me.

It didn't matter. A pattern was forming in the case, like a motif in discordant, angry music. I had the slimmest of leads, a sun-hat from a shop in Santa Monica. I also had the queer tumescent feeling you get when something is going to break.

I looked in on George before I left the house. He was snoring. I shouldn't have left him.

xxxxxxxxxx *chapter* 10

THE Taos Shop was a little tourist trap on the Coast Highway. It sold Navajo blankets and thunderbird necklaces and baskets and hats and pottery in an atmosphere of disordered artiness. A mouse blonde in a brown Indian blouse clicked her wampum at me languidly and asked me what I desired, a gift for my wife perhaps? I told her I was looking for another man's wife. She had romantic plum-colored eyes, and it seemed like the right approach. She said:

"How fascinating. Are you a detective?"

I said I was.

"How fascinating."

But when I told her about the hat, she shook her head regretfully. "I'm sorry. I'm sure it's one of ours, all right—we import them ourselves from Mexico. But we sell so many of them, I couldn't possibly—" She waved a willowy arm toward a tray piled with hats at the far end of the counter. "Perhaps if you described her?"

I described her. She shook her head dolefully. "I never could tell one Hollywood blonde from another."

"Neither could I."

"Ninety-nine and forty-four one-hundredths of them are blonde out of a bottle, anyway. I could be a blonde if I wanted to, just with a rinse now and then. Only I've got too much personal pride." She leaned toward me, and her wampum swung invitingly over the counter. "I'm sorry I can't help you."

"Thanks for trying. It was an off-chance anyway." I started out, and turned. "Her name is Hester Wall, by the way. That doesn't ring a bell?"

"Hester? I know of a Hester, but her last name isn't Wall. Her mother used to work here."

"What is her last name?"

"Campbell."

"She's the one. Campbell's her maiden name."

"Now, isn't that fascinating?" She smiled in dimpled glee, and her large eyes glowed. "The most exciting things happen to *people*, don't you think? I suppose you're looking for her about her inheritance?"

"Inheritance?"

"Yes. It's why Mrs. Campbell quit her job, on account of her daughter's inheritance. Don't tell me she's come into another fortune!"

"Who did she inherit the first one from?"

"Her husband, her late husband." She paused, and her soft mouth quivered. "It's sort of sad, when you realize, nobody inherits anything unless somebody else dies."

"That's true. And you say her husband died?"

"Yes. She married a wealthy husband in Canada, and he died."

"Is that what Hester told you?"

"No. Mrs. Campbell told me. I don't know Hester myself." Her face went blank suddenly. "I certainly hope it's not a false alarm. We were all so thrilled when Mrs. Campbell got the news. She's a dear, really, such a cute little duck for her age, and she used to have money, you know. Nobody begrudges her good fortune."

"When did she find out about it?"

"A couple of weeks ago. She only quit the beginning of this week. She's moving in with her daughter."

"Then she can tell me where her daughter is. If you'll tell me where *she* lives."

"I have her address someplace."

"Doesn't she have a phone?"

"No, she uses a neighbor's phone. Teeny Campbell's had hard sledding these last few years." She paused, and gave me a liquid look. "I'm not going to give you her address if it means trouble for her. Why are you looking for Hester?"

"One of her Canadian relatives wants to get in touch with her."

"One of her husband's relatives?"

"Yes."

"Cross your heart and hope to die."

"Cross my heart," I said. It felt like the kind of lie that would bring me bad luck. It was. "And hope to die."

Mrs. Campbell lived on a poor street of stucco and frame cottages half hidden by large, ancient oak trees. In their sunflecked shadows, pre-school children played their killing games: Bang bang, you're dead; I'm not dead; you are so dead. A garbage truck on its rounds started a chorus of dogs barking in resentment at the theft of their masters' garbage.

Mrs. Campbell's cottage stood behind a flaked stucco wall in which a rusty gate stood permanently open. There was a new cardboard FOR SALE sign wired to the gate. In the courtyard, red geraniums had thrust up through a couple of stunted lime trees and converted them into red-flowering bushes which seemed to be burning in the sun. The thorned and brighter fire of a bougainvillæa vine surged up the front porch and the roof.

I stepped in under its cool shade and knocked on the screen door, which was tufted with cotton to ward off flies. A tiny barred window was set in the inner door. Its shutter snapped open, and an eye looked out at me. It was a blue eye, a little faded, surrounded with curled lashes and equipped with a voice like the sparrows' in the oak trees:

"Good morning, are you from Mr. Gregory?"

I mumbled something indistinguishable which might have been, yes, I was.

"Goodie, I've been expecting you." She unlocked the door and opened it wide. "Come in, Mr.—?"

"Archer," I said.

"I'm absotively delighted to see you, Mr. Archer."

She was a small, straight-bodied woman in a blue cotton dress too short and frilly for her age. This would be about fifty, though everything about her conspired to deny it. For an instant in the dim little box of a hallway, her bird voice and quick graces created the illusion that she was an adolescent blonde.

In the sunlit living-room, the illusion died. The dry cracks of experience showed around her eyes and mouth, and she couldn't smile them away. Her ash-blond boyish bob was fading into gray, and her neck was withering. I kind of liked her, though. She saw that. She wasn't stupid.

She ankled around the small living-room, lifting clean ashtrays and setting them down again. "Do have a chair, or would you prefer to stand up and look around? How nice of you to be interested in my little nest. Please notice the sea view, which is one of the little luxuries I have. Isn't it lovely?"

She posed her trim, small body, extended her arm toward the window and held it stiff and still, slightly bent up at the elbow, fingers apart. There was a view of the sea: a meager blue ribbon, tangled among the oak-tree branches.

"Very nice." But I was wondering what ghostly audience or dead daddy she was playing to. And how long she would go on taking me for a prospective buyer.

The room was crammed with dark old furniture made for a larger room, and for larger people: a carved refectory table flanked by high-backed Spanish chairs, an overstuffed red plush divan, thick red drapes on either side of the window. These made a cheerless contrast with the plaster walls and ceiling, which were dark green and mottled with stains from old leaks in the roof.

She caught me looking at the waterstains. "It won't happen again, I can guarantee you that. I had the roof repaired last fall, and, as a matter of fact, I've been saving up to redecorate this room. When all of a sudden my big move came up. I've had the most wondrous good luck, you know, or should I say my daughter has." She paused in a dramatic listening attitude, as if she were receiving a brief message in code on her back fillings. "But let me tell you over coffee. Poor man, you look quite peaked. I know what house-hunting is."

Her generosity disturbed me. I hated to accept anything from her under false pretenses. But before I could frame an answer she'd danced away through a swinging door to the kitchen. She came back with a breakfast tray on which a silver coffee set shone proudly, laid it on the table, and hovered over it. It was a pleasure to watch her pour. I complimented the coffeepot.

"Thank you very mooch, kind sir. It was one of my wedding presents, I've kept it all these years. I've held on to a lot of things, and now I'm glad I did, now that I'm moving back into the big house." She touched her lips with her fingertips and chuckled musically. "But of course you can't know what I'm talking about, unless Mr. Gregory told you."

"Mr. Gregory?"

"Mr. Gregory the realtor." She perched on the divan beside me, confidentially. "It's why I'm willing to sell without a cent of profit, as long as I get my equity out of this place. I'm moving out the first of the week, to go and live with my daughter. You see, my daughter is flying to Italy for a month or so, and she wants me to be in the big house, to look after it while she's gone. Which I'll be very happy to do, I can tell you."

"You're moving into a larger house?"

"Yes indeedy I am. I'm moving back into my own house, the one my girls were born in. You might not think it to look around you, unless you have an eye for good furniture, but I used to live in a grand big house in Beverly Hills." She nodded her head vigorously, as though I'd contradicted her. "I lost it—we lost it way back before the war when my husband left us. But now that clever daughter of mine has bought it back! And she's asked me to live with her!" She hugged her thin chest. "How she must love her little mother! Eh? Eh?"

"She certainly must," I said. "It sounds as if she's come into some money."

"Yes." She plucked at my sleeve. "I *told* her it would happen, if she kept faith and worked hard and made herself agreeable to people. I told the girls the very day we moved out that someday we'd move back. And, sure enough, it's happened, Hester's come in to all this uranium money."

"She found uranium?"

"Mr. Wallingford did. He was a Canadian mining tycoon. Hester married an older man, just as I did in my time. Unfortunately the poor man died before they'd been married a year. I never met him."

"What was his name?"

"George Wallingford," she said. "Hester draws a substantial monthly income from the estate. And then she's got her movie money, too. Everything seems to have broken for her at once."

I watched her closely, but could see no sign that she was lying consciously.

"What does she do in the movies?"

"Many things," she said with a wavy flip of her hand. "She dances and swims and dives—she was a professional diver—and of course she acts. Her *father* was an actor, back in the good old days. You've heard of Raymond Campbell?"

I nodded. The name belonged to a swashbuckling silent-movie star who had tried to make the transition to the talkies and been tripped by advancing years and a tenor voice. I could remember a time in the early twenties when Campbell's serials filled the Long Beach movie houses on Saturday afternoons. Me they had filled with inspiration: his Inspector Fate of Limehouse series had helped to make me a cop, for good or ill. And when the cops went sour, the memory of Inspector Fate had helped to pull me out of the Long Beach force.

She said: "You *do* remember Raymond, don't you? Did you know him personally?"

"Just on the screen. It's been a long time. What ever happened to him?"

"He died," she said, "he died of a broken heart, way back

in the depression. He hadn't had a picture for years, his friends turned against him, he was terribly in debt. And so he died." Her eyes became glazed with tears, but she smiled bravely through them like one of Raymond Campbell's leading ladies. "I carried on the faith, however. I was an actress myself, before I subordinated my life to Raymond's, and I brought up my girls to follow in his footsteps, just as he would have wished. One of them, at least, has made the most of it."

"What does your other daughter do?"

"Rina? She's a psychiatric nurse, can you imagine? It's always been a wonder to me that two girls so close in age and looks could differ so in temperament. Rina actually doesn't *have* any temperament. With all the artistic training I gave her, she grew up just as cold and hard and practical as they come. Why, I'd drop dead with shock if Rina ever offered me a home. No!" she cried melodramatically. "Rina would rather spend her time with crazy people. Why would a pretty girl do a thing like that?"

"Maybe she wants to help them."

Mrs. Campbell looked blank. "She could have found a more feminine way. Hester brings real joy to others without demeaning herself."

A funny look must have crossed my face. She regarded me shrewdly, then snapped her eyelids wide and turned on her brights. "But I mustn't bore you with my family affairs. You came to look at the house. It's got just the three rooms, but it's *most* convenient, especially the kitchen."

"Don't bother with that, Mrs. Campbell. I've been imposing on your hospitality."

"Why, no you haven't. Not at all."

"I have, though. I'm a detective."

"A detective?" Her tiny fingers clawed at my arm and took hold. She said in a new voice, a full octave lower than her bird tones: "Has something happened to Hester?"

"Not that I know of. I'm simply looking for her."

"Is she in trouble?"

"She may be."

"I knew it. I've been so afraid that something would go wrong. Things never work out for us. Something goes wrong, always." She touched her face with her fingertips: it was like crumpled paper. "I'm in a damned hole," she said hoarsely. "I gave up my job on the strength of this, and I owe half the people in town. If Hester falls down on me now, I don't know what I'll do." She dropped her hands, and raised her chin. "Well, let's have the bad news. Is it all a bunch of lies?"

"Is what a bunch of lies?"

"What I've been telling you, what she told me. About the movie contract and the trip to Italy and the rich husband who died. I had my doubts about it, you know—I'm not that much of a fool."

"Part of it may be true. Part of it isn't. Her husband isn't dead. He isn't old, and he isn't rich, and he wants her back. Which is where I come in."

"Is that all there is to it? No." Her eyes regarded me with hard suspicion. The shock had precipitated a second personality in her, and I wondered how much of the hardness belonged to her, and how much to hysteria. "You're holding out on me. You admitted she's in trouble."

"I said she may be. What makes you so sure?"

"You're a hard man to get information out of." She stood up in front of me, planting her fists on her insignificant hips and leaning forward like a bantam fighter. "Now don't try to give me the runaround, though God knows I'm used to it after thirty years in this town. Is she or isn't she in trouble?"

"I can't answer that, Mrs. Campbell. So far as I know, there's nothing against her. All I want to do is talk to her."

"On what subject?"

"The subject of going back to her husband."

"Why doesn't she talk to her husband himself?"

"He intends to. At the moment he's a little under the weather. And we've had a lot of trouble locating her."

"Who is he?"

"A young newspaperman from Toronto. Name's George Wall."

"George Wall," she said. "George Wallingford."

"Yes," I said, "it figures."

"What sort of a man is this George Wall?"

"I think he's a good one, or he will be when he grows up."

"Is he in love with her?"

"Very much. Maybe too much."

"And what you want from me is her address?"

"If you know it."

"I ought to know it. I lived there for nearly ten years. 14 Manor Crest Drive, Beverly Hills. But if that's all you wanted, why didn't you say so? You let me beat my gums and make a fool of myself. Why do that to me?"

"I'm sorry. It wasn't very nice. But this may be more than a runaway-wife case. You suggested yourself that Hester's in trouble."

"Trouble is what the word detective means to me."

"Has she been in trouble before?"

"We won't go into that."

"Have you been seeing much of her this winter?"

"Very little. I spent one weekend with her—the weekend before last."

"In the Beverly Hills house?"

"Yes. She'd just moved in, and she wanted my advice about redecorating some of the rooms. The people who had it before Hester didn't keep it up—not like the days when we had our Japanese couple." Her blue gaze strained across the decades, and returned to the present. "Anyway, we had a good time together, Hester and I. A wonderful weekend all by our lonesomes, chatting and tending to her clothes and pretending it was old times. And it ended up with Hester inviting me to move in the first of the year."

"That was nice of her."

"Wasn't it? I was so surprised and pleased. We hadn't been close at all for several years. I'd hardly seen her, as a matter of fact. And then, out of the blue, she asked me to come and live with her."

"Why do you think she did?"

The question seemed to appeal to her realistic side. She sat on the edge of her chair, in thinking position, her fingertips to her temple. "It's hard to say. Certainly not on account of my beautiful blue eyes. Of course, she's going to be away and she needs someone to stay in the house and look after it. I think she's been lonely, too."

"And frightened?"

"She didn't act frightened. Maybe she was. She wouldn't tell me if she was. My girls don't tell me anything." She inserted the knuckle of her right thumb between her teeth, and wrinkled her face like a baby monkey. "Will I still be able to move the first of the year? Do you think I will?"

"I wouldn't count on it."

"But the house must belong to her. She wouldn't spend all that money on redecorating. Mr. Archer—is that your name? Archer?—where is all the money coming from?"

"I have no idea," I said, though I had several.

MANOR CREST DRIVE was one of those quiet palm-lined avenues which had been laid out just before the twenties went into their final convulsions. The houses weren't huge and fantastic like some of the rococo palaces in the surrounding hills, but they had pretensions. Some were baronial pseudo-Tudor with faked half-timbered façades. Others were imitation Mizener Spanish, thick-walled and narrow-windowed like stucco fortresses built to resist imaginary Moors. The street was good, but a little disappointed-looking, as though maybe the Moors had already been and gone.

Number 14 was one of the two-story Spanish fortresses. It sat well back from the street behind a Monterey cypress hedge. Water from a sprinkling system danced in the air above the hedge, rainbowed for an instant as I passed. A dusty gray Jaguar was parked in the driveway.

I left my car in front of one of the neighboring houses, walked back, and strolled down the driveway to the Jaguar. According to the white slip on the steering-post, it was registered to Lance Leonard.

I turned and surveyed the front of the house. Tiny gusts from the sprinkler wet my face. It was the only sign of life around. The black oak door was closed, the windows heavily draped. The pink tile roof pressed down on the house like a lid.

I mounted the stoop and pressed the bellpush and heard the electric buzzer sound deep inside the building. I thought I heard footsteps approaching the ironbound door. Then I thought I heard breathing. I knocked on the door and waited. The breathing on the other side of the door, if it was breathing, went away or ceased.

I knocked a few more times and waited some more, in vain. Walking back toward the driveway, I caught a movement from the corner of my eye. The drape in the end window twitched at the edge. When I looked directly at it, it had fallen back in place. I reached across a spiky pyracantha and tapped on the window, just for kicks. Kicks were all I got.

I returned to my car, U-turned at the next intersection, drove back past the pink-roofed house, and parked where I could watch its front in my rear-view mirror. The street was very quiet. Along both sides of it, the fronds of the palms hung in the air like static green explosions caught by a camera. In the middle distance, the tower of the Beverly Hills City Hall stood flat white against the flat blue sky. Nothing happened to mark the passage of time, except that the hands of my wristwatch bracketed two o'clock and moved on past.

About two ten, a car rolled into sight from the direction of the City Hall. It was an old black Lincoln, long and heavy as a hearse, with gray curtains over the rear windows completing the resemblance. A man in a black felt hat was at the wheel. He was doing about fifty in a twenty-five-mile zone. As he entered the block I was in, he started to slow down.

I reached for a yesterday's newspaper in the back seat and propped it up on the wheel to hide my face. Its headlines read like ancient history. The Lincoln seemed to take a long time to pass me. Then it did. Small-eyed, saddle-nosed, rubber-mouthed, its driver's face was unforgettable. Unforgettably ugly.

He turned into the driveway of Number 14, entering my rear-view mirror, and parked beside the Jaguar and got out. He moved quickly and softly, without swinging his arms. In a long charcoal-gray raglan topcoat, his slope-shouldered body looked like a torpedo sliding on its base.

The door opened before he knocked. I couldn't see who opened it. The door closed for a while, two or three long minutes, and then opened again.

Lance Leonard came out of the house. In a queer little hustling run, like a puppet jerked by wires, he descended the steps and crossed the lawn to the Jaguar, not noticing the sprinkler, though it wet his white silk open-necked shirt and spotted his light-beige slacks.

The Jaguar backed roaring into the street. As it raced past on squealing tires I caught a glimpse of Lance Leonard's face. His face was a blank, dead yellow. The nose and chin were drawn sharp. The eyes blazed black. They didn't see me.

The Jaguar plunged away into silence. I got out the .38 Special which I kept in the dash compartment and crossed the street. The Lincoln was registered to a Theodore Marfeld who lived at a Coast Highway address in South Malibu. Its black leather interior was shabby and smelled of cat. The back seat and floor were covered with sheets of heavy wrapping paper. The dashboard clock had stopped at eleven twenty.

I went to the door of the house and lifted my fist to knock and saw that the door was standing slightly ajar. I pushed it wider, stepped into a dim hall with a round Moorish ceiling. Ahead to my left a flight of red tile steps rose cumbrously through the ceiling. To the right, an inner door threw a bent fan of brightness across the floor and up the blank plaster side of the staircase.

A hatted shadow moved into the brightness and blotted most of it out. The head and shoulder of Saddlenose leaned from the doorway.

"Mr. Marfeld?" I said.

"Yeah. Who the hell are you? You got no right barging into a private residence. Get the hell out."

"I'd like to speak to Miss Campbell."

"What about? Who sent you?" he said mouthily.

"Her mother sent me, as a matter of fact. I'm a friend of the family. Are you a friend of the family?"

"Yeah. A friend of the family."

Marfeld raised his right hand to his face. His left hand was out of sight behind the door frame. I was holding the gun in my pocket with my finger on the trigger. Marfeld seemed puzzled. He took hold of the entire lower part of his face and pulled it sideways. There was a red smear on the ball of his thumb. It left a red thumbprint on the side of his indented nose.

"Cut yourself?"

He turned his hand around and looked at his thumb and closed his fist over it. "Yeah, I cut myself."

"I'm an expert at First Aid. If you're in pain, I have some monoacetic acid ester of salicylic acid in the car. I also have some five-per-cent tincture of iodine to offset the risk of blood-poisoning or other serious infection."

His right hand pushed the words away from his face. Neurosis cheeped surprisingly in his voice. "Shut up, God damn you, I can't stand doubletalk." He got himself under control and returned to his lower-register personality. "You heard me tell you to get out of here. What are you waiting for?"

"That's no way for a friend of the family to talk to another friend of the family."

He leaned round-shouldered out of the doorway, a metal rod glittering in his left hand. It was a brass poker. He shifted it to his right hand and lunged toward me, so close I could smell his breath. His breath was sour with trouble. "God-damn doublemouth."

I could have shot him through my pocket. Maybe I should have. The trouble was, I didn't know him well enough to shoot him. And I trusted the speed of my reflexes, forgetting Leonard's knockdown punch and the residue of languor in my legs.

Marfeld raised the poker. A dark drop flew from its hooked point and spattered the plaster wall like a splash of wet red paint. My eye stayed on it a millisecond too long. The poker seared and chilled the side of my head. It was a glancing blow, or I would have gone all the way out. As it was, the floor upended and rapped my knees and elbows and my forehead. The gun went skittering through a hole in the broken light.

I crawled up the steep floor toward it. Marfeld stamped at my fingers. I got my hands on one of his feet, my shoulder against his knee, and threw him over backward. He went down hard and lay whooping for breath.

I groped for the gun among jagged shards of light. The bright room beyond the doorway flashed on my angled vision with a hallucination's vividness. It was white and black and red. The blonde girl in the linen dress lay on a white rug in front of a raised black fireplace. Her face was turned away. An inkblot of red darkness spread around it.

Then there were footsteps behind me, and as I turned, the front end of the Sunset Limited hit the side of my head and knocked me off the rails into deep red darkness.

I came to, conscious of motion and a rumbling noise in my stomach which gradually detached itself from me and became the sound of a car engine. I was sitting propped up in the middle of the front seat. Shoulders were jammed against me on both sides. I opened my eyes and recognized the dashboard clock which had stopped at eleven twenty.

"People are dying to get in there," Marfeld said across me from the right.

My eyeballs moved grittily in their sockets. Marfeld had my gun on his knee. The driver, on my left, said:

"Brother, you kill me. You pull the same old gag out of the file every time you pass the place."

We were passing Forest Lawn. Its Elysian fields were distorted by moving curves, heat waves in the air or behind my eyes. I felt a craving nostalgia for peace. I thought how nice it would be to lie down in the beautiful cemetery and listen to organ music. Then I noticed the driver's hands on the wheel. They were large, dirty hands, with large, dirty fingernails, and they made me mad.

I reached for the gun on Marfeld's knee. Marfeld pulled it away like somebody taking candy from a baby. My reactions were so feeble and dull it scared me. He rapped my knuckles with the gun muzzle.

"How about that? The sleeper awakes."

My wooden tongue clacked around in my desiccated mouth and produced some words: "You jokers know the penalty for kidnapping?"

"Kidnapping?" The driver had a twisted little face which sprouted queerly out of a massive body. He gave me a corkscrew look. "I didn't hear of any kidnapping lately. You must of been dreaming."

"Yeah," Marfeld said. "Don't try to kid me, peeper. I was on the county cops for fifteen years. I know the law and what you can do and what you can't do. You can't go bulling into a private house with a deadly weapon. You was way out of line and I had a right to stop you. Christ, I could of killed you, they wouldn't even booked me."

"Count your blessings," the driver said. "You peepers, some of you, act like you think you can get away with murder."

"Somebody does."

Marfeld turned violently in the seat and pushed the gun muzzle into the side of my stomach. "What's that? Say that again. I didn't catch it."

My wits were still widely scattered around Los Angeles County. I had just enough of them with me to entertain a couple of ideas. They couldn't be sure, unless I told them, that I had seen the girl in the bright room. If she was dead and they knew I knew, I'd be well along on my way to a closed-coffin funeral.

"What was that about murder?"

Marfeld leaned hard on the gun. I tensed my stomach muscles against its pressure. The taste of the little seeds they put in rye bread rose in my throat. I concentrated on holding it down.

Marfeld got tired of prodding me after a while, and sat back with the gun on his knee. "Okay. You can do your talking to Mr. Frost."

He made it sound as if nothing worse could ever happen to me.

✖✖✖✖✖✖✖✖✖✖ *chapter* 12

LEROY FROST was not only the head of Helio-Graff's private police force. He had other duties, both important and obscure. In certain areas, he could fix a drunk-driving or narcotics rap. He knew how to bring pressure to settle a divorce suit or a statutory-rape charge out of court. Barbiturate suicides changed, in his supple hands, to accidental overdoses. Having served for a time as deputy security chief of a Washington agency, he advised the editorial department on the purchase of scripts and the casting department on hiring and firing. I knew him slightly, about as well as I wanted to.

The studio occupied a country block surrounded by a high white concrete wall on the far side of San Fernando. Twistyface parked the Lincoln in the semicircular drive. The white-columned colonial façade of the administration building grinned emptily into the sun. Marfeld got out and put my gun in his coat pocket and pointed the pocket at me.

"March."

I marched. Inside in the vestibule a blue-uniformed guard sat in a glass cage. A second uniformed guard came out of the white oak woodwork. He led us up a curved ramp, along a windowless corridor with a cork floor and a glass roof, past rows of bigger-than-life-size photographs: the heads that Graff and, before him, Heliopoulos had blown up huge on the movie screens of the world.

The guard unlocked a door with a polished brass sign: SECURITY. The room beyond was large and barely furnished with filing cabinets and typewriter desks, one of which was occupied by a man in earphones typing away like mad. We passed into an anteroom, with a single desk, unoccupied, and Marfeld disappeared through a further door which had Leroy Frost's name on it.

The guard stayed with me, his right hand near the gun on his hip. His face was heavy and blank and content to be heavy and blank. Its lower half stuck out like the butt end of a ham, in which his mouth was a small, meaningless slit. He stood with his chest pushed out and his stomach held in, wearing his unofficial uniform as though it was very important to him.

I sat on a straight chair against the wall and didn't try to make conversation. The dingy little room had the atmosphere of an unsuccessful dentist's waiting-room. Marfeld came out of Frost's office looking as if the dentist had told him he'd have to have all his teeth pulled. The uniform that walked like a man waved me in.

I'd never seen Leroy Frost's office. It was impressively large, at least the size of a non-producing director's on long-term contract. The furniture was heavy but heterogeneous, probably inherited from various other rooms at various times: leather chairs and a camel-backed English settee and a bulging rosewood Empire desk which was big enough for table tennis.

Frost sat behind the desk, holding a telephone receiver to his head. "Right now," he said into it. "I want you to contact her right now."

He laid the receiver in its cradle and looked up, but not at me. I had to be made to realize how unimportant I was.

He leaned back in his swivel chair, unbuttoned his waist-coat, buttoned it up again. It had mother-of-pearl buttons. There were crossed cavalry sabers on the wall behind him, and the signed photographs of several politicians.

In spite of all this backing, and the word on the outer door, Frost looked insecure. The authority that thick brown eyebrows lent his face was false. Under them, his eyes were glum and yellowish. He had lost weight, and the skin below his eyes and jaw was loose and quilted like a half-sloughed snakeskin. His youthful crewcut only emphasized the fact that he was sick and prematurely aging.

"All right, Lashman," he said to the guard. "You can wait outside. Lew Archer and me, we're buddy-buddy from way back."

His tone was ironic, but he also meant that I had eaten lunch at Musso's with him once and made the mistake of letting him pick up the tab because he had been on an expense account and I hadn't. He didn't invite me to sit down. I sat down anyway, on the arm of one of the leather chairs.

"I don't like this, Frost."

"*You* don't like it. How do you think I feel? Here I thought we were buddy-buddy like I said, I thought there was a basis of mutual live-and-let-live there. My God, Lew, people got to be able to have faith and confidence in each other, or the whole fabric comes to pieces."

"You mean the dirty linen you're washing in public?"

"Now what kind of talk is that? I want you to take me seriously, Lew, it offends my sense of fitness when you don't. Not that *I* matter personally. I'm just another joe working my way through life—a little cog in a big machine." He lowered his eyes in humility. "A *very* big machine. Do you know what our investment is, in plant and contracts and unreleased film and all?"

He paused rhetorically. Through the window to my right, I could see hangarlike sound stages and a series of open sets: Brownstone Front, Midwestern Town, South Sea Village, and the Western Street where dozens of celluloid heroes had taken the death walk. The studio seemed to be shut down, and the sets were deserted, dream scenes abandoned by the minds that had dreamed them.

"Close to fifteen million," Frost said in the tone of a priest revealing a mystery. "A huge investment. And you know what its safety depends on?"

"Sun spots?"

"It isn't sun spots," he said gently. "The subject isn't funny, fifteen million dollars isn't funny. I'll tell you what it depends on. You know it, but I'll tell you anyway." His fingers formed a Gothic arch a few inches in front of his nose. "Number one is glamour, and number two is goodwill. The two things are interdependent and interrelated. Some people think the public will swallow anything since the war—any stinking crud—but I know different. I'm a student of the problem. They swallow just so much, and then we lose them. Especially these days, when the industry's under attack from all sides. We got to keep our glamour dry for the public. We got to hold on to our strategic goodwill. It's psychological warfare, Lew, and I'm on the firing line."

"So you send your troopers out to push citizens around. You want a testimonial from me?"

"You're not just any old ordinary citizen, Lew. You get around so fast and you make so many mistakes. You go bucketing up to Lance Leonard's house and invade his privacy and throw your weight around. I was on the phone to Lance just now. It wasn't smart what you did, and it wasn't ethical, and nobody's going to forget it."

"It wasn't smart," I admitted.

"But it was brilliant compared with the rest of it. Merciful God, Lew, I thought you had some feeling for situations. When we get to the payoff—you trying to force your way into the house of a lady who shall be nameless—" He spread his arms wide and dropped them, unable to span the extent of my infamy.

"What goes on in that house?" I said.

He munched the inside corner of his mouth, watching my face. "If you were smart, as smart as I used to think, you wouldn't ask that question. You'd let it lie. But you're so interested in facts, I'll tell you the one big fact. The less you know, the better for you. The more you know, the worse for you. You got a reputation for discretion. Use it."

"I thought I was."

"Uh-uh, you're not that stupid, kiddo. Nobody is. Your neck's out a mile, and you know it. You follow the thought, or do I have to spell it out in words of one syllable?"

"Spell it out."

He got up from behind the desk. His sick yellow glance avoided mine as he moved around me. He leaned on the back of my chair. His allusive little whisper was scented with some spicy odor from his hair or mouth:

"A nice fellow like you that percolates around where he isn't wanted—he could stop percolating period."

I stood up facing him. "I was waiting for that one, Frost. I wondered when we were getting down to threats."

"Call me Leroy. Hell, I wouldn't threaten you." He repudiated the thought with movements of his shoulders and hands. "I'm not a man of violence, you know that. Mr. Graff doesn't like violence, and I don't like it. That is, when I can prevent it. The trouble with a high-powered operation like this one, sometimes it runs over people by accident when they keep getting in the way. It's our business to make friends, see, and we got friends all over, Vegas, Chicago, all over. Some of them are kind of rough, and they might get an idea in their little pointed heads—you know how it is."

"No. I'm very slow on the uptake. Tell me more."

He smiled with his mouth; his eyes were dull yellow flint. "The point is, I like you, Lew. I get a kick out of knowing that you're in town, in good health and all. I wouldn't want your name to be bandied about on the long-distance telephone."

"It's happened before. I'm still walking around, and feeling pretty good."

"Let's keep it that way. I owe it to you to be frank, as one old friend to another. There's a certain gun that would blast you in a minute if he knew what you been up to. For his own reasons he'd do it, in his own good time. And it could be he knows now. That's a friendly warning."

"I've heard friendlier. Does he have a name?"

"You'd know it, but we won't go into that." Frost leaned forward across the back of the chair, his fingers digging deep into the leather. "Get wise to yourself, Lew. You trying to get yourself killed and drag us down with you, or what?"

"What's all the melodrama about? I was looking for a woman. I found her."

"You found her? You mean you saw her—you talked to her?"

"I didn't get to talk to her. Your goon stopped me at the door."

"So you didn't actually see her?"

"No," I lied.

"You know who she is?"

"I know her name. Hester Campbell."

"Who hired you to find her? Who's behind this?"

"I have a client."

"Come on now, don't go fifth-amendment on me. Who hired you, Lew?"

I didn't answer.

"Isobel Graff? Did she sick you onto the girl?"

"You're way off in left field."

"I used to play left field. Let me tell you something, just in case it's her. She's nothing but trouble—schizzy from way back. I could tell you things about Isobel you wouldn't believe."

65

"Try me."

"Is she the one?"

"I don't know the lady."

"Scout's honor?"

"Eagle Scout's honor."

"Then where's the trouble coming from? I got to know, Lew. It's my job to know. I got to protect the Man and the organization."

"What do you have to protect them against?" I said experimentally. "A murder rap?"

The experiment got results. Fear crossed Leroy Frost's face like a shadow chased by shadows. He said very mildly and reasonably: "Nobody said a word about murder, Lew. Why bring up imaginary trouble? We got enough real ones. The trouble I'm featuring just this minute is a Hollywood peeper name of Archer who is half smart and half stupid and who has been getting too big for his goddam breeches." While he spoke, his fear was changing to malice. "You going to answer my question, Lew? I asked you who's your principal and why."

"Sorry."

"You'll be sorrier."

He came around the chair and looked me up and down and across like a tailor measuring me for a suit of clothes. Then he turned his back on me, and flipped the switch on his intercom.

"Lashman! Come in here."

I looked at the door. Nothing happened. Frost spoke into the intercom again, on a rising note:

"Lashman! Marfeld!"

No answer. Frost looked at me, his yellow eyes dilating.

"I wouldn't slug a sick old man," I said.

He said something in a guttural voice which I didn't catch. Outside the window, like his echo vastly amplified, men began to shout. I caught some words:

"He's comin' your way." And further off: "I see him."

A pink-haired man in a dark suit ran under the window, chasing his frenzied shadow across the naked ground. It was George Wall. He was running poorly, floundering from side to side and almost falling. Close behind him, like a second bulkier shadow struggling to make contact with his heels, Marfeld ran. He had a gun in his hand.

Frost said: "What goes on?"

He cranked open the casement window and shouted the same question. Neither man heard him. They ran on in the dust, up Western Street, through the fake tranquillity of Midwestern Town. George's legs were pumping weakly, and Marfeld was closing up the distance between them. Ahead of George, in South Sea Village, Lashman jumped into sight around the corner of a palm-thatched hut.

George saw him and tried to swerve. His legs gave under him. He got up, swaying in indecision as Lashman and Marfeld converged on him. Marfeld's shoulder took him in the side, and he went down again. Lashman dragged him up to his feet, and Marfeld's dark bulk blotted out his face.

Frost was leaning on the window sill, watching the distant figures. Marfeld's shoulder, leaning over George, moved in a jerky rhythm from side to side. I pushed Frost out of the way—he was light as straw—and went out through the window and across the lot.

Marfeld and Lashman were fascinated and oblivious. Marfeld was pistol-whipping George while Lashman held him up. Blood streaked his blind face and spotted his charcoal-gray suit. I noticed the irrelevant fact that the suit belonged to me: I'd last seen it hanging in my bedroom closet. I moved on them in ice-cold anger, got one hand on Marfeld's collar and the other on the slippery barrel of the gun. I heaved. The man and the gun came apart. The man went down backward. The gun stayed in my hand. It belonged to me, anyway. I reversed it and held it on Lashman:

"Turn him loose. Let him down easy."

The little, cruel mouth in his big jaw opened and closed. The fever left his eyes. He laid George out on the white imported sand. The boy was out, with the whites of his eyes glaring.

I took the revolver off Lashman's hip, stepped back and included Marfeld in the double line of fire. "What are you cookies up to, or you just do this for fun?"

Marfeld got to his feet, but he remained silent. Lashman answered the guns in my hands politely:

"The guy's a crackpot. He bust into Mr. Graff's office, threatened to kill him."

"Why would he do that?"

"It was something about his wife."

"Button it down," Marfeld growled. "You talk too much, Lashman."

There were muffled footsteps in the dust behind me. I circled Marfeld and Lashman, and backed against the bamboo wall of a hut. Frost and the guard from the vestibule were crossing the lot toward us. This guard had a carbine on his arm. He stopped, and raised it into firing position.

"Drop it," I said. "Tell him to drop it, Frost."

"Drop it," he said to the guard.

The carbine thudded on the ground and sent up a little dust cloud. The situation was mine. I didn't want it.

"What goes on?" Frost said in a querulous tone. "Who is he?"

"Hester Campbell's husband. Kick him around some more if you really want bad publicity."

"Jesus Christ!"

"You better get him to a doctor."

Nobody moved. Frost slid his hand up under his waistcoat and fingered his rib-cage to see if his heart had stopped. He said faintly:

"You brought him here?"

"You know better than that."

"The guy tried to kill Mr. Graff," Lashman said virtuously. "He was chasing Mr. Graff around the office."

"Is Graff all right?"

"Yeah, sure. I heard the guy yelling and run him out of there before he did any damage."

Frost turned to the guard who had dropped the carbine: "How did he get in?"

The man looked confused, then sullen. He broke his lips apart with difficulty:

"He had a press card. Said he had an appointment with Mr. Graff."

"You didn't clear it with me."

"You were busy, you said not to disturb—"

"Don't tell me what I said. Get out of here. You're finished here. Who hired you?"

"You did, Mr. Frost."

"I ought to be shot for that. Now get out of my sight." His voice was very mild. "Tell anybody about this, anybody at all, and you might as well leave town, it'll save you hospital bills."

The man's face had turned a grainy white, the color of rice pudding. He opened and closed his mouth several times without speaking, turned on his heel, and trudged toward the gate.

Frost looked down at the bloody man in the sand. He whined with pity, all of it for himself:

"What am I going to do with him?"

"Move your butt and get him an ambulance."

Frost turned his measuring look on me. Over it, he tried on a Santa Claus smile that didn't fit. A fluttering tic in one eyelid gave him the air of having a secret understanding with me:

"I talked a little rough back there in the office. Forget it,

Lew. I like you. As a matter of fact, I like you very much."

"Get him an ambulance," I said, "or you'll be needing one for yourself."

"Sure, in a minute." He rolled his eyes toward the sky like a producer having an inspiration. "I been thinking for some time, long before this came up, we can use you in the organization, Lew. How would you like to go to Italy, all expenses paid? No real work, you'll have men under you. It'll be a free vacation."

I looked at his sick, intelligent face and the cruel, stupid faces of the two men beside him. They went with the unreal buildings which stood around like the cruel, sick pretense of a city.

"I wouldn't let you pay my way to Pismo Beach. Now turn around and walk, Frost. You too, Marfeld, Lashman. Stay close together. We're going to a telephone and call the Receiving Hospital. We've wasted enough time."

I had very little hope of getting out of there and taking George out with me. I merely had to try. What hope I had died a sudden death. Two men appeared ahead of us in Midwestern Town, running stooped over behind a clean white picket fence. One was the guard Frost had fired. Both of them had Thompson guns at the ready.

They saw me and ducked behind a deep front porch with an old-fashioned glider on it. Frost and his goons stopped walking. I said to Frost's back:

"You're going to have to handle this with care. You'll be the first one drilled. Tell them to come out into the middle of the street and put their tommyguns down."

Frost turned to face me, shaking his head. Out of the tail of my left eye, I saw a third man running and crouching toward me, hugging the walls of the South Sea huts. He had a riot gun. I felt like a major strike was being broken. Frost made a mock-lugubrious face which fitted all his wrinkles.

"You'd never get out alive." He raised his voice. "Drop 'em, Lew. I'll count to three."

The man in the tail of my left eye was on his elbows and knees, crawling. He lay still and aimed as Frost began to count. I dropped the guns on the count of two. Marfeld and Lashman turned at the sound.

Frost nodded. "Now you're being smart."

Marfeld scooped up the guns. Lashman took a step forward. He had a black leather sap in his right hand. The man with the riot gun was on his feet now, trotting. The commandos behind the front porch came out from behind it, cautiously at first and then more quickly. The one Frost had fired had a silly, sickly grin on his face. He was

69

ashamed of what he was doing, but couldn't stop doing it.

Away off on the other side of the lot, Simon Graff stood in a doorway and watched Lashman swing his sap.

TIME began to tick again, in fits and starts. Pain glowed in my mind like lightning in a cloud, expanding and contracting with my heartbeat. I lay on my back on a hard surface. Somewhere above me, Lance Leonard said through flutter and wow:

"This is a neat layout Carlie's got himself here. I been out here plenty of times. He gives me the run of the place. I get the use of it any time he's away. It's swell for dames."

"Be quiet." It was Frost.

"I was just explaining." Leonard's voice was aggrieved. "I know this place like I know the back of my hand. Anything you want, any kind of booze or wine, I can get it for you."

"I don't drink."

"Neither do I. You on drugs?"

"Yah, I'm on drugs," Frost said bitterly. "Now shut it off. I'm trying to think."

Leonard subsided. I lay in the unblessed silence for a while. Sunlight was hot on my skin and red through my eyelids. When I raised my eyelids slightly, scalpels of light probed the inside of my head.

"His eyelids just fluttered," Leonard said.

"Better take a look at him."

Boots scraped concrete. I felt a toe in my side. Leonard squatted and pulled open one of my eyelids. I had turned up my eyes.

"He's still out."

"Throw some water on him. There's a hose on the other side of the pool."

I waited, and felt its stream gush into my face, hot from the sun, then lukewarm. I let a little of the water run into my dry mouth.

70

"Still out," Leonard said glumly. "What if he don't wake up? What do we do then?"

"That's your friend Stern's problem. He will, though. He's a hardhead, bone all the way through. I almost wish he wouldn't."

"Carlie ought to been here long ago. You think his plane crashed?"

"Yah, I think his plane crashed. Which makes you a goddam orphan." There was a rattlesnake buzz in Frost's voice.

"You're stringing me, ain't you? Aren't you?" Leonard was dismayed.

Frost failed to answer him. There was another silence. I kept my eyes shut, and sent a couple of messages down the red-lit avenues behind them. The first one took a long time getting there, but when it arrived it flexed the fingers of my right hand. I willed my toes to wiggle, and they wiggled. It was very encouraging.

A telephone rang behind a wall.

"I bet that's Carlie now," Leonard said brightly.

"Don't answer it. We'll sit here and guess who it is."

"You don't have to get sarcastic. Flake can answer it. He's in there watching television."

The telephone hadn't rung again. A sliding wall hissed in its grooves and bumped. Twistyface's voice said:

"It's Stern. He's in Victorville, wants to be picked up."

"Is he still on the line?" Leonard asked.

"Yeah, he wants to talk to you."

"Go and talk to him," Frost said. "Put him out of his misery."

Footsteps receded. I opened my eyes, looked up into glaring blue sky in which the declining sun hung like an inverted hot-plate. I raised my pulsating head, a little at a time. A winking oval pool was surrounded on three sides by a blue Fiberglas fence, on the fourth side by the glass wall of an adobe-colored desert house. Between me and the pool, Frost sat lax in a long aluminum chair under a blue patio umbrella. He was half-turned away from me, listening to a murmur of words from the house. An automatic hung from his limp right hand.

I sat up slowly, leaning my weight on my arms. My vision had a tendency to blur. I focused on Frost's neck. It looked like a scrawny plucked rooster's, easy to wring. I gathered my legs under me. They were hard to control, and one shoe scraped the concrete.

Frost heard the little sound it made. His eyes swiveled toward me. His gun came up. I crawled toward him anyway, dripping reddish water. He scrambled out of the long chair and backed toward the house.

"Flake! Come out here."

Twistyface appeared in the opening of the wall. I wasn't thinking well, and my movements were sluggish. I got up, made a staggering lunge for Frost, and fell short, onto my knees. He aimed a kick at my head, which I was too slow to avoid. The sky broke up in lights. Something else hit me, and the sky turned black.

I swung in black space, supported by some kind of sky hook above the bright scene. I could look down and see everything very clearly. Frost and Leonard and Twistyface stood over a prostrate man, palavering in doubletalk. At least, it sounded like doubletalk to me. I was occupied with deep thoughts of my own. They flashed on my mind like brilliant lantern slides: Hollywood started as a meaningless dream, invented for money. But its colors ran, out through the holes in people's heads, spread across the landscape and solidified. North and south along the coast, east across the desert, across the continent. Now we were stuck with the dream without a meaning. It had become the nightmare that we lived in. Deep thoughts.

I realized with some embarrassment that the body on the deck belonged to me. I climbed air down to it and crawled back in, a rat who lived in a scarecrow. It was familiar, even cozy, except for the leaks. But something had happened to me. I was hallucinating a little bit, and self-pity opened up in front of me like a blue, inviting pool where a man could drown. I dove in. I swam to the other side, though. There were barracuda in the pool, hungry for my manhood. I climbed out.

Came to my senses and saw I hadn't moved. Frost and Leonard had gone away. Twistyface sat in the aluminum chair and watched me sit up. He was naked to the waist. Black fur made tufted patterns on his torso. He had breasts like a female gorilla. The inevitable gun was in his paw.

"That's better," he said. "I don't know about you, but ole Flake feels like going in and watching some TV. It's hotter than the hinges out here."

It was like walking on stilts, but I made it inside, across a large, low room, into a smaller room. This was paneled in dark wood and dominated by the great blind eye of a television set. Flake pointed with his gun at the leather armchair beside it.

"You sit there. Get me a Western movie."

"What if I can't?"

"There's always a Western movie at this time of day."

He was right. I sat for what seemed a long time and listened to the clop-clop and bang-bang. Flake sat close up in front of the screen, fascinated by simple virtue conquering simple evil with fists and guns and rustic philosophy. The old plot repeated itself like a moron's recurrent wish-fulfillment dream. The pitchman in the intervals worked hard to build up new little mechanical wishes. Colonel Risko says buy Bloaties, they're yum-yum delicious, yum-yum nutritious. Get your super-secret badge of membership. You'll ell-oh-vee-ee Bloaties.

I flexed my arms and legs from time to time and tried to generate willpower. There was a brass lamp on top of the television set. It had a thick base, and looked heavy enough to be used as a weapon. If I could find the will to use it, and if Flake would forget his gun for two consecutive seconds.

The movie ended in a chaste embrace which brought tears to Flake's eyes. Or else his eyes were watering from eyestrain. The gun sagged between his spread knees. I rose and got hold of the lamp. It wasn't as heavy as it looked. I hit him on the head with it anyway.

Flake merely looked surprised. He fired in reflex. The pitchman on the television screen exploded in the middle of a deathless sentence. In a hail of glass I kicked at the gun in Flake's hand. It hopped through the air, struck the wall, and went off again. Flake lowered his little dented head and charged me.

I sidestepped. His wild fist cracked a panel in the wall. Before he recovered his balance, I got a half-nelson on him and then a full nelson.

He was a hard man to bend. I bent him, and rapped his head on the edge of the television box. He lunged sideways, dragging me across the room. I retained my hold, clenched hands at the back of his neck. I rapped his head on the steel corner of an air-conditioning unit set in the window. He went soft, and I dropped him.

I got down on my knees and found the gun and had a hard time getting up again. I was weak and trembling. Flake was worse off, snoring through a broken nose.

I found my way to the kitchen and had a drink of water and went outside. It was already evening. There were no cars in the carport, just a flat-tired English bicycle and a motor scooter that wouldn't start. Not for me it wouldn't. I thought of waiting there for Frost and Leonard and Stern, but all I could think of to do with them was shoot them. I was sick and tired of violence. One more piece of violence and they could reserve my room at Camarillo, in one of the back wards. Or such was my opinion at the time.

I started down the dusty private road. It descended a low rise toward the bed of a dry stream in the middle of a wide, flat valley. There were mountain ranges on two sides of the valley, high in the south and medium high in the west. On the slopes of the southern range, drifts of snow gleamed impossibly white between the deep-blue forests. The western range was jagged black against a sky where the last light was breaking up into all its colors.

I walked toward the western range. Pasadena was on the other side of it. On my side of it, in the middle of the valley, tiny cars raced along a straight road. One of them turned toward me, its headlights swinging up and down on the bumps. I lay down in the sage beside the road.

It was Leonard's Jaguar, and he was driving it. I caught a glimpse of the face in the seat beside him: a pale, flat oval like a dish on which flat eyes were painted, a pointed chin resting on a spotted bow tie. I'd seen that old-young face before, in the papers after Siegel died, on television during the Kefauver hearings, once or twice at nightclub tables flanked by bodyguards. Carl Stern.

I stayed off the road, cutting at an angle across the high desert toward the highway. The air was turning chilly. In the darkness rising from the earth and spreading across the sky, the evening star hung alone. I was a bit lightheaded, and from time to time I thought that the star was something I had lost, a woman or an ideal or a dream.

Self-pity stalked me, snuffing at my spoor. He was invisible, but I could smell him, a catty smell. Once or twice he fawned on the backs of my legs, and once I kicked at him. The joshua trees waved their arms at me and tittered.

xxxxxxxx *chapter* 14

THE fourth car I thumbed stopped for me. It was a cut-down jalopy with a pair of skis strapped to the top, driven by a college boy on his way back to Westwood. I told him I'd turned my car over on a back road. He was young enough to accept my story without too many questions, and decent enough to let me go to sleep in the back seat.

He took me to the ambulance entrance of St. John's Hospital. A resident surgeon put some stitches in my scalp, gave me quiet hell, and told me to go to bed for a couple of days. I took a taxi home. Traffic was sparse and rapid on the boulevard. I sat back in the seat and watched the lights go by, flashing like thrown knives. There were nights when I hated the city.

My house looked shabby and small. I turned on all the lights. George Wall's dark suit lay like a crumpled man on the bedroom floor. To hell with him, I thought, and repeated the thought aloud. I took a bath and turned off all the lights and went to bed.

It didn't do any good. A nightmare world sprang up around the room, a world of changing faces which wouldn't hold still. Hester's face was there, refracted through George Wall's mind. It changed and died and came alive and died again smiling, staring with loveless eyes out of the red darkness. I thrashed around for a while and gave up. Got up and dressed and went out to my garage.

It hit me then, and not until then, that I was minus a car. If the Beverly Hills cops hadn't hauled it away, my car was parked on Manor Crest Drive, across the street from Hester's house. I called another taxi and asked to be let off on a corner half a block from the house. My car was where I had left it, with a parking ticket under the windshield-wiper.

I crossed the street for a closer look at the house. There was no car in the drive, no light behind the windows. I climbed the front steps and leaned on the bellpush. Inside, the electric bell chirred like a cricket on an abandoned hearth. The nobody-home sound, the empty-house girl-gone one-note blues.

I tried the door. It was locked. I glanced up and down the street. Lights shone at the intersections and from the quiet houses. The people were all inside. They had given up night walks back in the cold war.

Call me trouble looking for a place to happen. I went around to the side of the house, through a creaking wooden gate into a walled patio. The flagstone paving was uneven under my feet. Crab grass grew rank in the spaces between the stones. I made my way among wrought-iron tables and disemboweled chaises to a pair of French doors set into the wall.

My flashlight beam fell through dirty glass into a lanai full of obscene shadows. They were cast by rubber plants and cacti growing in earthenware pots. I reversed the light and used its butt to punch out one of the panes, drew back a reluctant bolt, and forced the door open.

The house was mostly front, like the buildings on Graff's sets. Its rear had been given over to ghosts and spiders. Spiders had rigged the lanai's bamboo furniture and black oak rafters with loops and hammocks and wheels of dusty webbing. I felt like an archæologist breaking into a tomb.

The door at the end of the lanai was unlocked. I passed through a storeroom full of once-expensive junk: high, unsittable Spanish chairs, a grand piano with grinning yellow keys, brownish oil paintings framed in gilt: through another door, into the central hallway of the house. I crossed to the door of the living-room.

White walls and a half-beamed ceiling rose in front of me, supported by the upward beam from my light. I lowered it to the floor, which was covered with ivory carpeting. White and black sectional furniture, low-slung and cubistic, was grouped in angular patterns around the room. The fireplace was faced with black tile and flanked by a square white leather hassock. On the other side of the fireplace, a faint dark patch showed in the carpet.

I got down on my knees and examined it. It was a wet spot the size of a large dinner plate, of no particular color. Through the odor of detergent, and under the other odors in the room, perfume and cigarette smoke and sweet mixed drinks, I could smell blood. The odor of blood was persistent, no matter how you scrubbed.

Still on my knees, I turned my attention to the raised fireplace. It was equipped with a set of brass fire tools in a rack: brush, shovel, a pair of leather bellows with brass handles. The set was new, and looked as if it had never been used or even touched. Except that the poker was missing.

Beyond the fireplace there was a doorless arch which probably opened into the dining-room. Most of the houses of this style and period had similar floor plans, and I had been in a lot of them. I moved to the arch, intending to go over the rest of the downstairs, then the upstairs.

A motor droned in the street. Light washed the draped front windows and swept past. I went to the end window and looked out through the narrow space between the drape and the window frame. The old black Lincoln was standing in the driveway. Marfeld was at the wheel, his face grotesquely shadowed by the reflection of the headlights. He switched them off and climbed out.

Leroy Frost got out on the far side. I knew him by his hurrying feeble walk. The two men passed within three or four feet of me, headed for the front door. Frost was carrying a glinting metal rod which he used as a walking-stick.

I went through the archway into the next room. In its center a polished table reflected the wan light filtered through lace-curtained double windows. A tall buffet stood against the wall inside the arch, a chair in the corner behind it. I sat down in the deep shadow, with my flashlight in one hand and my gun in the other.

I heard a key turn in the front door, then Leroy Frost's voice, jerking with strain:

"I'll take the key. What happened to the other key?"

"Lance give it to the pig."

"That was a sloppy way to handle it."

"It was your idea, chief. You told me not to talk to her myself."

"All right, as long as she got it." Frost mumbled something indistinguishable. I heard him shuffling in the entrance to the living-room. Suddenly he exploded: "Where is the goddam light? You been in and out of this house, you expect me to grope around in the dark all night?"

The lights went on in the living-room. Footsteps crossed it. Frost said:

"You didn't do a very good job on the rug."

"I did the best I could in the time. Nobody's gonna go over it with a fine-tooth comb, anyway."

"You hope. You better bring that hassock over here, cover it up until it dries. We don't want her to see it."

Marfeld grunted with effort. I heard the hassock being dragged across the carpet.

"Fine," Frost said. "Now wipe my prints off the poker and put it where it belongs."

There was the sound of metal coming in contact with metal.

"You sure you got it clean, chief?"

"Don't be a birdbrain, it isn't the same poker. I found a match for it in the prop warehouse."

"I be damned, you think of everything." Marfeld's voice was moist with admiration. "Where did you ditch the other one?"

"Where nobody's going to find it. Not even you."

"Me? What would I want with it?"

"Skip it."

"Hell, don't you *trust* me, chief?"

"I trust nobody. I barely trust myself. Now let's get out of here."

"What about the pig? Don't we wait for her?"

"No, she won't be here for a while. And the less she sees of us, the better. Lance told her what she's supposed to do, and we don't want her asking us questions."

"I guess you're right."

"I don't need you to tell me I'm right. I know more about heading off blackmail than any other two men in this town. Bear it in mind in case you develop any ideas."

"I don't get it, chief. What kind of ideas you mean?" Marfeld's voice was full of injured innocence.

"Ideas of retiring, maybe, with a nice fat pension."

"No, sir. Not me, Mr. Frost."

"I guess you know better, at that. You try to put the bite on me or any friend of mine—it's the quickest way to get a hole in the head to go with the hole in the head you already got."

"I know that, Mr. Frost. Christ amighty, I'm *loyal*. Didn't I prove it to you?"

"Maybe. Are you sure you saw what you said you saw?"

"When was that, chief?"

"This afternoon. Here."

"Christ, yes." Marfeld's plodding mind caught the implication and was stung by it. "Christ, Mr. Frost, I wouldn't lie to you."

"You would if you did it yourself. That would be quite a trick, to do a murder and con the organization into covering for you."

"Aw now, chief, you wouldn't accuse me. Why would I kill anybody?"

"For kicks. You'd do it for kicks, any time you thought you could get away with it. Or to make yourself into a hero, if you had a few more brains."

Marfeld whined adenoidally: "Make myself into a hero?"

"Yah, Marfeld to the rescue, saving the company's cookies for it again. It's kind of a coincidence that you been in on both killings, Johnny-on-the-spot. Or don't you think so?"

"That's crazy, chief, honest to God." Marfeld's voice throbbed with sincerity. It ran down, and began on a new note: "I been loyal all my life, first to the sheriff and then to you. I never asked for anything for myself."

"Except a cash bonus now and then, eh?" Frost laughed. Now that Marfeld was jittery, too, Frost was willing to forgive him. His laughter rustled like a Santa Ana searching among dry leaves. "Okay, you'll get your bonus, if I can get it past the comptroller."

"Thank you, chief. I mean it very sincerely."

"Sure you do."

The light went out. The front door closed behind them. I

78

waited until the Lincoln was out of hearing, and went upstairs. The front bedroom was the only room in use. It had quilted pink walls and a silk-canopied bed, like something out of a girl's adolescent dream. The contents of the dressing-table and closet told me that the girl had been spending a lot of money on clothes and cosmetics, and hadn't taken any of it with her.

xxxxxxxxxx *chapter* 15

I LEFT the house the way I had entered, and drove up into the Canyon. A few sparse stars peered between the streamers of cloud drifting along the ridge. Houselights on the slopes islanded the darkness through which the road ran white under my headlight beam. Rounding a high curve, I could see the glow of the beach cities far below to my left, phosphorescence washed up on the shore.

Lance Leonard's house was dark. I parked on the gravel shoulder a hundred yards short of the entrance to his driveway. Its steep grade was slippery with fog. The front door was locked, and nobody answered my knock.

I tried the garage door. It opened easily when I lifted the handle. The Jaguar had returned to the fold, and the motorcycle was standing in its place. I moved between them to the side entrance. This door wasn't locked.

The concentric ovals of light from my flash slid ahead of me across the floor of the utility room, the checkerboard linoleum in the kitchen, the polished oak in the living-room, up along the glass walls on which the gray night pressed heavily, around and over the fieldstone-faced fireplace, where a smoking log was disintegrating into talc-like ash and dull-red flakes of fire. The mantel held a rack of pipes and a tobacco jar, an Atmos clock which showed that it was three minutes to eleven, a silver-framed glamour shot of Lance Leonard smiling with all his tomcat charm.

Lance himself was just inside the front door. He wore a plaid evening jacket and midnight-blue trousers and dull-blue dancing-pumps, but he wasn't going anywhere. He lay on his back with his toes pointing at opposite corners of the ceiling. One asphalt eye looked into the light, unblinking. The other had been broken by a bullet.

I put on gloves and got down on my knees and saw the second bullet wound in the left temple. It was bloodless. The hair around it was singed, the skin peppered with powder marks. I covered the floor on my hands and knees. Pushing aside one of the stiff legs, I found a used copper shellcase, medium caliber. Apparently it had rebounded from the wall or from the murderer's clothes and rolled across the floor where Leonard fell on it.

It took me a long time to find the second shell. I opened the front door, finally, and saw it glinting in the crack between the lintel and the concrete stoop. I squatted in the doorway with my back to the dead man and tried to reconstruct his murder. It looked simple enough. Someone had knocked on the door, waited with a gun for Lance to open it, shot him in the eye, shot him again after he fell to make certain, and gone away, closing the door behind him. The door had a self-locking mechanism.

I left the shells where they were, and shook down the rest of the house. The living-room was almost as impersonal as a hotel room. Even the pipes on the mantel had been bought by the set, and only one of them had ever been smoked. The tobacco in the jar was bone dry. There was nothing but tobacco in the jar, nothing but wood in the woodbox. The portable bar in one corner was well stocked with bottles, most of which were unopened.

I went into the bedroom. The blond oak chests of drawers were stuffed with loot from the Miracle Mile haberdasheries: stacks of shirts custom-made out of English broadcloth and wool gabardine and Madras, hand-painted ties, Argyle socks, silk scarves, a rainbow of cashmere sweaters. A handkerchief drawer contained gold cufflinks and monogrammed tie-bars; a gold identification bracelet engraved with the name Lance Leonard; a tarnished medal awarded to Manuel Torres (it said on the back) for the Intermediate Track and Field Championships, Serena Junior High School, 1945; five expensive wristwatches and a stopwatch. The boy had been running against time.

I looked into the closet. A wooden shoe-rack held a dozen pairs of shoes to go with the dozen suits and jackets hanging above them. A double-barreled shotgun stood in a corner beside a two-foot pile of comic books and crime magazines. I leafed through some of the top ones: Fear, Lust, Horror, Murder, Passion.

On the shelves at the head of the bed there were some

other books of a different kind. A morocco-bound catechism inscribed in a woman's hand: "Manuel Purificación Torres, 1943." An old life of Jack Dempsey, read to pieces, whose flyleaf bore the legend: "Manny 'Terrible' Torres, 1734 West Nopal Street, Los Angeles, California, The United States, The Western Hemisfear, the World, The Universe." A manual of spoken English whose first few pages were heavily underscored in pencil. The name on the flyleaf of this one was Lance Leonard.

The fourth and final book was a stamped-leather album of clippings. The newspaper picture on the first page showed a boyish Lance leaning wide-shouldered and wasp-waisted into the camera. The caption stated that Manny Torres was being trained by his Uncle Tony, veteran club-fighter, and experts conceded him an excellent chance of capturing the lightweight division of the Golden Gloves. There was no follow-up to this. The second entry was a short account of Lance Torres' professional debut; he had knocked out another welterweight in two minutes of the second round. And so on for twenty fights, through six-rounders up to twelve. None of the clippings mentioned his arrest and suspension.

I replaced the album on the shelf and went back to the dead man. His breast pocket contained an alligator billfold thick with money, a matching address book filled with girls' names and telephone numbers scattered from National City to Ojai. Two of the names were Hester Campbell and Rina Campbell. I wrote down their Los Angeles telephone numbers.

There was a gold cigarette case full of reefers in the side pocket of his dinner jacket. In the same pocket, I found an engraved invitation in an envelope addressed to Lance Leonard, Esq., at the Coldwater Canyon address. Mr. and Mrs. Simon Graff requested his presence at a Roman Saturnalia to be held at the Channel Club tonight.

I put everything back and stood up to leave, turned at the door for a final look at the boy. He lay exhausted by his incredible leap from nowhere into the sun. His face was old-ivory in the flashlight beam. I switched it off and let the darkness take him.

"Lance Manuel Purificación Torres Leonard," I said out loud by way of epitaph.

Outside, a wisp of cloud dampened my face like cold and meager tears. I climbed on heavy legs to my car. Before I started the motor, I heard another motor whining up the grade from the direction of Ventura Boulevard. Headlights climbed the hanging cloud. I left my own lights off.

The headlights swerved around the final curve, projected

by a dark sedan with a massive chrome cowcatcher. Without hesitating, they entered Leonard's driveway and lit up the front of his house. A man got out of the driver's seat and waded through the flowing light to the front door. He wore a dark raincoat belted tight at the waist, and he stepped lightly, with precision. All I could see of his head was the short, dark crewcut that surmounted it.

Having knocked and got no answer, he pulled out a flashing keyring and opened the door. The lights came on in the house. A minute later, half muffled by its redwood walls, a man's voice rose in a scream which sounded like a crow cawing. The lights went out again. The cawing continued for some time in the dark interior of the house.

There was an interval of silence before the door was opened. The man stepped out into the glare of his own headlights. He was Carl Stern. In spite of the crewcut and the neat bow tie, his face resembled an old woman's who had been bereaved.

He turned his sedan rather erratically and passed my car without appearing to notice it. I had to start and turn my car, but I caught him before he reached the foot of the hill. He went through boulevard stops as if he had a motorcycle escort. So did I. I had him.

Then we were on Manor Crest Drive, and I was completing the circuit of the roller-coaster. There was a difference, though. Hester's house was lighted upstairs and down. On the the second floor, a woman's shadow moved across a blind. She moved like a young woman, with an eager rhythm.

Stern left his sedan in the driveway with the motor running, knocked and was admitted, came out again before I'd decided what to do. He got in and drove away. I didn't follow him. It was beginning to look as though Hester was home again.

I WENT in by the broken lanai door and through to the front. Feet were busy on the floor over my head. I heard quick, clacking heels and a girl's tuneless humming. I climbed the stairs, leaning part of my weight on the banister. At the end of the upstairs hallway, light spilled from the doorway of the front bedroom. I moved along the wall to a point from which I could see into the room.

The girl was standing by the canopied bed with her back to me. She was very simply dressed in a tweed skirt and a short-sleeved white blouse. Her bright hair was brushed slick around the curve of her skull. A white leather suitcase with a blue silk lining lay open on the bed. She was folding some kind of black dress into it, tenderly.

She straightened and went to the far side of the room, her hips swinging from a flexible small waist. She opened the mirrored door of a closet and entered its lighted interior. When she came out, with more clothes in her arms, I was in the room.

Her body went stiff. The bright-colored dresses fell to the floor. She stepped backward against the mirrored door, which closed with a snap.

"Hello, Hester. I thought you were dead."

Her teeth showed, and she pressed her knuckles against them. She said behind the knuckles: "Who are you?"

"The name is Archer. Don't you remember me from this morning?"

"Are you the detective—the one that Lance had a fight with?"

I nodded.

"What do you want with me?"

"A little talk."

"You get out of here." She glanced at the ivory telephone on the bedside table, and said uncertainly: "I'll call the police."

"I doubt that very much."

She took her hand away from her mouth and laid it against her side below the swell of her breast, as though she felt a pain there. Anger and anxiety wrenched at her face, but she was one of those girls who couldn't look ugly. There was a sculptured beauty built into her bones, and she held herself with a sense that her beauty would look after her.

"I warn you," she said, "some friends of mine are coming here, any minute now."

"Fine. I'd like to meet them."

"You think so?"

"I think so."

"Stick around if you like, then," she said. "Do you mind if I go on with my packing?"

"Go right ahead, Hester. You are Hester Campbell, aren't you?"

She didn't answer me or look at me. She picked up the fallen dresses, carried the rustling sheaf to the bed, and began to pack.

"Where are you going at this time of night?" I said.

"It's no concern of yours."

"Cops might be interested."

"Might they? Go and tell them, why don't you? Do anything you like."

"That's kind of reckless talk for a girl on the lam."

"I'm not on the lam, as you put it, and you don't frighten me."

"You're just going away for a weekend in the country."

"Why not?"

"I heard you tell Lance this morning that you wanted out."

She didn't react to the name as I'd half suspected she would. Her deft hands went on folding the last of the dresses. I liked her courage, and distrusted it. There could be a gun in the suitcase. But when she finally turned she was empty-handed.

"Wanted out of what?" I said.

"I don't know what you're talking about, and I couldn't care less." But she cared.

"These friends of yours who are coming here—is Lance Leonard one of them?"

"Yes, and you better get out before he does come."

"You're sure he's coming?"

"You'll see."

"It ought to be something to see. Who's going to carry the basket?"

"The basket?" she said in a high little voice.

"Lance isn't getting around much any more. They have to carry him in a basket."

Her hand went to her side again. The pain had risen higher. Her body moved angrily, hips and shoulders, trying to pass through the narrow space between the bed and me. I blocked her way.

"When did you see him last?"

"Tonight."

"What time tonight?"

"I don't know. Several hours ago. Does it matter?"

"It matters to you. How was he when you left him?"

"He was fine. Why, has something happened to him?"

"You tell me, Hester. You leave a trail of destruction like Sherman marching through Georgia."

"What happened? Is he hurt?"

"Badly hurt."

"Where is he?"

"At home. He'll soon be in the morgue."

"He's dying?"

"He's dead. Didn't Carl Stern tell you?"

She shook her head. It was more of a convulsion than a denial. "Lance couldn't be dead. You're crazy."

"Sometimes I think I'm the only one who isn't."

She sat down on the edge of the bed. A row of tiny droplets stood along her peaked hairline. She brushed at them with her hand, and her right breast rose with the movement of her arm. She looked up at me, her eyes sleepy with shock. She was a very good actress, if she was acting.

I didn't think she was. "Your good friend is dead," I said. "Somebody shot him."

"You're lying."

"Maybe I should have brought along the body. Shall I tell you where he took the slugs? One in the temple, one in the eye. Or do you know all this? I don't want to bore you to death."

Her forehead crinkled. Her mouth stretched in the tragic rectangle.

"You're horrible. You're making all this up, trying to make me tell you things. You said the same thing about—about me —that I was dead." Tears started in her eyes. "You'd say anything to make me talk."

"What kind of things could you tell me if you did?"

"I don't have to answer your questions, any of them."

"Give it a little thought, and you might want to. It looks as though they're using you for a patsy."

She gave me a bewildered look.

"You're kind of naïve, aren't you, in view of the company you keep? Nice company. They're setting you up for a murder rap. They saw a chance to kill two birds with one stone, to knock off Lance and fix you at the same time."

I was playing by ear, but it was a familiar tune to me, and she was listening hard. She said in a hushed voice:

"Who would do such a thing?"

"Whoever talked you into taking a trip."

"Nobody talked me into it. I wanted to."

"Whose idea was it? Leroy Frost's?"

Her gaze flickered and dimmed.

"What did Frost tell you to do? Where did he tell you to go?"

"It wasn't Mr. Frost. It was Lance who contacted me. So

what you say can't be true. He wouldn't plan his own murder."

"Not if he knew what the plan was. Obviously he didn't. They conned him into it the same way they conned you."

"Nobody conned me," she said stubbornly. "Why would anybody try to con me?"

"Come off it, Hester, you're no ingenue. You know better than I do what you've been doing."

"I haven't done anything wrong."

"People have different standards, don't they? Some of us think that blackmail is the dirtiest game in the world."

"Blackmail?"

"Look around you, and stop pretending. Don't tell me Graff's been giving you things because he likes the way you do your hair. I've seen a lot of blackmail in this town, it's got so I can smell it on people. And you're in it up to your neck."

She fingered her neck. Her resistance to suggestion was wearing thin. She looked around at the pink walls and slowly turned their color. It was an authentic girlish blush, the first I had seen for some time, and it made me doubtful. She said:

"You're inventing all this."

"I have to. You won't tell me anything. I go by what I see and hear. A girl leaves her husband, takes up with a washed-up fighter who runs with mobsters. In no time at all, you're in the chips. Lance has a movie contract, you have your nice big house in Beverly Hills. And Simon Graff turns out to be your fairy godmother. Why?"

She didn't answer. She looked down at her hands twisting in her lap.

"What have you been selling him?" I said. "And what has Gabrielle Torres got to do with it?"

The color had drained out of her face, leaving it wan, blue-shadowed around the eyes. Her gaze turned inward on an image in her mind. The image seemed to appall her.

"I think you know who killed her," I said. "If you do, you'd better tell me. It's time to break these things out into the open, before more people are killed. Because you'll be next, Hester."

Her lips flew open like a dummy's controlled by a ventriloquist: "I'm not—" Her will took over, biting the sentence off.

She shook her head fiercely, dislodging tears from her eyes. She covered her streaked face with her hands and flung herself sideways on the bed. Fear ran through her, silent and rigorous as an electric current, shaking her entire body. Something that felt like pity rose from the center of mine. The

86

trouble with pity was that it always changed to something else—repulsion or desire. She lay still now, one hip arching up in a desolate slope.

"Are you going to tell me about Gabrielle?"

"I don't know anything to tell you." Her voice was small and muffled.

"Do you know who shot Lance?"

"No. Leave me alone."

"What did Carl Stern say to you?"

"Nothing. We had a date. He wanted to postpone it, that's all."

"What kind of a date?"

"It's none of your business."

"Is he going to take you for a ride?"

"Perhaps." She seemed to miss the implication.

"A one-way ride?"

This time she caught it, and sat up almost screaming: "Get away from me, you sadist. I know your kind. I've seen police detectives, and the way they torment helpless people. If you're a man at all, you'll get out of here."

Her torso was twisted sideways, her breasts sharp under the white blouse. Her red lips curled, and her eyes sparked blue. She was an extraordinarily good-looking girl, but there was more to her than that. She sounded like a straight one.

I caught myself doubting my premises, doubting that she could be any kind of hustler. Besides, there was just enough truth in her accusation, enough cruelty in my will to justice, enough desire in my pity, to make the room uncomfortable for me. I said good-night and left it.

The problem was to love people, try to serve them, without wanting anything from them. I was a long way from solving that one.

xxxxxxxxxx *chapter* 17

THERE was no guard on duty when I got to the Channel Club. The gate was open, though, and the party was still going on. Music and light spilled from one wing of the building. Several dozen cars stood in the parking-lot. I left mine between a black Porsche and a lavender Cadillac convertible with wine-colored leather upholstery and gold trim; and went in under the inverted red Christmas tree. It seemed to be symbolic of something, but I couldn't figure out what.

I knocked on Bassett's office door and got no answer. The pool was a slab of green brilliance, lit from below by under-water floodlights and spotlit from above. People were gathered at the far end under the aluminum-painted diving tower. I went down a shallow flight of steps and along the tiled edge toward the people.

Most of them were Hollywood fillies, sleek and self-con-scious in strapless evening gowns or bathing suits not intended for the water. Among the men, I recognized Simon Graff and Sammy Swift and the Negro lifeguard I had talked to in the morning. Their faces were turned up toward a girl who stood absolutely still on the ten-meter platform.

She ran and took off into the light-crossed air. Her body bowed and turned in a smooth flip-and-a-half, changed from a bird to a fish as it entered the water. The spectators ap-plauded. One of them, an agile youth in a dinner jacket and his middle forties, took a flashbulb picture as she came drip-ping up the ladder. She shook the water out of her short black hair contemptuously, and retired to a corner to dry herself. I followed her.

"Nice dive."

"You think so?" She turned up her taut brown face and I saw that she wasn't a girl and hadn't been for years. "I wouldn't give myself a score of three. My timing was way off. I can do it with a twist when I'm in shape. But thank you anyway."

She toweled one long brown leg, and then the other, with a kind of impersonal affection, like somebody grooming a racehorse.

"You dive competitively?"

"I did at one time. Why?"

"I was just wondering what makes a woman do it. That tower's high."

"A person has to be good at something, and I'm not pretty." Her smile was thin and agonized. "Dr. Frey—he's a psychiatrist friend of mine—says the tower is a phallic symbol. Anyway, you know what the swimmers say—a diver is a swimmer with her brains knocked out."

"I thought a diver was a swimmer with guts."

"That's what the *divers* say. Do you know many divers?"

"No, but I'd like to. Would Hester Campbell be a friend of yours?"

Her face became inert. "I know Hester," she said cautiously. "I wouldn't call her a friend."

"Why not?"

"It's a long story, and I'm cold." She turned brusquely and trotted away toward the dressing-room. Her hips didn't bounce.

"Quiet, everyone," a loud voice said. "You are about to witness the wonder of the century, brought to you at fabulous expense."

It came from a gray-haired man on the five-meter platform of the tower. His legs were scrawny, his chest pendulous, his belly a brown leather ball distending his shorts. I looked again and saw it was Simon Graff.

"Ladies and gentlemen." Graff shaded his eyes with a hand and looked around facetiously. "Are there any ladies present? Any gentlemen?"

The women tittered. The men guffawed. Sammy Swift, who was standing near me, looked more than ever like a ghost who had seen a goblin.

"Watch it, boys and girls," Graff shouted in a high, unnatural voice. "The Great Graffissimo, in his unique and death-defying leap."

He took a flat-footed little run and launched himself with his arms at his sides in what boys used to call a dead-soldier dive. His people waited until he came to the surface and then began to applaud, clapping and whistling.

Sammy Swift noticed my silence and moved toward me. He didn't recognize me until I called him by name. I could have set fire to his breath.

"Lew Archer, by damn. What are you doing in this *galère?*"

"Slumming."

"Yah, I bet. Speaking of slumming, did you get to see Lance Leonard?"

"No. My friend got sick and we gave up on the interview."

"Too bad, the boy's had quite a career. He'd make a story."

"Fill me in."

"Uh-uh." He wagged his head. "You tell your friend to take it up with Publicity. There's an official version and an unofficial version, I hear."

"What do you hear in detail?"

"I didn't know you did leg work for newspapers, Lew. What's the pitch, you trying to get something on Leonard?"

His fogged eyes had cleared and narrowed. He wasn't as

drunk as I'd thought, and the subject was touchy. I backed away from it:

"Just trying to give a friend a lift."

"You looking for Leonard now? I haven't seen him here tonight."

Graff raised his voice again:

"*Achtung*, everyone. Time for lifesaving practice." His eyes were empty and his mouth was slack. He stepped toward the twittering line of girls and pointed at one who was wearing a silver gown. His forefinger dented her shoulder. "You! What is your name?"

"Martha Matthews." She smiled in an agony of delight. The lightning was striking her.

"You're a cute little girl, Martha."

"Thank you." She towered over him. "Thank you very much, Mr. Graff."

"Would you like me to save your life, Martha?"

"I'd simply adore it."

"Go ahead, then. Jump in."

"But what about my dress?"

"You can take it off, Martha."

Her smile became slightly dazed. "I can?"

"I just said so."

She pulled the dress off over her head and handed it to one of the other girls. Graff pushed her backward into the pool. The agile photographer took a shot of the action. Graff went in after her and towed her to the ladder, his veined hand clutching her flesh. She smiled and smiled. The lifeguard watched them with no expression at all on his black face.

I felt like slugging somebody. There wasn't anybody big enough around. I walked away, and Sammy Swift tagged along. At the shallow end of the pool, we leaned against a raised planter lush with begonia, and lit cigarettes. Sammy's face was thin and pale in the half-light.

"You know Simon Graff pretty well," I stated.

His light eyes flickered. "You got to know him well to feel the way I do about him. I been making a worm's-eye study of the Man for just about five years. What I don't know about him isn't worth knowing. What I do know about him isn't worth knowing, either. It's interesting, though. You know why he pulls this lifesaving stunt, for instance? He does it every party, just like clockwork, but I bet I'm the only one around who's got it figured out. I bet Sime doesn't even know, himself."

"Tell me."

90

Sammy assumed an air of wisdom. He said in the jargon of the parlor analyst:

"Sime's got a compulsion neurosis, he has to do it. He's fixated on this girl that got herself killed last year."

"What girl would that be?" I said, trying to keep the excitement out of my voice.

"The girl they found on the beach with the bullets in her. It happened just below here." He gestured toward the ocean, which lay invisible beyond the margin of the light. "Sime was stuck on her."

"Interesting if true."

"Hell, you can take my word for it. I was with Sime that morning when he got the news. He's got a ticker in his office—he always wants to be the first to know—and when he saw her name on the tape he turned as white as a sheet, to coin a simile. Shut himself up in his private bathroom and didn't come out for an hour. When he finally did come out, he passed it off as a hangover. Hangover is the word. He hasn't been the same since the girl died. What was her name?" He tried to snap his fingers, unsuccessfully. "Gabrielle something."

"I seem to remember something about the case. Wasn't she a little young for him?"

"Hell, he's at the age when they really go for the young ones. Not that Sime's so old. It's only the last year his hair turned gray, and it was the girl's death that did it to him."

"You're sure about this?"

"Sure, I'm sure. I saw them together a couple of times that spring, and I got X-ray eyes, boy, it's one thing being a writer does for you."

"Where did you see them?"

"Around, and once in Vegas. They were lying beside the pool of one of the big hotels, smoking the same cigarette." He looked down at the glowing butt of his own cigarette, and threw it spinning into the water. "Maybe I shouldn't be telling tales out of school, but you won't quote me, and it's all in the past, anyway. Except that he keeps going through these crazy lifesaving motions. He's re-enacting her death, see, trying to save her from it. Only please note that he does it in a heated pool."

"This is your own idea, no doubt."

"Yeah, but it makes sense," he said with some fanaticism. "I been watching him for years, like you watch the flies on the wall, and I *know* him. I can read him like a book."

"Who wrote the book? Freud?"

Sammy didn't seem to hear me. His gaze had roved to the

far end of the pool, where Graff was posing for more pictures with some of the girls. I wondered why picture people never got tired of having their pictures taken. Sammy said:

"Call me Œdipus if you want to. I really hate that bastard."

"What did he do to you?"

"It's what he does to Flaubert. I'm writing the Carthage script, version number six, and Sime Graff keeps breathing down my neck." His voice changed; he mimicked Graff's accent: "Matho's our juvenile lead, we can't let him die on us. We got to keep him alive for the girl, that's basic. I got it. I got it. She nurses him back to health after he gets chopped up, how about that? We lose nothing by the gimmick, and we gain heart, the quality of heart. Salammbô rehabilitates him, see? The boy was kind of a revolutionary type before, but he is saved from himself by the influence of a good woman. He cleans up on the barbarians for her. The girl watches from the fifty-yard line. They clinch. They marry." Sammy resumed his own voice: "You ever read *Salammbô?*"

"A long time ago, in translation. I don't remember the story."

"Then you wouldn't see what I'm talking about. *Salammbô* is a tragedy, its theme is dissolution. So Sime Graff tells me to tack a happy ending onto it. And I write it that way. Jesus," he said in a tone of surprise, "this is the way I've written it. What makes me do it to myself and Flaubert? I used to worship Flaubert."

"Money?" I said.

"Yeah. Money. Money." He repeated the word several times, with varying inflections. He seemed to be finding new shades of meaning in it, subtle drunken personal meanings which brought the tears into his voice. But he was too chancy and brittle to hold the emotion. He slapped himself across the eyes, and giggled. "Well, no use crying over spilled blood. How about a drink, Lew? How about a drink of Danziger Goldwasser, in fact?"

"In a minute. Do you know a girl called Hester Campbell?"

"I've seen her around."

"Lately?"

"No, not lately."

"What's her relation to Graff, do you know?"

"No, I wouldn't know," he answered sharply. The subject disturbed him, and he took refuge in clowning: "Nobody tells me anything, I'm just an intellectual errand boy around here. An ineffectual intellectual errand boy. Song." He began to sing in a muffled tenor to an improvised tune: "He's so reprehensible yet so indispensable he makes things comprehensible he's my joy. That intellectual—ineffectual—but oh so sexual—intellectual errand boy. Whom nothing can alloy. . . . Dig that elegant whom."

"I dug it."

"It's the hallmark of genius, boy. Did I ever tell you I was a genius? I had an I.Q. of 183 when I was in high school in Galena, Illinois." His forehead crinkled. "What ever happened to me? Wha' happen? I used to like people, by damn, I used to have talent. I didn't know what it was worth. I came out here for the kicks, going along with the gag—seven fifty a week for playing word games. Then it turns out that it isn't a gag. It's for keeps, it's your life, the only one you've got. And Sime Graff has got you by the short hairs and you're not inner-directed any more. You're not yourself."

"Who are you, Sam?"

"That's my problem." He laughed, and almost choked. "I had a vision of myself last week, I could see it as plain as a picture. Dirty word, picture, but let it pass. I was a rabbit running across a desert. Rear view." He laughed and coughed again. "A goddam white-tailed bunny rabbit going lickety-split across the great American desert."

"Who was chasing you?"

"I don't know," he said with a lopsided grin. "I was afraid to look."

xxxxxxxxx *chapter* **18**

GRAFF came strutting toward us along the poolside, trailed by his twittering harem and their eunuchs. I wasn't ready to talk to him, and turned my back until he'd passed. Sammy was yawning with hostility.

"I really need a drink," he said. "My eyes are focusing. How's about joining me in the bar?"

"Later, maybe."

"See you. Don't quote me on anything."

I promised that I wouldn't, and Sammy went away toward the lights and the music. At the moment the pool was deserted except for the Negro lifeguard, who was moving around under the diving tower. He trotted in my direction with a double armful of soiled towels, took them into a lighted room at the end of the row of *cabañas*.

I went over and tapped on the open door. The lifeguard turned from a canvas bin where he had dumped the towels. He had on gray sweat-clothes with CHANNEL CLUB stenciled across the chest.

"Can I get you something, sir?"

"No, thanks. How are the tropical fish?"

He gave me a quick grin of recognition. "No tropical-fish trouble tonight. People trouble is all. There's always people trouble. Why they want to go swimming on a night like this! I guess it's the drinking they do. The way they pour it down is a revelation."

"Speaking of pouring it down, your boss is pretty good at it."

"Mr. Bassett? Yeah, he's been drinking like a fish lately, ever since his mother died. A tropical fish. Mr. Bassett was very devoted to his mother." The black face was smooth and bland, but the eyes were sardonic. "He told me she was the only woman he ever loved."

"Good for him. Do you know where Bassett is now?"

"Circulating." He stirred the air with his finger. "He circulates around at all the parties. You want me to find him for you?"

"Not just now, thanks. You know Tony Torres?"

"Know him well. We worked together for years."

"And his daughter?"

"Some," he said guardedly. "She worked here, too."

"Would Tony still be around? He isn't on the gate."

"No, he goes off at night, party or no party. His fill-in didn't show up tonight. Maybe Mr. Bassett forgot to call him."

"Where does Tony live, do you know?"

"I ought to. He lives under your feet, practically. He's got a place next to the boiler room, he moved in there last year. He used to get so cold at night, he told me."

"Show me, will you?"

He didn't move, except to look at his wristwatch. "It's half past one. You wouldn't want to wake him up in the middle of the night."

"Yes," I said. "I would."

He shrugged and took me along a corridor filled with a soapy shower-room odor, down a flight of concrete steps into hothouse air, through a drying-room where bathing suits hung like sloughed snakeskins on wooden racks, between the two great boilers which heated the pool and the buildings. Behind them, a room-within-a-room had been built out of two-by-fours and plywood.

"Tony lives here because he wants to," the lifeguard said rather defensively. "He won't live in his house on the beach any more, he rents it out. I wish you wouldn't wake him up. Tony's an old man, he needs his rest."

But Tony was already awake. His bare feet slithered on the floor. Light came on, blazing through all the cracks in the plywood walls and framing the door. Tony opened it and blinked at us, a big-bellied little old man in long underwear with a religious locket hanging around his neck.

"Sorry to get you out of bed. I'd like to talk to you."

"What about? What's the trouble?" He scratched at his tousled, graying hair.

"No trouble." Just two murders in his family, one of which I wasn't supposed to know about. "May I come in?"

"Sure thing. Matter 'fact, I been thinking I'd like to talk to you."

He pushed the door wide and stepped back with a gesture that was almost courtly. "You comin' in, Joe?"

"I got to get back upstairs," the lifeguard said.

I thanked him and went in. The room was hot and small, lit by a naked bulb on an extension cord. I'd never seen a monk's cell, but the room could probably have served as one. A blistered oak-veneer bureau, an iron cot, a kitchen chair, a doorless cardboard wardrobe containing a blue serge suit, a horsehide windbreaker, and a clean uniform. Faded blue flannelette sheets covered the cot, and an old brass-fitted suitcase protruded from underneath it. Two pictures shared the wall above the head of the bed. One was a hand-tinted studio photograph of a pretty dark-eyed girl in a white dress that looked like a high-school graduation dress. The other was a Virgin in four colors, holding a blazing heart in her extended hand.

Tony indicated the kitchen chair for me, and sat on the bed himself. Scratching his head again, he looked down at the floor, his eyes impassive as anthracite. The big knuckles of his right hand were jammed and swollen.

"Yeah, I been thinkin'," he repeated, "All day and half of the night. You're a detective, Mr. Bassett says."

"A private one."

"Yeah, private. That's for me. These county cops, who can trust 'em? They run around in their fancy automobiles and arrest people for no-taillight or throw-a-beer-can-in-the-highway-ditch. Something real bad happens, they ain't there."

"They're usually there, Tony."

"Maybe. I seen some funny things in my time. Like what happened last year, right in my own family." His head turned slowly to the left, under intangible but irresistible pressure, until he was looking at the girl in the white dress. "I guess you heard about Gabrielle, my daughter."

"Yes. I heard."

"Shot on the beach, I found her. March twenty-first, last year. She was gone all night supposed to be with a girl friend. I found her in the morning, eighteen years old, my only daughter."

"I'm sorry."

His black glance probed my face, gauging the depth of my sympathy. His wide mouth was wrenched by the pain of truth-telling: "I ain't no bleeding heart. It was my fault, I seen it coming. How could I bring her up myself? A girl without a mother? A pretty young girl?" His gaze rotated in a quarter-circle again, and returned to me. "What could I tell her what to do?"

"What happened to your wife, Tony?"

"My wife?" The question surprised him. He had to think for a minute. "She run out on me, many years now. Run away with a man, last I heard she's in Seattle, she's always crazy for men. My Gabrielle took after her, I think. I went to Catholic Welfare, ask them what I should do, my girl is running out of control like a loco mare in heat—I didden say that to the Father, not them words.

"The Father says, put her in a convent school, but it was too much money. Too much money to save my daughter's life. All right, I saved the money, I got the money in the bank, nobody to spend it for." He turned and said to the Virgin: "I am a dirty old fool."

"You can't live their life for them, Tony."

"No. What I could do, I coulda kept her locked up with good people looking after her. I coulda kept Manuel out of my house."

"Did he have something to do with her death?"

"Manuel is in jail when it happens. But he was the one started her running wild. I didden catch on for a long time, he taught her to lie to me. It was high-school basketball, or swimming team, or spend-the-night-with-a-friend. Alla time she was riding around on the back of motorcycles from Oxnard, learning to be a dirty—" His mouth clamped down on an unspoken word.

After a pause, he went on more calmly: "That girl I seen with Manuel on the Venice Speedway in the low-top car. Hester Campbell. She's the one Gabrielle's supposed to spend the night with, the night that she got killed. Then you come here this morning asking about Manuel. It started me thinking, about who done it to her. Manuel and the blondie girl, why do they get together, can you tell me?"

"Later on I may be able to. Tell me, Tony, is thinking all you've been doing?"

"Huh?"

"Did you leave the Club today or tonight? Did you see your nephew Manuel?"

"No. No to both questions."

"How many guns do you have?"

"Just the one."

"What caliber?"

"Forty-five Colt revolver." His mind was one-track and too preoccupied to catch the inference. "Here."

He reached behind the mashed pillow and handed me his revolver. Its chambers were full, and it showed no signs of having been fired recently. In any case, the shells I had found beside his nephew's body were medium-caliber, probably thirty-two's.

I hefted the Colt. "Nice gun."

"Yeah. It belongs to the Club. I got a permit to carry it."

I gave it back to him. He pointed it at the floor, sighting along the barrel. He spoke in a very old voice, dry, sexless, dreadful:

"If I ever know who killed her, this is what he gets. I don't wait for crooked cops to do my business." He leaned forward and tapped my arm with the barrel, very lightly: "You're a detective, mister, find me who killed my girl, you can have all I got. Money in the bank, over a thousand dollars, I *save* my money these days. Piece of rented property onna beach, mortgage all paid off."

"Keep it that way. And put the gun away, Tony."

"I was a gunner's mate in the World War Number One. I know how to handle guns."

"Prove it. Too many people would get a boot out of it if I got myself drilled in a shooting accident."

He slipped the revolver under the pillow and stood up. "It's too late, huh? Nearly two years, a long time. You are not interested in wild-duck cases, you got other business."

"I'm very much interested. In fact, this is why I wanted to talk to you."

"It's what you call a coincidence, eh?" He was proud of the word.

"I don't believe much in coincidences. If you trace them back far enough, they usually have a meaning. I'm pretty sure this one has."

"You mean," he said slowly, "Gabrielle and Manuel and Manuel's blondie?"

"And you, and other things. They all fit together."

"Other things?"

"We won't go into them now. What did the cops tell you last March?"

"No evidence, they said. They poked around here a few days and closed down the case. They said some robber, but I dunno. What robber shoots a girl for seventy-five cents?"

"Was she raped?"

Something like dust gathered on the surface of his anthracite eyes. The muscles stood out in his face like walnuts of various sizes in a leather bag, altering its shape. I caught a glimpse of the gamecock passion that had held him up for six rounds against Armstrong in the old age of his legs.

"No rape," he said with difficulty. "Doctor at the autopsy says a man was with her some time in the night. I don't wanna talk about it. Here."

He stooped and dragged the suitcase out from under the bed, flung it open, rummaged under a tangle of shirts. Stood up breathing audibly with a dog-eared magazine in his hand.

"Here," he said violently. "Read it."

It was a lurid-covered true-crime book which fell open to an article near the middle entitled "The Murder of the Violated Virgin." This was an account of the murder of Gabrielle Torres, illustrated with photographs of her and her father, one of which was a smudgy reproduction of the photograph on the wall. Tony was shown in conversation with a sheriff's plainclothesman identified in the caption as Deputy Theodore Marfeld. Marfeld had aged since March of the previous year. The account began:

It was a balmy Spring night at Malibu Beach, gay playground of the movie capital. But the warm tropical wind that whipped the waves shoreward seemed somehow threatening to Tony Torres, onetime lightweight boxer and now watchman at the exclusive Channel Club. He was not easily upset after many years in the squared circle, but tonight Tony was desperately worried about his gay young teen-aged daughter, Gabrielle.

What could be keeping her? Tony asked himself again and again. She had promised to be in by midnight at the latest. Now it was three o'clock in the morning, now it was four o'clock, and still no Gabrielle. Tony's inexpensive alarm clock ticked remorselessly on. The waves that thundered on the beach below his modest seaside cottage seemed to echo in his ears like the very voice of doom itself. . . ."

I lost patience with the clichés and the excess verbiage, which indicated that the writer had nothing much to say. He hadn't. The rest of the story, which I scanned in a hurry, leered a great deal under a veil of pseudo-poetic prose, on the strength of a few facts:

Gabrielle had a bad reputation. There had been men in her life, unnamed. Her body had been found to contain male seed and two bullets. The first bullet had inflicted a superficial wound in her thigh. This had bled considerably. The implication was that several minutes at least had elapsed between the firing of the first bullet and the firing of the second. The second had entered her back, found its way through the ribs, and stopped her heart.

Both slugs were twenty-two long, and had been fired from the same long-barreled revolver, location unknown. That is what the police ballistics experts said. Theodore Marfeld said —the quotation ended the article: "Our daughters must be protected. I am going to solve this hideous crime if it takes me the rest of my life. At the moment I have no definite clues."

I looked up at Tony. "Nice fellow, Marfeld."

"Yah." He heard the irony. "You know him, huh?"

"I know him."

I stood up. Tony took the magazine from my hand, tossed it into the suitcase, kicked the suitcase under the bed. He reached for the string that controlled the light, and jerked the grief-stricken room downward into darkness.

꿈꿈꿈꿈꿈꿈 *chapter* 19

I WENT upstairs and along the gallery to Bassett's office. He still wasn't in it. I went in search of a drink. Under the half-retracted roof of a great inner court, dancers were sliding around on the waxed tiles to the music of a decimated orchestra. JEREMY CRANE AND HIS JOY BOYS was the legend on the drum. Their sad musicians' eyes looked down their noses at the merrymaking squares. They were playing lilting melancholy Gershwin: "Someone to Watch Over Me."

My diving friend whose hips didn't bounce was dancing with the perennial-bachelor type who loved taking pictures. Her diamonds glittered on his willowy right shoulder. He didn't like it when I cut in, but he departed gracefully.

She had on a tiger-striped gown with a slashed neckline and a flaring skirt which didn't become her. Her dancing was rather tigerish. She plunged around as if she was used to leading. Our dance was politely intense, like an amateur wrestling match, with no breath wasted on words. I said when it ended:

"Lew Archer is my name. May I talk to you?"

"Why not?"

We sat at one of several marble-topped tables separated by a glass windscreen from the pool. I said:

"Let me get you a drink."

"Thank you, I don't drink. You're not a member, and you're not one of Sime Graff's regulars. Let me guess." She fingered her pointed chin, and her diamonds flashed. "Reporter?"

"Guess again."

"Policeman?"

"You're very acute, or am I very obvious?"

She studied me from between narrowed eyelids, and smiled narrowly. "No, I wouldn't say you're obvious. It's just you asked me something about Hester Campbell before. And it kind of made me wonder if you were a policeman."

"I don't follow your line of reasoning."

"Don't you? Then how does it happen that you're interested in her?"

"I'm afraid I can't tell you that. My lips are sealed."

"Mine aren't," she said. "Tell me, what is she wanted for? Theft?"

"I didn't say she was wanted."

"Then she ought to be. She's a thief, you know." Her smile had a biting edge. "She stole from me. I left my wallet in the dressing-room in my *cabaña* one day last summer. It was early in the morning, no one was around except the staff, so I didn't bother locking up the place. I did a few dives and showered, and when I went to dress, my wallet was gone."

"How do you know she took it?"

"There's no doubt whatever that she did. I saw her slinking down the shower-room corridor just before I found it missing. She had something wrapped in a towel in her hand, and a guilty smirk on her face. She didn't fool me for a minute. I went to her afterwards and asked her point-blank if she had it. Of course she denied it, but I could see the deceitful look in her eyes."

"A deceitful look is hardly evidence."

"Oh, it wasn't only that. Other members have suffered losses, too, and they always coincided with Miss Campbell's being around. I know I sound prejudiced, but I'm not, really. I'd done my best to help the girl, you see. I considered her almost a protégée at one time. So it rather hurt when I caught her stealing from me. There was over a hundred dollars in the wallet, and my driver's license and keys, which had to be replaced."

"You say you caught her."

"Morally speaking, I did. Of course she wouldn't admit a thing. She'd cached the wallet somewhere in the meantime."

"Did you report the theft?" My voice was sharper than I intended.

She drummed on the tabletop with blunt fingertips. "I must say, I hardly expected to be cross-questioned like this. I'm voluntarily giving you information, and I'm doing so completely without malice. You don't understand, I *liked* Hester. She had bad breaks when she was a kid, and I felt sorry for her."

"So you didn't report it."

"No, I didn't, not to the authorities. I did take it up with Mr. Bassett, which did no good at all. She had him thoroughly hoodwinked. He simply couldn't believe that she'd do wrong—until it happened to him."

"What happened to him?"

"Hester stole from him, too," she said with a certain complacency. "That is, I can't swear that she did, but I'm morally certain of it. Miss Hamblin, his secretary, is a friend of mine, and I hear things. Mr. Bassett was dreadfully upset the day she left." She leaned toward me across the table: I could see the barred rib-cage between her breasts. "And Miss Hamblin said he changed the combination of his safe that very day."

"All this is pretty tenuous. Did he report a theft?"

"Of course he didn't. He never said a word to anybody. He was too ashamed of being taken in by her."

"And you've never said a word to anybody, either?"

"Until now."

"Why bring it all out now?"

She was silent, except for her drumming fingers. The lower part of her face set in a dull, thick expression. She had turned her head away from the source of light, and I couldn't see her eyes. "You asked me."

"I didn't ask you anything specific."

"You talk as if you were a friend of hers. Are you?"

"Are *you?*"

She covered her mouth with her hand, so that her whole face was hidden, and mumbled behind it: "I thought she was my friend. I could have forgiven her the wallet, even. But I saw her last week in Myrin's. I walked right up to her, prepared to let bygones be bygones, and she snubbed me. She pretended not to know me." Her voice became deep and harsh, and the hand in front of her mouth became a fist. "So I thought, if she's suddenly loaded, able to buy clothes at Myrin's, the least she can do is repay me my hundred dollars."

"You need the money, do you?"

Her fist repelled the suggestion, fiercely, as if I'd accused her of having a moral weakness or a physical disease. "Of course I don't need the money. It's the principle of the thing." After a thinking pause she said: "You don't like me the least little bit, do you?"

I hadn't expected the question, and I didn't have an answer ready. She had the peculiar combination of force and meanness you often find in rich, unmarried women. "You're loaded," I said, "and I'm not, and I keep remembering the difference. Does it matter?"

"Yes, it matters. You don't understand." Her eyes emerged from shadow, and her meager breast leaned hard against the table edge. "It isn't the money, so much. Only I thought Hester *liked* me. I thought she was a true friend. I used to coach her diving, I let her use Father's pool. I even gave a party for her once—a birthday party."

"How old was she?"

"It was her eighteenth birthday. She was the prettiest girl in the world then, and the nicest. I can't understand—what happened to all her niceness?"

"It's happening to a lot of people."

"Is that a crack at me?"

"At me," I said. "At all of us. Maybe it's atomic fallout or something."

Needing a drink more than ever, I thanked her and excused myself and found my way to the drinking-room. A curved mahogany bar took up one end of it. The other walls were decorated with Hollywood-Fauvist murals. The large room contained several dozen assorted couples hurling late-night insults at each other and orders at the Filipino bartenders. There were actresses with that numb and varnished look, and would-be actresses with that waiting look; junior-executive types hacking diligently at each other with their profiles; their wives watching each other through smiles; and others.

I sat at the bar between strangers, wheedled a whisky-and-water out of one of the white-coated Filipinos, and listened to the people. These were movie people, but a great deal of their talk was about television. They talked about communications media and the black list and the hook and payment for second showings and who had money for pilot films and what their agents said. Under their noise, they gave out a feeling of suspense. Some of them seemed to be listening hard for the rustle of a dropping option. Some of their eyes were knowing previews of that gray, shaking hangover dawn when all the mortgage payments came due at once and the options fell like snow.

The man on my immediate right looked like an old actor and sounded like a director. Maybe he was an actor turned director. He was explaining something to a frog-voiced whisky blonde: "It means it's happening to you, you see. You're the one in love with the girl, or the boy, as the case may be. It's not the girl on the screen he's making a play for, it's you."

"Empathy-schwempathy," she croaked pleasantly. "Why not just call it sex?"

"It isn't sex. It includes sex."

"Then I'm for it. Anything that includes sex, I'm for it. That's my personal philosophy of life."

"And a fine philosophy it is," another man said. "Sex and television are the opium of the people."

"I thought marijuana was the opium of the people."

"Marijuana is the *marijuana* of the people."

There was a girl on my left. I caught a glimpse of her profile, young and pretty and smooth as glass. She was talking earnestly to the man beside her, an aging clown I'd seen in twenty movies.

"You said you'd catch me if I fell," she said.

"I was feeling stronger then."

"You said you'd marry me if it ever happened."

"You got more sense than to take me seriously. I'm two years behind on alimony now."

"You're very romantic, aren't you?"

"That's putting it mildly, sweetheart. I got some sense of responsibility, though. I'll do what I can for you, give you a telephone number. And you can tell him to send the bill to me."

"I don't want your dirty telephone number. I don't want your dirty money."

"Be reasonable. Think of it like it was a tumor or something—that is, if it really exists. Another drink?"

"Make mine prussic acid," she said dully.

"On the rocks?"

I left half my drink standing. It was air I needed. At one of the marble-topped tables in the court, under the saw-toothed shadow of a banana tree, Simon Graff was sitting with his wife. His gray hair was still dark and slick from the shower. He wore a dinner jacket with a pink shirt and a red cummerbund. She wore a blue mink coat over a black gown figured with gold which was out of style. His face was brown and pointed, talking at her. I couldn't see her face. She was looking out through the windscreen at the pool.

I had a contact mike in my car, and I went out to the parking-lot to get it. There were fewer cars than there had been, and one additional one: Carl Stern's sedan. It had Drive-Yourself registration. I didn't take time to go over it.

Graff was still talking when I got back to the poolside. The pool was abandoned now, but wavelets still washed the sides, shining in the underwater light. Hidden from Graff by the banana tree, I moved a rope chair up against the wind-screen and pressed the mike to the plate glass. The trick had worked before, and it worked again. He was saying:

"Oh, yes, certainly, everything is my fault, I am your personal *bête noire*, and I apologize deeply."

"Please, Simon."

"Simon who? There is no Simon here. I am Mephisto Bête Noire, the famous hell husband. No!" His voice rose sharply on the word. "Think a minute, Isobel, if you have any mind left to think with. Think of what I have done for you, what I have endured and continue to endure. Think where you would be if it weren't for my support."

"This is support?"

"We won't argue. I know what you want. I know your purpose in attacking me." His voice was smooth as butter salted with tears. "You have suffered, and you want me to suffer. I refuse to suffer. You cannot make me suffer."

"God damn you," she said in a rustling whisper.

"God damn me, eh? How many drinks have you had?"

"Five or ten or twelve. Does it signify?"

"You know you cannot drink, that alcohol is death for you. Must I call Dr. Frey and have you locked up again?"

"No!" She was frightened. "I'm not drunk."

"Of course not. You are sobriety personified. You are the girl ideal of the Women's Christian Temperance Union, *mens sana in corpore sano*. But let me tell you one thing, Mrs. Sobriety. You are not going to ruin my party, no matter what.

If you cannot or will not act as hostess, you will take yourself off, Toko will drive you."

"Get *her* to be your hostess, why don't you?"

"Who? Who are you talking about?"

"Hester Campbell," she said. "Don't tell me you're not seeing her."

"For business purposes. I have seen her for business purposes. If you have hired detectives, you will regret it."

"I don't need detectives, I have my sources. Did you give her the house for business purposes? Did you buy her those clothes for business purposes?"

"What do you know about that house? Have you been in that house?"

"It's none of your business."

"Yes." The word hissed like steam escaping from an overloaded pressure system. "I make it my business. Were you in that house today?"

"Maybe."

"Answer me, crazy woman."

"You can't talk to me like that." She began to call him names in a low, husky voice. It sounded like something tearing inside of her, permitting the birth of a more violent personality.

She rose suddenly, and I saw her walking across the patio in a straight line, moving among the dancers as though they were phantoms, figments of her mind. Her hip bumped the door frame as she went into the bar.

She came right out again, by another door. I caught a glimpse of her face in the light from the pool. It was white and frightened-looking. Perhaps the people frightened her. She skirted the shallow end of the pool, clicking along on high heels, and entered the *cabaña* on the far side.

I strolled toward the other end of the pool. The diving tower rose gleaming against a bank of fog that hid the sea. The ocean end was surrounded by a heavy wire fence. From a locked gate in the fence, a flight of concrete steps led down to the beach. High tides had gnawed and crumbled the lower steps.

I leaned on the gatepost and lit a cigarette. I had to cup the match against the stream of cold air which flowed upward from the water. This and the heavy sky overhead created the illusion that I was on the bow of a slow ship, and the ship was headed into foggy darkness.

xxxxxxxxxx *chapter* 20

SOMEWHERE behind me, a woman's voice rose sharp. A man's voice answered it and drowned it out. I turned and looked around the bright, deserted pool. The two were standing close together at the wavering margin of the light, so close they might have been a single dark and featureless body. They were at the far end of the gallery, maybe forty yards away from me, but their voices came quite clearly across the water.

"No!" she repeated. "You're crazy. I did not."

I crossed to the gallery and walked toward them, keeping in its shadow.

"I'm not the one who is crazy," the man was saying. "We know who's crazy, sweetheart."

"Leave me alone. Don't touch me."

I knew the woman's voice. It belonged to Isobel Graff. I couldn't place the man's. He was saying:

"You bitch. You dirty bitch. Why did you do it? What did he do to you?"

"I didn't. Leave me alone, you filth." She called him other names which reflected on his ancestry and her vocabulary.

He answered her in a low, blurred voice I didn't catch. There were Lower East Side marbles in his mouth. I was close enough to recognize him now. Carl Stern.

He let out a feline sound, a mewling growl, and slapped her face, twice, very hard. She reached for his face with hooked fingers. He caught her by the wrists. Her mink coat slid from her shoulders and lay on the concrete like a large blue animal without a head. I started to run on my toes.

Stern flung her away from him. She thudded against the door of a *cabaña* and sat down in front of it. He stood over her, dapper and broad in his dark raincoat. The greenish light from the pool lent his head a cruel bronze patina.

"Why did you kill him?"

She opened her mouth and closed it and opened it, but no sound came. Her upturned face was like a cratered moon. He leaned over her in silent fury, so intent on her that he didn't know I was there until I hit him.

I hit him with my shoulder, pinned his arms, palmed his flanks for a gun. He was clean, in that respect. He bucked and snorted like a horse, trying to shake me off. He was almost as strong as a horse. His muscles cracked in my grip. He kicked at my shins and stamped my toes and tried to bite my arm.

I released him and, when he turned, chopped at the side of his jaw with my right fist. I didn't like men who bit. He spun and went down with his back to me. His hand dove up under his trouser-leg. He rose and turned in a single movement. His eyes were black nailheads on which his face hung haggard. A white line surrounded his mouth and marked the edges of his black nostrils, which glared at me like secondary eyes. Protruding from the fist he held at the center of his body was the four-inch blade of the knife he carried on his leg.

"Put it away, Stern."

"I'll carve your guts." His voice was high and rasping, like the sound of metal being machined.

I didn't wait for him to move. I threw a sneak right hand which crashed into his face and rocked him hard. His jaw turned to meet the left hook that completed the combination and finished Stern. He swayed on his feet for a few seconds, then collapsed on himself. The knife clattered and flashed on the concrete. I picked it up and closed it.

Footsteps came trotting along the gallery. It was Clarence Bassett, breathing rapidly under his boiled shirt. "What on earth?"

"Cat fight. Nothing serious."

He helped Mrs. Graff to her feet. She leaned on the wall and straightened her twisted stockings. He picked up her coat, brushing it carefully with his hands, as though the mink and the woman were equally important.

Carl Stern got up groggily. He gave me a dull-eyed look of hatred. "Who are you?"

"The name is Archer."

"You're the eye, uh?"

"I'm the eye who doesn't think that women should be hit."

"Chivalrous, eh? You're going to hate yourself for this, Archer."

"I don't think so."

"I think so. I got a lot of friends. I got connections. You're through in L.A., you know that? All finished."

"Put it in writing, will you? I've been wanting to get out of the smog."

"Speaking of connections," Bassett said quietly to Stern, "you're not a member of this club."

"I'm a guest of a member. And you're going to get crucified, too."

"Oh, my, yes. What fun. Whose guest would you happen to be?"

"Simon Graff's. I want to see him. Where is he?"

"We won't bother Mr. Graff just now. And may I make a suggestion? It's getting latish, more for some than for others. Don't you think you'd better leave?"

"I don't take orders from servants."

"Don't you indeed?" Bassett's smile was a toothy mask which left his eyes sad. He turned to me.

I said: "You want to be hit again, Stern? It would be a pleasure."

Stern glared at me for a long moment, red lights dancing on his shallow eyes. The lights went out. He said:

"All right. I'll leave. Give me back my knife."

"If you promise to cut your throat with it."

He tried to go into another fury, but lacked the energy. He looked sick. I tossed him the closed knife. He caught it and put it in the pocket of his coat, turned and walked away toward the entrance. He stumbled several times. Bassett marched behind him, at a distance, like a watchful policeman.

Mrs. Graff was fumbling with a key at the door of the *cabaña*. Her hands were shaking, out of control. I turned the key for her and switched on the light. It was indirect, and shone from four sides on a bellying brown fishnet ceiling. The room was done in primitive Pacific style, with split-bamboo screens at the windows, grass matting on the floor, rattan armchairs and chaise longues. Even the bar in one corner was rattan. Beside it, at the rear of the room, two louvered doors opened into the dressing-rooms. The walls were hung with tapa cloths and Douanier Rousseau reproductions, bamboo-framed.

The only discordant note was a Matisse travel poster lithographed in brilliant colors and advertising Nice. Mrs. Graff paused in front of it, and said to no one in particular:

"We have a villa near Nice. Father gave it to us as a wedding present. Simon was all for it in those days. All for me, and all for one." She laughed, for no good reason. "He won't even take me to Europe with him any more. "He says I always make trouble for him when we go away together, any more. It isn't true, I'm as quiet as a quilt. He flies away on his trans-polar flights and leaves me here to rot in the heat and cold."

She clasped her head with both hands, tightly, for a long moment. Her hair stuck up between her fingers like black, untidy feathers. The silent pain she was fighting to control was louder than a scream.

"Are you all right, Mrs. Graff?"

I touched her blue mink back. She sidestepped away from my touch, whirled the coat off, and flung it on a studio bed. Her back and shoulders were dazzling, and her breast overflowed the front of her strapless dress like whipped cream. She held her body with a kind of awkward pride mixed with shame, like a young girl suddenly conscious of her flesh.

"Do you like my dress? It isn't new. I haven't been to a party for years and years and years. Simon doesn't take me any more."

"Nasty old Simon," I said. "Are you all right, Mrs. Graff?"

She answered me with a bright actress's smile which didn't go with the stiffness of the upper part of her face, the despair in her eyes:

"I'm wonderful. Wonderful."

She did a brief dance-step to prove it, snapping her fingers at the end of rigid arms. Bruises were coming out on her white forearms, the size and color of Concord grapes. Her dancing was mechanical. She stumbled and lost a gold slipper. Instead of putting it on again, she kicked off the other slipper. She sat on one of the bar stools, wriggling her stockinged feet, clasping and rubbing them together. They looked like blind, flesh-colored animals making furtive love under the hem of her skirt:

"Incidentally," she said, "and accidentally, I haven't thanked you. I thank you."

"What for?"

"For saving me from a fate worse than life. That wretched little drug-peddler might have killed me. He's terribly strong, isn't he?" She added resentfully: "They're not supposed to be strong."

"Who aren't? Drug-peddlers?"

"Pansies. All pansies are supposed to be weak. Like all bullies are cowards, and all Greeks run restaurants. That isn't a good example, though. My father was a Greek, at least he was a Cypriot, and, by God, he ran a restaurant in Newark, New Jersey. Great oaks from little acorns grow. Miracles of modern science. From a greasy spoon in Newark to wealth and decadence in one easy generation. It's the new accelerated pace, with automation."

She looked around the alien room. "He might as well have stayed in Cyprus, for God's sake. What good did it do me?

I ended up in a therapy room making pottery and weaving rugs like a God-damn cottage industry. Except that *I* pay them. I always do the paying."

Her contact seemed to be better, which encouraged me to say: "Do you always do the talking, too?"

"Am I talking too much?" She gave me her brilliant, disorganized smile again, as if her mouth could hardly contain her teeth. "Am I making any sense, for God's sake?"

"From time to time you are, for God's sake."

Her smile became slightly less intense and more real. "I'm sorry, I get on a talking jag sometimes and the words come out wrong and they don't mean what I want them to. Like in James Joyce, only to me it just *hap*pens. Did you know his daughter was schizzy?" She didn't wait for an answer. "So sometimes I'm a wit and sometimes I'm a nit-wit, so they tell me." She extended her bruise-mottled arm: "Sit down and have a drink and tell me who *you* are."

"Archer," she repeated thoughtfully, but she wasn't interested in me. Memory flared and smoked inside of her like a fire in changing winds: "I'm nobody in particular, either. I used to think I was. My father was Peter Heliopoulos, at least that's what he called himself, his real name was longer than that and much more complicated. And I was much more complicated, too. I was the crown princess, my father *called* me Princess. So now—" her voice jangled harshly off-key— "so now a cheap Hollywood drug-peddler can push me around and get away with it. In my father's day they would have flayed him alive. So what does my husband do? He goes into business with him. They're palsy-walsies, cerebral palsy-walsies."

"Do you mean Carl Stern, Mrs. Graff?"

"Who else?"

"What kind of business are they in?"

"Whatever people do in Las Vegas, gambling and helling around. I never go there myself, never go anywhere."

"How do you know he's a drug-peddler?"

"I bought drugs from him myself when I ran out of doctors —yellow jackets and demerol and the little kind with the red stripe. I'm off drugs now, however. Back on liquor again. It's one thing Dr. Frey did for me." Her eyes focused on my face, and she said impatiently: "You haven't made yourself a drink. Go ahead and make yourself a drink, and make one for me, too."

"Do you think that's a good idea, Isobel?"

"*Don't* talk to me as though I were a child. I'm not drunk. I can hold my liquor." The bright smile gashed her face. "The only trouble with me is that I am somewhat crazy. But not at

110

the moment. I was upset there for a moment, but you're very soothing and smoothing, aren't you? Kind of kind of kind." She was mimicking herself.

"Any more," I said.

"Any more. But you won't make fun of me, will you? I get so mad sometimes—angry-mad, I mean—when people mock my dignity. I may be going into a wind-up, I don't know, but I haven't taken off yet. On my trans-polar flight," she added wryly, "into the wild black yonder."

"Good for you."

She nodded in self-congratulation. "That was one of the wit ones, wasn't it? It isn't really true, though. When it happens, it isn't like flying or any sort of arrival or departure. The *feel* of things changes, that's all, and I can't tell the difference between me and other things. Like when Father died and I saw him in the coffin and had my first breakdown. I thought *I* was in the coffin. I felt dead, my flesh was cold. There was embalming fluid in my veins, and I could smell myself. At the same time I was lying dead in the coffin and sitting in the pew in the Orthodox Church, mourning for my own death. And when they buried him, the earth—I could hear the earth dropping on the coffin and then it smothered me and I was the earth."

She took hold of my hand and held it, trembling. "Don't let me talk so much. It does me harm. I almost *went*, just then."

"Where did you go?" I said.

"Into my dressing-room." She dropped her hand and gestured toward one of the louvered doors. "For a second I was in there, watching us through the door and listening to myself. *Please* pour me a drink. It does me good, honestly. Scotch on the rocks."

I moved around behind the bar and got ice cubes out of the small beige refrigerator and opened a bottle of Johnnie Walker and made a couple of drinks, medium strength. I felt more comfortable on the wrong side of the bar. The woman disturbed me basically, the way you can be disturbed by starvation in a child, or a wounded bird, or a distempered cat running in yellow circles. She seemed to be teetering on the verge of a psychotic episode. Also, she seemed to know it. I was afraid to say anything that might push her over the edge.

She raised her glass. The steady tremor in her hand made the brown liquor slosh around among the ice cubes. As if to demonstrate her self-control, she barely sipped at it. I sipped at mine, leaned on my elbow across the formica counter in the attitude of a bartender with a willing ear.

"What was the trouble, Isobel?"

"Trouble? You mean with Carl Stern?"

"Yes. He got pretty rough."

"He hurt me," she said, without self-pity. A taste of whisky had changed her mood, as a touch of acid will change the color of blue litmus paper. "Interesting medical facts. I bruise very easily." She exhibited her arms. "I bet my entire body is covered with bruises."

"Why would Stern do it to you?"

"People like him are sadists, at least a lot of them are."

"You know a lot of them?"

"I've known my share. I attract them, apparently, I don't know why. Or maybe I do know why. Women like me, we don't expect too much. *I* don't expect *anything*."

"Lance Leonard one of them?"

"How should I know? I guess so. I hardly knew—I hardly knew the little mackerel."

"He used to be a lifeguard here."

"I don't mess with lifeguards," she said harshly. "What is this? I thought we were going to be friends, I thought we were going to have fun. I never have any *fun*."

"Any more."

She didn't think it was funny. "They lock me up and punish me, it isn't fair," she said. "I did one terrible thing in my life, and now they blame me for everything that happens. Stern's a filthy liar. I never touched his lover-boy, I didn't even know that he was dead. Why would I shoot him? I have enough on my conscious—on my conscience."

"Such as?"

She peered at my face. Hers was as stiff as a board. "Such as, you're trying to pump me, aren't you, such as? Trying to dig things out of me?"

"Yes, I am. What terrible thing did you do?"

Something peculiar happened to her face. One of her eyes became narrow and sly, one became hard and wide. On the sly side, her upper lip lifted and her white teeth gleamed under it. She said: "I'm a naughty, naughty, naughty girl. I watched them doing it. I stood behind the door and watched them doing it. Miracles of modern science. And I was in the room and behind the door."

"What did you do?"

"I killed my mother."

"How?"

"By wishing," she said slyly. "I wished my mother to death. Does that take care of your questions, Mr. Questionnaire? Are you a psychiatrist? Did Simon hire you?"

"The answer is no and no."

"I killed my father, too. I broke his heart. Shall I tell you

112

my other crimes? It's quite a decalogue. Envy and malice and pride and lust and rage. I'd sit at home and plan his death, by hanging, burning, shooting, drowning, poison. I'd sit at home and imagine him with them, all the young girls with their bodies and waving white legs. I sat at home and tried to have men friends. It never seemed to work out. They were exhausted by the heat and cold or else I frightened them. One of them told me I frightened him, the lousy little nance. They'd drink up my liquor and never come back." She sipped from her glass. "Go ahead," she said. "Drink up your liquor."

"Drink up yours, Isobel. I'll take you home. Where do you live?"

"Quite near here, on the beach. But I'm not going home. You won't make me go home, will you? I haven't been to a party for so long. Why don't we go and dance? I am very ugly to look at, but I am a good dancer."

"You are very beautiful, but I am a lousy dancer."

"I'm ugly," she said. "You mustn't mock me. I know how ugly I am. I was born ugly through and through, and nobody ever loved me."

The door opened behind her, swinging wide. Simon Graff appeared in the opening. His face was stony.

"Isobel! What kind of *Walpurgisnacht* is this? What are you doing here?"

Her reaction was slow, almost measured. She turned and rose from the stool. Her body was tense and insolent. The drink was shaking in her hand.

"What am I doing? I'm telling my secrets. I'm telling all my dirty little secrets to my dear friend."

"You fool. Come home with me."

He took several steps toward her. She threw her glass at his head. It missed him and dented the wall beside the door. Some of the liquid spattered his face.

"Crazy woman," he said. "You come home now with me. I will call Dr. Frey."

"I don't have to go with you. You're not my father." She turned to me, the look of lopsided cunning still on her face. "Do I have to go with him?"

"I don't know. Is he your legal guardian?"

Graff answered: "Yes, I am. You will keep out of this." He said to her: "There is nothing but grief for you, for all of us, if you try to break loose from me. You would be really lost." There was a new quality in his voice, a largeness and a darkness and an emptiness.

"I'm lost now. How lost can a woman get?"

"You will find out, Isobel. Unless you come with me and do as I say."

"Svengali," I said. "Very old-hat."

"Keep out of this, I warn you." I felt his glance like an icicle parting my hair. "This woman is my wife."

"Lucky her."

"Who are you?"

I told him.

"What are you doing in this club, at this party?"

"Watching the animals."

"I expect a specific answer."

"Try using a different tone, and you might get one." I came around the end of the bar and stood beside Isobel Graff. "You've been spoiled by all those yes-men in your life. I happen to be a no-man."

He looked at me in genuine shock. Maybe he hadn't been contradicted for years. Then he remembered to be angry, and turned on his wife:

"Did he come here with you?"

"No." She sounded intimidated. "I thought he was one of your guests."

"What is he doing in this *cabaña?*"

"I offered him a drink. He helped me. A man hit me." Her voice was monotonous, threaded by a whine of complaint.

"What man hit you?"

"Your friend Carl Stern," I said. "He slapped her around and pushed her down. Bassett and I threw him out."

"You threw him out?" Graff's alarm turned to anger, which he directed against his wife again: "You permitted this, Isobel?"

She hung her head and assumed an awkward, ugly posture, standing on one leg like a schoolgirl.

"Didn't you hear me, Graff? Or don't you object to thugs pushing your wife around?"

"I will look after my wife in my own way. She is mentally disturbed, sometimes she requires to be firmly handled. You are not needed. Get out."

"I'll finish my drink first, thank you." I added conversationally: "What did you do with George Wall?"

"George Wall? I know no George Wall."

"Your strong-arm boys do—Frost and Marfeld and Lashman."

The names piqued his interest. "Who is this George Wall?"

"Hester's husband."

"I am not acquainted with any Hester."

His wife gave him a swift, dark look, but said nothing. I fixed him with my steeliest glance and tried to stare him down. It didn't work. His eyes were like holes in a wall; you looked through them into a great, dim, empty place.

"You're a liar, Graff."

His face turned purple and white. He went to the door and called Bassett in a loud, trembling voice. When Bassett appeared, Graff said: "I want this man thrown out. I don't permit party-crashers—"

"Mr. Archer is not exactly a party-crasher," Bassett said coolly.

"Is he a friend of yours?"

"I think of him as a friend, yes. A friend of brief standing, shall we say. Mr. Archer is a detective, a private detective I hired for personal reasons."

"What reasons?"

"A crackpot threatened me last night. I hired Mr. Archer to investigate the matter."

"Instruct him, then, to leave my friends alone. Carl Stern is an associate of mine. I want him treated with respect."

Bassett's eyes gleamed wetly, but he stood up to Graff. "I am manager of this club. As long as I am, I'll set the standards for the behavior of the guests. No matter whose friends they are."

Isobel Graff laughed tinnily. She had sat down on her coat, and was plucking at the fur.

Graff clenched his fists at his sides and began to shake. "Get out of here, both of you."

"Come along, Archer. We'll give Mr. Graff a chance to recover his manners."

Bassett was white and scared, but he carried it off. I didn't know he had it in him.

xxxxxxxxx *chapter* 21

WE went along the gallery to his office. His walk was a stiff-backed, high-shouldered march step. His movements seemed to be controlled by a system of outside pressures that fitted him like a corset.

He brought glasses out of his portable bar and poured me

a stiff slug of whisky, a stiffer one for himself. The bottle was a different bottle from the one I had seen in the morning, and it was nearly empty. Yet the long day's drinking, like a passage of years, had improved Bassett in some ways. He'd lost his jaunty self-consciousness, and he wasn't pretending to be younger than he was. The sharp skull pressed like a death mask behind the thin flesh of his face.

"That was quite a performance," I said. "I thought you were a little afraid of Graff."

"I am, when I'm totally sober. He's on the board of trustees, and you might say he controls my job. But there are limits to what a man can put up with. It's rather wonderful not to feel frightened, for a change."

"I hope I didn't get you into trouble."

"Don't worry about me. I'm old enough to look after myself." He waved me into a chair and sat behind his desk with the half-glass of neat whisky in his hand. He drank from it and regarded me over the rim. "What brings you here, old man? Has something happened?"

"Plenty has happened. I saw Hester tonight."

He looked at me as though I'd said that I had seen a ghost. "You saw her? Where?"

"In her house in Beverly Hills. We had some conversation, which got us nowhere—"

"Tonight?"

"Around midnight, yes."

"Then she's alive!"

"Unless she was wired for sound. Did you think she was dead?"

It took him a while to answer. His eyes were wet and glassy. Behind them, something obscure happened to him. I guessed he was immensely relieved. "I was mortally afraid that she was dead. I've been afraid all day that George Wall was going to kill her."

"That's nonsense. Wall has disappeared himself. He may be in a bad way. Graff's people may have killed him."

Bassett wasn't interested in Wall. He came around the desk and laid a tense hand on my shoulder. "You're not lying to me? You're certain that Hester's all right?"

"She was all right, physically, a couple of hours ago. I don't know what to make of her. She looks and talks like a nice girl, but she's involved with the crummiest crew in the Southwest. Carl Stern, for instance. What do you make of her, Bassett?"

"I don't know what to make of her. I never have."

He leaned on the desk, pressed his hand to his forehead,

and stroked his long horse face. His eyelids lifted slowly. I could see the dull pain peering out from under them.

"You're fond of her, aren't you?"

"Very fond of her. I wonder if you can understand my feeling for the girl. It's what you might call an avuncular feeling. There's nothing—nothing fleshly about it at all. I've known Hester since she was an infant, her and her sister, too. Her father was one of our members, one of my dearest friends."

"You've been here a long time."

"Twenty-five years as manager. I was a charter member of the Club. There were twenty-five of us originally. Each of us put up forty thousand dollars."

"You put up forty thousand?"

"I did. Mother and I were fairly well fixed at one time, until the crash of '29 wiped us out. When that happened, my friends in the Club offered me the post of manager. This is the first and only job I've ever had."

"What happened to Campbell?"

"He drank himself to death. As I am doing, on a somewhat retarded schedule." Grinning sardonically, he reached for his glass and drained it. "His wife was a silly woman, completely impractical. Lived up Topanga Canyon after Raymond's death. I did what I could for the fatherless babes."

"You didn't tell me all this yesterday morning."

"No. I was brought up not to boast of my philanthropies."

His speech was very formal, and slightly blurred. The whisky was getting to him. He looked from me to the bottle, his eyes swiveling heavily. I shook my head. He poured another quadruple shot for himself, and sipped at it. If he drank enough of it down, there would be no more pain behind his eyelids. Or the pain would take strange forms. That was the trouble with alcohol as a sedative. It floated you off reality for a while, but it brought you back by a route that meandered through the ash-dumps of hell.

I threw out a question, a random harpoon before he floated all the way down to Lethe: "Did Hester doublecross you?"

He looked startled, but he handled his alcohol-saturated words with care: "What in heaven's name are you talking about?"

"It was suggested to me that Hester stole something from you when she left here."

"Stole from me? Nonsense."

"She didn't rob your safe?"

"Good Lord, no. Hester wouldn't do a thing like that. Not that I have anything worth stealing. We handle no cash at the club, you know, all our business is done by chit—"

"I'm not interested in that. All I want is your word that Hester didn't rob your safe in September."

"Of course she didn't. I can't imagine where you got such a notion. People have such poisonous tongues." He leaned toward me, swaying slightly. "Who was it?"

"It doesn't matter."

"I say it does matter. You should check your sources, old man. It's character-assassination. What kind of a girl do you think Hester is?"

"It's what I'm trying to find out. You knew her as well as anyone, and you say she isn't capable of theft."

"Certainly not from me."

"From anyone?"

"I don't know what she's capable of."

"Is she capable of blackmail?"

"You ask the weirdest questions—weirder and weirder."

"Earlier in the day, you didn't think blackmail was so far-fetched. You might as well be frank with me. Is Simon Graff being blackmailed?"

He wagged his head solemnly. "What could Mr. Graff be blackmailed for?"

I glanced at the photograph of the three divers. "Gabrielle Torres. I've heard that there was a connection between her and Graff."

"What kind of connection?"

"Don't pretend to be stupid, Clarence. You're not. You knew the girl—she worked for you. If there was a thing between her and Graff, you'd probably know it."

"If there was," he said stolidly, "it never came to my knowledge." He meditated for a while, swaying on his feet. "Good Lord, man, you're not suggesting he *killed* her?"

"He could have. But Mrs. Graff was the one I had in mind."

Bassett gave me a stunned and murky look. "What a perfectly dreadful notion."

"That's what you'd say if you were covering for them."

"But thish ish utterly—" He grimaced and started over: "This is utterly absurd and ridiculous—"

"Why? Isobel is crazy enough to kill. She had a motive."

"She isn't crazy. She was—she did have serious emotional problems at one time."

"Ever been committed?"

"Not committed, I don't believe. She's been in a private sanitorium from time to time. Dr. Frey's in Santa Monica."

"When was she in last?"

"Last year."

"What part of last year?"

118

"All of it. So you shee—" He waved his hand in front of his face, as if a buzzing fly had invaded his mouth. "You see, it's quite impossible. Isobel was incarcerated at the time the girl was shot. Absolutely imposhible."

"Do you know this for a fact?"

"Shertainly I do. I visited her regularly."

"Isobel is another old friend of yours?"

"Shertainly is. Very dear old friend."

"Old enough and dear enough to lie for?"

"Don't be silly. Ishobel wouldn't harm a living creashur."

His eyes were clouding up, as well as his voice, but the glass in his hand was steady. He raised it to his mouth and drained it, then sat down rather abruptly on the edge of his desk. He swayed gently from side to side, gripping the empty glass in both hands as though it was his only firm support.

"Very dear old friend," he repeated sentimentally. "Poor Ishbel, hers is a tragic story. Her mother died young, her father gave her everything but love. She needed sympathy, someone to talk to. I tried to be that shomeone."

"You did?"

He gave me a shrewd, sad look. The jolt of whisky had partly and temporarily sobered him, but he had reached the point of diminishing returns. His face was the color of boiled meat, and his thin hair hung lank at the temples. He detached one hand from its glass anchor and pushed his hair back.

"I know it sounds unlikely. Remember, this was twenty years ago. I wasn't always an old man. At any rate, Isobel liked older men. She was devoted to her father, but he couldn't give her the understanding she needed. She'd just flunked out of college, for the third or fourth time. She was terribly withdrawn. She used to spend her days here, alone on the beach. Gradually she discovered that she could talk to me. We talked all one summer and into the fall. She wouldn't go back to school. She wouldn't leave me. She was in love with me."

"You're kidding."

I was deliberately needling him, and he reacted with alcoholic emotionalism. Angry color seeped into his capillaries, stippling his gray cheeks with red:

"It's true, she loved me. I'd had emotional problems of my own, and I was the only one who understood her. And she respected me! I am a Harvard man, did you know that? I spent three years in France in the first war. I was a stretcher-bearer."

That would make him about sixty, I thought. And twenty years ago he would have been forty to Isobel's twenty, say.

"How did you feel about her?" I said. "Avuncular?"

"I loved her. She and my mother were the only two women I ever loved. And I'd have married her, too, if her father hadn't stood in the way. Peter Heliopoulos disapproved of me."

"So he married her off to Simon Graffff."

"To Simon Graff, yah." He shuddered with the passion of a weak and timid man who seldom lets his feelings show. "To a climber and a pusher and a whoremonger and a cheat. I knew Simon Graff when he was an immigrant nobody, a nothing in this town. Assistant director on quickie Westerns with one decent suit to his name. I liked him, he pretended to like me. I lent him money, I got him a guest membership in the Club, I introduced him to people. I introduced him to Heliopoulos, by heaven. Within two years he was producing for Helio, and married to Isobel. Everything he has, everything he's done, has come out of that marriage. And he hasn't the common decency to treat her decently!"

He stood up and made a wide swashbucking gesture which carried him sideways all the way to the wall. Dropping the glass, he spread the fingers of both hands against the wall to steady himself. The wall leaned toward him, anyway. His forehead struck the plaster. He jackknifed at the hips and sat down with a thud on the carpeted floor.

He looked up at me, chuckling foolishly. One of his boiled blue eyes was straight, and one had turned outward. It gave him the appearance of mild, ridiculous lunacy.

"There's a seavy hea running," he said.

"We'll hatten down the batches."

I took him by the arms and set him on his feet and walked him to his chair. He collapsed in it, hands and jaw hanging down. His divided glance came together on the bottle. He reached for it. Five or six ounces of whisky swished around in the bottom. I was afraid that another drink might knock him out, or maybe even kill him. I lifted the bottle out of his hands, corked it, and put it away. The key of the portable bar was in the lock. I turned it and put it in my pocket.

"By what warrant do you sequester the grog?" Working his mouth elaborately around the words, Bassett looked like a camel chewing. "This is illegal—false seizure. I demand a writ of habeas corpus."

He leaned forward and reached for my glass. I snatched it away. "You've had enough, Clarence."

"Make those decisions myself. Man of decision. Man of distinction. Bottle-a-day man, by God. Drink you under table."

120

"I don't doubt it. Getting back to Simon Graff, you don't like him much?"

"Hate him," he said. "Lez be frank. He stole away only woman I ever loved. 'Cept Mother. Stole my maître dee, too. Best maître dee in Southland, Stefan. They offered him double shallery, spirited him away to Las Vegas."

"Who did?"

"Graff and Stern. Wanted him for their slo-called club."

"Speaking of Graff and Stern, why would Graff be fronting for a mobster?"

"Sixty-four-dollar question, *I* don't know the ansher. Wouldn't tell *you* if did know. *You* don't like me."

"Buck up, Clarence. I like you fine."

"Liar. Cruel and inhuman." Two tears detached themselves from the corners of his eyes and crawled down his grooved cheeks like little silver slugs. "Won't give me a drink. Trying to make me talk, withholding my grog. 'Snot fair, 'snot humane."

"Sorry. No more grog tonight. You don't want to kill yourself."

"Why not? All alone in the world. Nobody loves me." He wept suddenly and copiously, so that his whole face was wet. Transparent liquid streamed from his nose and mouth. Great sobs shook him like waves breaking in his body.

It wasn't a pretty sight. I started out.

"Don't leave me," he said between sobs. "Don't leave me alone."

He came around the desk, buckled at the knees as if he'd struck an invisible wire, and lay full-length on the carpet, blind and deaf and dumb. I turned his head sideways so that he wouldn't smother and went outside.

chapter 22

THE air was turning chilly. Laughter and other party sounds still overflowed the bar, but the music in the court had ceased. A car toiled up the drive to the highway, and then another. The party was breaking up.

There was light in the lifeguard's room at the end of the row of *cabañas*. I looked in. The young Negro was sitting inside, reading a book. He closed it when he saw me, and stood up. The name of the book was *Elements of Sociology*.

"You're a late reader."

"Better late than never."

"What do you do with Bassett when he passes out?"

"Is he passed out again?"

"On the floor of his office. Does he have a bed around?"

"Yeah, in the back room." He made a resigned face. "Guess I better put him in it, eh?"

"Need any help?"

"No, thanks, I can handle him myself, I had plenty of practice." He smiled at me, less automatically than before. "You a friend of Mr. Bassett's?"

"Not exactly."

"He give you some kind of a job?"

"You could say that."

"Working around the Club here?"

"Partly."

He was too polite to ask what my duties were. "Tell you what, I'll pour Mr. Bassett in bed, you stick around, I'll make you a cup of coffee."

"I could use a cup of coffee. The name is Lew Archer, by the way."

"Joseph Tobias." His grip was the kind that bends horseshoes. "Kind of an unusual name, isn't it? You can wait here, if you like."

He trotted away. The storeroom was jammed with folded beach umbrellas, piled deckchairs, deflated plastic floats and beach balls. I set up one of the deckchairs for myself and stretched out on it. Tiredness hit me like pentothal. Almost immediately, I went to sleep.

When I woke up, Tobias was standing beside me. He had opened a black iron switchbox on the wall. He pulled a series of switches, and the glimmering night beyond the open door turned charcoal gray. He turned and saw that I was awake.

"Didn't like to wake you up. You look tired."

"Don't you ever get tired?"

"Nope. For some reason I never do. Only time in my life I got tired was in Korea. There I got bone-tired, pushing a jeep through that deep mud they have. You want your coffee now?"

"Lead me to it."

He led me to a brightly lighted white-walled room with SNACK BAR over the door. Behind the counter, water was

122

bubbling in a glass coffee-maker. An electric clock on the wall was taking spasmodic little bites of time. It was a quarter to four.

I sat on one of the padded stools at the counter. Tobias vaulted over the counter and landed facing me with a dead-pan expression.

"Cuchulain the Hound of Ulster," he said surprisingly. "When Cuchulain was weary and exhausted from fighting battles, he'd go down by the riverside and exercise. That was his way of resting. I turned the fire on under the grill in case we wanted eggs. I could use a couple of eggs or three, personally."

"Me, too."

"Three?"

"Three."

"How's about some tomato juice to start out with? It clarifies the palate."

"Fine."

He opened a large can and poured two glasses of tomato juice. I picked up my glass and looked at it. The juice was thick and dark red in the fluorescent light. I put the glass down again.

"Something the matter with the juice?"

"It looks all right to me," I said unconvincingly.

He was appalled by this flaw in his hospitality. "What is it—dirt in the juice?" He leaned across the counter, his forehead wrinkled with solicitude. "I just opened the can, so if there's something in it, it must be the cannery. Some of these big corporations think that they can get away with murder, especially now that we have a businessmen's administration. I'll open another can."

"Don't bother."

I drank the red stuff down. It tasted like tomato juice.

"Was it all right?"

"It was very good."

"I was afraid there for a minute that there was something the matter with it."

"Nothing the matter with it. The matter was with me."

He took six eggs out of the refrigerator and broke them onto the grill. They sputtered cozily, turning white at the edges. Tobias said over his shoulder:

"It doesn't alter what I said about the big corporations. Mass production and mass marketing do make for some social benefits, but sheer size tends to militate against the human element. We've reached the point where we should count the human cost. How do you like your eggs?"

"Over easy."

"Over easy it is." He flipped the six eggs with a spatula, and inserted bread in the four-hole toaster. "You want to butter your own toast, or you want me to butter it for you? I have a butter brush. Personally, I prefer that, myself."

"You butter it for me."

"Will do. Now how do you like your coffee?"

"At this time in the morning, black. This is a very fine service you have here."

"We endeavor to please. I used to be a snack-bar bus boy before I switched over to lifeguard. Lifeguard doesn't pay any better, but it gives me more time to study."

"You're a student, are you?"

"Yes, I am." He dished up our eggs and poured our coffee. "I bet you're surprised at the facility with which I express myself."

"You took the words right out of my mouth."

He beamed with pleasure, and took a bite of toast. When he had chewed and swallowed it, he said: "I don't generally let the language flow around here. People, the richer they get, the more they dislike to hear a Negro express himself in well-chosen words. I guess they feel there's no point in being rich unless you can feel superior to somebody. I study English on the college level, but if I talked that way I'd lose my job. People are very sensitive."

"You go to U.C.L.A.?"

"Junior College. I'm working up to U.C.L.A. Heck," he said, "I'm only twenty-five, I've got plenty of time. 'Course I'd be way ahead of where I am now if I'd of caught on sooner. It took a hitch in the Army to jolt me out of my unthinking complacency." He rolled the phrase lovingly on his tongue. "I woke up one night on a cold hill on the way back from the Yalu. And suddenly it hit me—wham!—I didn't know what it was all about."

"The war?"

"Everything. War and peace. Values in life." He inserted a forkful of egg into his mouth and munched at me earnestly. "I realized I didn't know who *I* was. I wore this kind of mask, you know, over my face and over my mind, this kind of blackface mask, and it got so I didn't know who I was. I decided I had to find out who I was and be a man. If I could make it. Does that sound like a foolish thing for a person like me to decide?"

"It sounds sensible to me."

"I thought so at the time. I still do. Another coffee?"

"Not for me, thanks. You have another."

"No, I'm a one-cup man, too. I share your addiction for moderation." He smiled at the sound of the words.

124

"What do you plan to do in the long run?"

"Teach school. Teach and coach."

"It's a good life."

"You bet it is. I'm looking forward to it." He paused, taking time out to look forward to it. "I love to tell people important things. Especially kids. I love to communicate values, ideas. What do you do, Mr. Archer?"

"I'm a private detective."

Tobias looked a little disappointed in me. "Isn't that kind of a dull life? I mean, it doesn't bring you into contact with ideas very much. Not," he added quickly, for fear he had hurt my feelings, "not that I place *ideas* above other values. Emotions. Action. Honorable action."

"It's a rough life," I said. "You see people at their worst. How's Bassett, by the way?"

"Dead to the world. I put him to bed. He sleeps it off without any trouble, and *I* don't mind putting him to bed. He treats me pretty well.

"How long have you worked here?"

"Over three years. I started out in the snack bar here, and shifted over to lifeguard summer before last.

"You knew Gabrielle here, then."

He answered prefunctorily: "I knew her. I told you that."

"At the time that she was murdered?"

His face closed up entirely. The brightness left his eyes like something quick and timid retreating into its hole. "I don't know what you're getting at."

"Nothing to do with you. Don't run out on me, Joseph, just because I asked you a couple of questions."

"I'm not running out." But his voice was dull and singsong. "I already answered all the questions there are."

"What do you mean?"

"You know what I mean, if you're a detective. When Gabrielle—when Miss Torres was killed, I was the very first one that they arrested. They took me down to the sheriff's station and questioned me in relays, all day and half the night."

He hung his head under the weight of the memory. I hated to see him lose his fine *élan*.

"Why did they pick on you?"

"For no good reason." He raised his hand and turned it before his eyes. It was burnished black in the fluorescent light.

"Didn't they question anybody else?"

"Sure, when I proved to them I was at home all night. They picked up some winoes and sex deviates that live around

Malibu and up the canyons, and some hoboes passing through. And they asked Miss Campbell some questions."

"Hester Campbell?"

"Yes. She was the one that Gabrielle was supposed to be spending the evening with."

"How do you know?"

"Tony said so."

"Where did she really spend the evening?"

"How would I know that?"

"I thought you might have some idea."

"You thought wrong, then." His gaze, which had been avoiding mine, returned slowly to my face. "Are you reopening that murder case? Is that what Mr. Bassett hired you to do?"

"Not exactly. I started out investigating something else, but it keeps leading me back to Gabrielle. How well did you know her, Joseph?"

He answered carefully: "We worked together. Weekends, she took orders for sandwiches and drinks around the pool and in the *cabañas*. She was too young to serve the drinks herself, so I did that. Miss Torres was a very nice young lady to work with. I hated to see the thing that happened to her."

"You saw what happened to her?"

"I don't mean that. I didn't see what happened to her when it happened. But I was right here in this room when Tony came up from the beach. Somebody shot her, I guess you know that, shot her and left her lying just below the Club. Tony lived down the shore a piece from here. He expected Gabrielle home by midnight. When she didn't come home, he phoned the Campbell's house. They said they hadn't seen her, so he went out looking for her. He found her in the morning with bulletholes in her, the waves splashing up around her. She was supposed to be helping Mrs. Lamb that day, and Tony came up here first thing to tell Mrs. Lamb about it."

Tobias licked his dry lips. His eyes looked through me at the past. "He stood right there in front of the counter. For a long time he couldn't say a word. He couldn't open his mouth to tell Mrs. Lamb that Gabrielle was dead. She could see that he needed comfort, though. She walked around the end of the counter and put her arms around him and held him for a while like he was a child. Then he told her. Mrs. Lamb sent me to call the police."

"You called them yourself?"

"I was going to. But Mr. Bassett was in his office. He called them. I went down to the end of the pool and peeked down

126

through the fence. She was lying there in the sand, looking up at the sky. Tony had pulled her up out of the surf. I could see sand in her eyes, I wanted to go down and wipe the sand out of her eyes, but I was afraid to go down there."

"Why?"

"She had no clothes on. She looked so *white*. I was afraid they'd come and catch me down there and get a crazy idea about me. They went ahead and got their ideas anyway. They arrested me right that very morning. I was half expecting it."

"You were?"

"People have to blame somebody. They've been blaming us for three hundred years now. I guess I had it coming. I shouldn't have let myself get—friendly with her. And then, to make it worse, I had this earring belonging to her in my pocket."

"What earring was that?"

"A little round earring she had, made of mother-of-pearl. It was shaped like a lifesaving belt, with a hole in the middle, and U.S.S. Malibu printed on it. The heck of it was, she was still—the other earring that matched it was still on her ear."

"How did you happen to have the earring?"

"I just picked it up," he said, "and I was going to give it back to her. I found it alongside the pool," he added after a moment.

"That morning?"

"Yes. Before I knew she was dead. That Marfeld and the other cops made a big deal about it. I guess they thought they had it made, until I proved out my alibi." He made a sound which was half snort and half groan. "As if I'd lay a hand on Gabrielle to hurt her."

"Were you in love with her, Joseph?"

"I didn't say that."

"It's true, though, isn't it?"

He rested his elbow on the counter and his chin on his hand, as though to steady his thinking. "I could have been," he admitted, "if I'd had a chance with her. Only there was no mileage in it. She was only half Spanish-American, and she never really saw me as a human being."

"That could be a motive for murder."

I watched his face. It lengthened, but it showed no other sign of emotion. The planes of his cheeks, his broad lips, had the look of a carved and polished mask balanced on his palm.

"You didn't kill her yourself, Joseph?"

He winced, but not with surprise, as though I'd pressed on the scar of an old wound. He shook his head sadly. "I wouldn't hurt a hair on her head, and you know it."

"All right. Let it pass."

"I won't let it pass. You can take it back or get out of here."

"All right. I take it back."

"You shouldn't have said it in the first place. She was my friend. I thought you were my friend."

"I'm sorry, Joseph. I have to ask these questions."

"Why do you have to? Who makes you? You should be careful what you say about who did what around here. Do you know what Tony Torres would do if he thought I killed his girl?"

"Kill you."

"That's right. He threatened to kill me when the police turned me loose. It was all I could do to talk him out of it. He gets these fixed ideas in his head, and they stick there like a bur. And he's got a lot of violence in him yet."

"So do we all."

"I know it, Mr. Archer. I know it in myself. Tony's got more than most. He killed a man with his fists once, when he was young."

"In the ring?"

"Not in the ring, and it wasn't an accident. It was over a woman, and he meant to do it. He asked me down to his room one night and got drunk on muscatel and told me all about it."

"When was this?"

"A couple of months ago. I guess it was really eating him up. Gabrielle's mother was the woman, you see. He killed the man that she was running with, and she left him. The other man had a knife, so the judge in Fresno called it self-defense, but Tony blamed himself. He connected it up with Gabrielle, said that what happened to her was God's punishment on him. Tony's very superstitious."

"You know his nephew Lance?"

"I know him." Joseph's tone defined his attitude. It was negative. "He used to have the job I have a few years back, when I started in the snack bar. I heard he's a big wheel now, it's hard to believe. He was so bone lazy he couldn't even hold a lifeguard job without his uncle filling in for him. Tony used to do his clean-up work while Lance practiced fancy diving."

"How does Tony feel about him now?"

Joseph scratched his tight hair. "He finally caught on to him. I'd say he almost hates him."

"Enough to kill him?"

"What's all this talk about killing, Mr. Archer? Did somebody get killed?"

128

"I'll tell you, if you can keep a secret."

"I can keep a secret."

"See that you do. Your friend Lance was shot last night."

He didn't lift his eyes from the counter. "He was no friend of mine. He was nothing in my life."

"He was in Tony's."

He shook his head slowly from side to side. "I shouldn't have told you what I did about Tony. He did something once when he was young and crazy. He wouldn't do a thing like that again. He wouldn't hurt a flea, unless it was biting him."

"You can't have it both ways at once, Joseph. You said he hated Lance."

"I said almost."

"Why did he hate him?"

"He had good reason."

"Tell me."

"Not if you're going to turn it against Tony. That Lance isn't fit to tie his shoelaces for him."

"You think yourself that Tony may have shot him."

"I'm not saying what I think, I don't think anything."

"You said he had good reason. What was the reason?"

"Gabrielle," he said to the floor. "Lance was the first one she went with, back when she was just a kid in high school. She told me that. He started her drinking, he taught her all the ways of doing it. If Tony shot that *pachuco*, he did a good service to the world."

"Maybe, but not to himself. You say Gabrielle told you all these things?"

He nodded, and his black, despondent shadow nodded with him.

"Were you intimate with her?"

"I never was, not if you mean what I think you mean. She treated me like I had no human feelings. She used to torture me with these things she told me—the things he taught her to do." His voice was choked. "I guess she didn't know she was torturing me. She just didn't know I had feelings."

"You've got too many feelings."

"Yes, I have. They break me up inside sometimes. Like when she told me what he wanted her to do. He wanted her to go to L.A. with him and live in a hotel, and he would get her dates with men. I blew my top on that one, and went to Tony with it. That was when he broke off with Lance, got him fired from here and kicked him out of the house."

"Did Gabrielle go with him?"

"No, she didn't. I thought with him out of the way, maybe she'd straighten out. But it turned out to be too late for her. She was already gone."

"What happened to her after that?"

"Listen, Mr. Archer," he said in a tight voice. "You could get me in trouble. Spying on the members is no part of my job."

"What's a job?"

"It isn't the job. I could get another job. I mean really bad trouble."

"Sorry. I didn't mean to frighten you. I thought you wanted to be serviceable."

xxxxxxxxx *chapter* **23**

HE looked up at the light. His face was smooth. No moral strain showed. But I could feel the cracking tension in him.

"Gabrielle is dead," he said to the unblinking light. "What service can I do her by talking about her?"

"There are other girls, and it could happen to them."

His silence stretched out. Finally he said:

"I'm not as much of a coward as you think. I tried to tell the policemen, when they were asking me questions about the earring. But they weren't interested in hearing about it."

"Hearing about what?"

"If I've got to say it, I'll say it. Gabrielle used to go in one of the *cabañas* practically every day and stay there for an hour or more."

"All by herself?"

"You know I don't mean that."

"Who was with her, Joseph?"

I was almost certain what his answer would be.

"Mr. Graff used to be with her."

"You're sure of that?"

"I'm sure. You don't understand about Gabrielle. She was young and silly, proud that a man like Mr. Graff would take an interest in her. Besides, she wanted me to cover for her by taking orders in the other *cabañas* when she was—otherwise occupied. She wasn't ashamed for me to know," he added bitterly. "She was just ashamed for Mrs. Lamb to know."

130

"Did they ever meet here at night?" I said. "Graff and Gabrielle?"

"Maybe they did. I don't know. I never worked at night in those days."

"She was in the Club the night she was killed," I said. "We know that."

"How do we know that? Tony found her on the beach."

"The earring you found. Where was it you found it?"

"On the gallery in front of the *cabañas*. But she could have dropped it there any time."

"Not if she was still wearing the other one. Do you know for a fact that she was, or is this just what they told you?"

"I know it for a fact. I saw it myself. When they were asking me questions, they took me down to where she was. They opened up the drawer and made me look at her. I saw the little white earring on her ear."

Tears started in his eyes, the color of blue-black ink. Memory had given him a sudden stab. I said:

"Then she must have been in the Club shortly before she was killed. When a girl loses one earring, she doesn't go on wearing the other one. Which means that Gabrielle didn't have time to notice the loss. It's possible that she lost it at the precise time that she was being killed. I want you to show me where you found it, Joseph."

Outside, first light was washing the eastern slopes of the sky. The sparse stars were melting in it like grains of snow on stone. Under the dawn wind, the pool was gray and restless like a coffined piece of the sea.

Tobias led me along the gallery, about half the length of the pool. We passed the closed doors of half-a-dozen *cabañas*, including Graff's. I noticed that the spring had gone out of his walk. His sneakered feet slapped the concrete disconsolately. He stopped and turned to me:

"It was right about here, caught in this little grid." A circular wire grating masking a drain was set into a shallow depression in the concrete. "Somebody'd hosed down the gallery and washed it into the drain. I just happened to see it shine."

"How do you know somebody hosed the gallery?"

"It was still wet in patches."

"Who did it, do you know?"

"Could have been anybody, anybody that worked around the pool. Or any of the members. You never can tell what the members are going to do."

"Who worked around the pool at that time?"

"Me and Gabrielle, mostly, and Tony and the lifeguard.
. . . No, there wasn't any lifeguard just then—not until I

131

took over in the summer. Miss Campbell was filling in as lifeguard."

"Was she there that morning?"

"I guess she was. Yes, I remember she was. What are you trying to get at, Mr. Archer?"

"Who killed Gabrielle, and why and where and how."

He leaned against the wall, his shoulders high. His eyes and mouth gleamed in his black basalt face. "For God's sake, Mr. Archer, you're not pointing the finger at me again?"

"No. I'd like your opinion. I think that Gabrielle was killed in the Club, maybe right on this spot. The murderer dragged her down to the beach, or else she crawled there under her own power. She left a trail of blood, which had to be washed away. And she dropped an earring, which didn't get washed away."

"A little earring isn't much to go on."

"No," I said. "It isn't."

"You think Miss Campbell did all this?"

"It's what I want your opinion about. Did she have any reason, any motive?"

"Could be she had." He licked his lips. "She made a play for Mr. Graff herself, only he didn't go for her."

"Gabrielle told you this?"

"She told me Miss Campbell was jealous of her. She didn't have to tell me. I can see things for myself."

"What did you see?"

"The dirty looks between them, all that spring. They were still friends in a way, you know how girls can be, but they didn't like each other the way they used to. Then, right after it happened, right after the inquest, Miss Campbell took off for parts unknown."

"But she came back."

"More than a year later she came back, after it all died down. She was still very interested in the case, though. She asked me a lot of questions this last summer. She gave me a story that her and her sister Rina were going to write it up for a magazine, but I don't think that was their interest."

"What kind of questions did they ask?"

"I don't know," he said wearily. "Some of the ones you asked me, I guess. You've asked me about a million of them now."

"Did you tell her about the earring?"

"Maybe I did. I don't remember. Does it matter?" He pushed himself away from the wall, shuffled across the gallery, and looked up at the whitening sky. "I got to go home and get some sleep, Mr. Archer. I go back on duty at nine o'clock."

132

"I thought you never got tired."

"I get depressed. You stirred up a lot of things I want to forget. In fact, you've been giving me kind of a hard time."

"I'm sorry. I'm tired, too. It'll be worth it, though, if we can solve this murder."

"Will it? Say you do, then what will happen?" His face was grim in the gray light, and his voice drew on old reserves of bitterness. "The same thing will happen that happened before. The cops will take over your case and seal it off and nothing will happen, nobody get arrested."

"Is that what happened before?"

"I'm telling you it did. When Marfeld saw he couldn't railroad me, he suddenly lost interest in the case. Well, I lost interest, too."

"I can go higher than Marfeld if I have to."

"What if you do? It's too late for Gabrielle, too late for me. It was always too late for me."

He turned on his heel and walked away. I said after him: "Can I drop you someplace?"

"I have my own car."

ᴍᴍᴍᴍᴍᴍᴍᴍ *chapter* 24

I SHOULD have handled it better. I walked to the end of the pool, the last man at the party, feeling that early-morning ebb of heart when the blood runs sluggish and cold. The fog had begun to blow out to sea. It foamed and poured in a slow cataract toward the obscure west. Black-marble patches of ocean showed through here and there.

I must have seen it and known what it was before I was conscious of it. It was a piece of black driftwood with a twist of root at one end, floating low in the water near the shore. It rode in slowly and discontinuously, pushed by a series of breaking waves. Its branches were very flexible for a log. A wave lodged it on the wet brown sand. It was a man in a dark, belted overcoat, lying face-down.

The gate in the fence was padlocked. I picked up a DO

NOT RUN sign with a heavy concrete base and swung it at the padlock. The gate burst open. I went down the concrete steps and turned Carl Stern over onto his back. His forehead was deeply ridged where it had struck or been struck by a hard object. The wound in his throat gaped like a toothless mouth shouting silently.

I went to my car, remembering from my bottom-scratching days that there was a southward current along this shore, about a mile an hour. Just under three miles north of the Channel Club, a paved view-point for sightseers blistered out from the highway to the fenced edge of a bluff which overhung the sea. Stern's rented sedan was parked with its heavy chrome front against the cable fence. Blood spotted the windshield and dashboard and the front seat. Blood stained the blade of the knife which lay on the floormat. It looked like Stern's own knife.

I didn't mess with any of it. I wanted no part of Stern's death. I drove home on automatic pilot and went to bed. I dreamed about a man who lived by himself in a landscape of crumbling stones. He spent a great deal of his time, without much success, trying to reconstruct in his mind the monuments and the buildings of which the scattered stones were the only vestiges. He vaguely remembered some kind of oral tradition to the effect that a city had stood there once. And a still vaguer tradition: or perhaps it was a dream inside of the dream: that the people who had built the city, or their descendants, were coming back eventually to rebuild it. He wanted to be around when the work was done.

xxxxxxxxx *chapter* 25

MY answering service woke me at seven thirty. "Rise and shine, Mr. Archer!"

"Do I have to shine? I'm feeling kind of dim. I got to bed about an hour ago."

"I haven't been to bed yet. And, after all, you could have canceled your standing order."

"I hereby cancel it, forever." I was in one of those drained and chancy moods when everything seems either laughable or weepworthy, depending on the position you hold your head in. "Now hang the hell up and let me get back to sleep. This is cruel and unusual punishment."

"My, but we're in splendid spirits this morning!" Her secretarial instinct took over: "Wait now, don't hang up. Couple of long-distance calls for you, both from Las Vegas. First at one forty, young lady, seemed very anxious to talk to you, but wouldn't leave her name. She said she'd call back, but she never did. Got that? Second at three fifteen, Dr. Anthony Reeves, intern at the Memorial Hospital, said he was calling on behalf of a patient named George Wall, picked up at the airport with head injuries."

"The Vegas airport?"

"Yes. Does that mean anything to you?"

It meant a surge of relief, followed by the realization that I was going to have to drag myself out to International Airport and crawl aboard a plane. "Make me a reservation, will you, Vera?"

"First plane to Vegas?"

"Right."

"One other call, yesterday afternoon. Man named Mercero from the CHP, said the Jag was registered to Lance Leonard. Is that the actor that got himself shot last night?"

"It's in the morning papers, eh?"

"Probably. I heard it on the radio."

"What else did you hear?"

"That was all. It was just a flash bulletin."

"No," I said. "It wasn't the same one. What did you say the name was again?"

"I forget." She was a jewel among women.

Shortly before ten o'clock I was talking to Dr. Anthony Reeves in his room in the Southern Nevada Hospital. He'd had the night duty on Emergency, and had given George Wall a preliminary examination when George was brought in by the Sheriff's men. They had found him wandering around McCarran Airfield in a confused condition. He had a fractured cheekbone, probably a brain concussion, and perhaps a fractured skull. George had to have absolute quiet for at least a week, and would probably be laid up for a month. He couldn't see anyone.

It was no use arguing with young Dr. Reeves. Butter wouldn't melt in his mouth. I went in search of a susceptible nurse, and eventually found a plump little redhead in an L.A. General cap who was impressed by an old Special Deputy badge I carried. On the strength of it, she led me to a semi-private room with a NO VISITORS sign on the door.

George was the only occupant, and he was sleeping. I promised not to wake him.

The window shades were tightly drawn, and there was no light on in the room. It was so dim that I could barely make out George's white-bandaged head against the pillow. I sat in an armchair between his bed and the empty one, and listened to the susurrus of his breathing. It was slow and steady. After a while I almost went to sleep myself.

I was startled out of it by a cry of pain. I thought at first it was George, but it was a man on the other side of the wall. He cried loudly again.

George stirred and groaned and sat up, raising both hands to his half-mummified face. He swayed and threatened to fall out of bed. I held him by the shoulders.

"Take it easy, boy."

"Let me go. Who are you?"

"Archer," I said. "The indigent's Florence Nightingale."

"What happened to me? Why can't I see?"

"You've pulled the bandages down over your eyes. Also, it's dark in here."

"Where is here? Jail? Am I in jail?"

"You're in the hospital. Don't you remember asking Dr. Reeves to phone me long-distance?"

"I'm afraid I don't remember. What time is it?"

"It's Saturday morning, getting along towards noon."

The information hit him hard. He lay back quietly for a while, then said in a puzzled tone:

"I seem to have lost a day."

"Relax. You wouldn't want it back."

"Did I do something wrong?"

"I don't know what you did. You ask too many questions, George."

"You're just letting me down easy, aren't you?" Embarrassment thickened in his throat like phlegm. "I suppose I made a complete ass of myself."

"Most of us do from time to time. But hold the thought."

He groped for the light-switch at the head of the bed, found the cord, and pulled it. Fingering the bandages on his face, he peered at me through narrow slits in them. Below the bandages, his puffed lips were dry and cracking. He said with a kind of awe in his voice:

"That little pug in the pajamas—did he do this to me?"

"Part of it. When did you see him last, George?"

"You ought to know, you were with me. What do you mean, part of it?"

"He had some help."

"Whose help?"

"Don't you remember?"

"I remember something." He sounded childishly uncertain. Physical and moral shock had cut his ego down small. "It must have been just a nightmare. It was like a jumble of old movies running through my head. Only I was in it. A man with a gun was after me. The scene kept changing—it couldn't have been real."

"It was real. You got into a hassle with the company guards at Simon Graff's studio. Does the name Simon Graff mean anything to you?"

"Yes, it does. I was in bed in some wretched little house in Los Angeles, and someone talking on the telephone said that name. I got up and called a taxicab and asked the driver to take me to see Simon Graff."

"It was me on the telephone, George. In my house."

"Have I ever been in your house?"

"Yesterday." His memory seemed to be functioning very conveniently. I didn't doubt his sincerity, but I was irritated. "You also lifted a wretched little old charcoal-gray suit of mine which cost me one-two-five."

"Did I? I'm sorry."

"You'll be sorrier when you get the bill. But skip it. How did you get from the Graff studio to Vegas? And what have you been doing between then and now?"

The mind behind his blood-suffused eyes groped dully in limbo. "I think I came on a plane. Does that make any sense?"

"As much as anything does. Public or private plane?"

After a long pause, he said: "It must have been private. There were just the two of us, me and another fellow. I think it was the same one who chased me with the gun. He told me that Hester was in danger and needed my help. I blacked out, or something. Then I was walking down a street with a lot of signs flashing in my eyes. I went into this hotel where she was supposed to be, but she had gone, and the desk clerk wouldn't tell me where."

"Which hotel?"

"I'm not sure. The sign was in the shape of a wineglass. Or a martini glass. The Dry Martini? Does that sound possible?"

"There is one in town. When were you there?"

"Some time in the course of the night. I'd lost all track of time. I must have spent the rest of the night looking for her. I saw a number of girls who resembled her, but they always turned out to be someone different. I kept blacking out and coming to in another place. It was awful, with those lights in my eyes and the people milling about. They thought I was drunk. Even the policeman thought I was drunk."

"Forget it, George. It's over now."

"I won't forget it. Hester is in danger. Isn't that so?"

"She may be, I don't know. Forget about her, too, why don't you? Fall in love with the nurse or something. With your win-and-loss record, you ought to marry a nurse anyway. And, incidentally, you better lie down or the nurse will be reaming both of us."

Instead of lying down, he sat up straighter, his shoulders arching under the hospital shirt. Between the bandages, his red eyes were fixed on my face. "Something has happened to Hester. You're trying to keep me from knowing."

"Don't be crazy, kid. Relax. You've sparked enough trouble."

He said: "If you won't help me, I'm getting up and walking out of here now. Somebody has to do something."

"You wouldn't get far."

For answer, he threw off the covers, swung his legs over the edge of the high bed, reached for the floor with his bare feet, and stood up tottering. Then he fell forward onto his knees, his head swinging loose, slack as a killed buck. I hoisted him back onto the bed. He lay inert, breathing rapidly and lightly.

I pressed the nurse's signal, and passed her on my way out.

xxxxxxxxx *chapter* 26

THE DRY MARTINI was a small hotel on the edge of the older downtown gambling district. Two old ladies were playing Canasta for money in the boxlike knotty-pine lobby. The desk clerk was a fat man in a rayon jacket. His red face was set in the permanently jovial expression which people expect of fat men.

"What can I do for you, sir?"

"I have an appointment with Miss Campbell."

"I'm very much afraid Miss Campbell hasn't come in yet."

"What time did she go out?"

He clasped his hands across his belly and twiddled his thumbs. "Let's see, I came on at midnight, she checked in about an hour after that, stayed long enough to change her dress, and away she went again. Couldn't've been much later than one."

"You notice things."

"A sexburger like her I notice." The tip of his tongue protruded between his teeth, which were a good grade of plastic.

"Was anybody with her, going or coming?"

"Nope. She came and went by herself. You're a friend of hers, eh?"

"Yeah."

"Know her husband? Big guy with light-reddish hair?"

"I know him."

"What goes with him? He came in here in the middle of the night looking like the wrath of God. Big welts on his face, blood in his hair, yackety-yacking like a psycho. He had some idea in his head that his wife was in trouble and I was mixed up in it. Claimed I knew where she was. I had a hell of a time getting rid of him."

I looked at my watch. "She could be in trouble, at that. She's been gone eleven hours."

"Think nothing of it. They stay on the town for twenty-four, thirty-six hours at a time, some of them. Maybe she hit a winning streak and's riding it out. Or maybe she had a date. Somebody must've clobbered the husband. He *is* her husband, isn't he?"

"He is, and several people clobbered him. He has a way of leading with his chin. Right now he's in the hospital, and I'm trying to find her for him."

"Private dick?"

I nodded. "Do you have any idea where she went?"

"I can find out, maybe, if it's important." He looked me over, estimating the value of my clothes and the contents of my wallet. "It's going to cost me something."

"How much?"

"Twenty." It was a question.

"Hey, I'm not buying you outright."

"All right, ten," he said quickly. "It's better than getting poked in the eye with a carrot."

He took the bill and waddled into a back room, where I heard him talking on the telephone to somebody named Rudy. He came back looking pleased with himself:

"I called her a taxi last night, was just talking to the dispatcher. He's sending over the driver that took the call."

"How much is he going to cost me?"

"That's between you and him."

I waited inside the glass front door, watching the noon traffic. It came from every state in the Union, but most of the license plates belonged to Southern California. This carney town was actually Los Angeles's most farflung suburb.

A shabby yellow cab detached itself from the westbound stream and pulled up at the curb. The driver got out and started across the sidewalk. He wasn't old, but he had a drooping face and posture like a hound that had been fed too long on scraps. I stepped outside.

"You the gentleman interested in the blondie?"

"I'm the one."

"We're not supposed to give out information about our fares. Unless it's official—"

"A sawbuck official enough?"

He stood at attention and parodied a salute. "What was it you wanted to know, bud?"

"You picked her up what time?"

"One fifteen. I checked it on my sheet."

"And dropped her where?"

He gave me a yellow-toothed grin and pushed his peaked cap back. It hung almost vertically on the peaked rear of his skull. "Don't rush me, bud. Let's see the color of your money first."

I paid him.

"I set her out on the street," he said. "I didn't like to do it that time of night, but I guess she knew what she was doing."

"Where was this?"

"It's out past the Strip a piece. I can show you if you want. It's a two-dollar fare."

He opened the back door of his cab, and I got in. According to his identification card, his name was Charles Meyer. He told me about his troubles as we drove out past the Disney-Modern fronts where Hollywood and Times Square names decoyed for anonymous millionaires. Charles Meyer had many troubles. Drink had been his downfall. Women had wrecked his life. Gambling had ruined him. He told me in his singsong insistent whine:

"Three months I been hacking in this goddam burg trying to get together a stake to buy some clothes and a crate, get out of here. Last week I thought I had it made, two hundred and thirty bucks and all my debts paid off. So I went into the drugstore to get my insulin and they give me my change in silver, two dollars and a four-bits piece, and just for kicks I fed them in the machines and that was going

140

to be that." He clucked. "There went two thirty. It took me a little over three hours to drop it. I'm a fast worker."

"You could buy a bus ticket."

"No, sir. I'm sticking here until I get a car, a postwar like the one I lost, and a suit of decent clothes. I'm not dragging my tail back to Dago looking like a bum."

We passed several buildings under construction, identified by signs as additional club-hotels with fancy names. One of them was Simon Graff's Casbah. Their girders rose on the edge of the desert like armatures for people to build their glad bad dreams on.

The Strip degenerated into a long line of motels clinging to the fringes of glamour. Charles Meyer U-turned and stopped in front of one of them, the Fiesta Motor Court. He draped his hound face over the seat back:

"This is where I set her off."

"Did anybody meet her?"

"Not that I saw. She was all by herself on the street when I pulled away."

"But there was traffic?"

"Sure, there's always some traffic."

"Did she seem to be looking for anybody?"

"How could I tell? She wasn't making much sense, she was in a kind of a tizzy."

"What kind of a tizzy?"

"You know. Upset. Hysterical-like. I didn't like to leave her alone like that, but she says beat it. I beat it."

"What was she wearing?"

"Red dress, dark cloth coat, no hat. One thing, she had on real high heels. I thought at the time, she wouldn't walk far with them on."

"Which way did she walk?"

"No way, she just stood there on the curb, long as I could see her. You want to go back to the Martini now?"

"Stick around for a few minutes."

"Okay, but I keep my meter running."

The proprietor of the Fiesta Motor Court was sitting at an umbrella table in the small patio beside his office. He was smoking a waterpipe and fanning himself with a frayed palm-leaf fan. He looked like a happy Macedonian or a disappointed Armenian. In the background several dark-eyed girls who could have been his daughters were pushing linen carts in and out of the tiny cottages.

No, he hadn't seen the young lady in the red dress. He hadn't seen anything after eleven thirty, got his NO VACANCY up at eleven twenty-five and went straight to bed. As I moved away he barked commands at one of the dark-eyed girls, as

141

if to teach me by example how to keep my females out of trouble.

The Colonial Inn, next door, had a neat little office presided over by a neat little man with a clipped mustache and a north-by-northeast accent with asthmatic overtones. No, he certainly had not noticed the young lady in question, having better things to do with his time. He also had better things to do than answer questions about other people's wives.

Moving toward town and the unlit neon silo of the Flamingo, I tried the Bar-X Tourist Ranch and the Welcome Traveller and the Oasis. I got three different answers, all negative. Charles Meyer trailed me in his taxi, with many grins and nods.

The Rancho Eldorado was a double row of pastel chicken coops festooned with neon tubing. There was no one in the office. I rang until I got an answer, because it was close to the street and on a corner. A woman opened the door and looked at me down her nose, which was long and pitted with ancient acne craters. Her eyes were black and small, and her hair was up in pincurls. She was so homely that I felt sorry for her. It was practically an insult to offer her a description of a beautiful blonde in a red dress.

"Yes," she said. "I saw her." Her black eyes glinted with malice. "She stood on the corner for ten or twelve minutes last night. I don't set myself up as a judge of other people, but it made me mad to see her out there flaunting herself, deliberately trying to get herself picked up. I can tell when a girl's trying to get herself picked up. But it didn't work!" Her voice twanged triumphantly. "Men aren't as easily taken in as they used to be, and nobody stopped for her."

"What did she do to you?"

"Nothing, I just didn't like the way she flaunted herself under the light on my corner. That sort of thing is bad for business. This is a family motel. So I finally stepped outside and told her to move along. I was perfectly nice about it. I simply told her in a quiet way to peddle her papers elsewhere." Her mouth closed, lengthening in a horizontal line with right angles at the corners. "She's a friend of yours, I suppose?"

"No. I'm a detective."

Her face brightened. "I see. Well, I saw her go into the Dewdrop Inn, that's the second place down from here. It's about time somebody cleaned out that den of iniquity. Are you after her for some *crime?*"

"Third-degree pulchritude."

She chewed on this like a camel, then shut the door in my face. The Dewdrop Inn was a rundown stucco ell with

142

sagging shutters and doors that needed paint. Its office door was opened by a woman who was holding a soiled bathrobe tight around her waist. She had frizzled red hair. Her skin had been seared by blowtorch suns, except where her careless breast gleamed white in the V of her robe. She caught and returned my dipping glance, letting the V and the door both open wider.

"I'm looking for a woman."

"What a lucky coincidence. I'm looking for a man. It's just it's just a leetle early for me. I'm still a teensy bit drunky from last night."

Yawning, she cocked one fist and stretched the other arm straight up over her head. Her breath was a blend of gin and fermenting womanhood. Her bare feet were dirty white.

"Come on in, I won't bite you."

I stepped up into the office. She held herself in the doorway so that I brushed against her from shoulder to knee. She wasn't really interested, just keeping in practice. The room was dirty and disordered, with a couple of lipsticky glasses on the registration desk, confession magazines scattered on the floor.

"Big night last night?" I said.

"Oh, sure. Big night. Drink cocktails until four and wake up at six and you can't get back to sleep. This divorce kick—well, it isn't all it's cracked up to be."

I braced myself for another life-story. Something about my face, maybe a gullible look, invited them. But she spared me:

"Okay, Joe, we won't beat around the bush. You want the girlie in the red dress."

"You catch on very quick."

"Yeah. Well, she isn't here. I don't know where she is. You a mobster or what?"

"That's a funny question."

"Yeah, sure, uproarious. You got a hand gun in your armpit, and you're not Davy Crockett."

"You shatter my illusions."

She gave me a hard and murky look. Her eyes resembled mineral specimens, malachite or copper sulphate, which had been gathering dust on somebody's back shelf. "Come on, now, what's it all about? The kid said there was mobsters after her. You're no mobster, are you?"

"I'm a private dick. Her husband hired me to find her." I realized suddenly that I was back where I'd started, twenty-eight hours later and in another state. It felt more like twenty-eight days.

The woman was saying: "You find her for him, what's he plan to do with her? Beat her up?"

"Look after her. She needs it."

"That could be. Was it all malarkey about the mobsters? I mean, was she stringing me?"

"I don't think so. Did she mention any names?"

She nodded. "One. Carl Stern."

"You know that name?"

"Yeah. The *Sun* dug into his record and spread it on the front page last fall when he put in for a gambling license. *He* wouldn't be her husband?"

"Her husband's a nice boy from Toronto. George Wall. Some of Stern's friends put him in the hospital. I want to get to his wife before they do it to her."

"No kidding?"

"I mean it."

"What did she do to Stern?"

"It's a question I want to ask her. Where is she now?"

She gave me the mineral look again. "Let's see your license. Not that a license means much. The guy that got me my divorce was a licensed private detective, and he was a prime stinker if I ever saw one."

"I'm not," I said with the necessary smile, and showed her my photostat.

She looked up sharply. "Your name is Archer?"

"Yes."

"Is this a funny coincidence or what? She tried to phone you last night, person to person. Knocked on the door along towards two o'clock, looking pretty white and shaky, and asked to use my phone. I asked her what the trouble was. She broke down and told me that there were mobsters after her, or there soon would be. She wanted to call the airport, catch a plane out right away quick. I put in a call for her, but I couldn't get her on a flight till morning. So then she tried to call you."

"What for?"

"She didn't tell me. If you're a friend of hers, why didn't you say so? *Are* you a friend of Rina Campbell's?"

"Who?" I said.

"Rina Campbell. The girl we're talking about."

I made a not very smooth recovery. "I think I am. Is she still here?"

"I gave her a nembutal and put her to bed myself. I haven't heard a peep out of her. She's probably still sleeping, poor dearie."

"I want to see her."

"Yeah, you made that clear. Only, this is a free country,
144

and if she don't want to see you there's no way you can make her."

"I'm not planning to push her around."

"You better not, brother. Try anything with the kid, and I'll shoot you personally."

"You like her, do you?"

"Why not? She's a real good girl, as good as they come. I don't care what she's done."

"You're doing all right yourself."

"Am I? That I doubt. I had it once, when I was Rina's age. I tried to save a little of it for an emergency. If you can't pass on a little loving-kindness in this world, you might as well be a gopher in a hole."

"What did you say your name was?"

"I didn't say. My name is Carol, Mrs. Carol Busch." She offered me a red, unlovely hand. "Remember, if she changed her mind about wanting to see you, you amscray."

She opened an inner door, and shut it firmly behind her. I went outside where I could watch the exits. Charles Meyer was waiting in his cab.

"Hiyah. Any luck?"

"No luck. I'm quitting. How much do I owe you?"

He leaned sideways to look at the meter. "Three seventy-five. Don't you want a ride downtown? I'll let you have it for half-price."

"I'll walk. I need the exercise."

His look was sad and canine. He knew that I was lying, and he knew the reason: I didn't trust him. Mrs. Carol Busch called me from the doorway of the unit adjoining the office. "Okay, she's up, she wants to talk to you."

xxxxxxxxx *chapter* 27

MRS. BUSCH stayed outside and let me go in alone. The room was dim and cool. Blackout blinds and heavy drapes kept the sunlight out. A shaded bedside lamp was the only source of light. The girl sat on the foot of the unmade Hollywood bed with her face turned away from the lamp.

I saw the reason for this when she forgot her pose and looked up at me. Nembutal or tears had swollen her eyelids. Her bright hair was carelessly groomed. She wore her red wool dress as if it were burlap. Overnight, she seemed to have lost her assurance that her beauty would look after her. Her voice was small and high:

"Hello."

"Hello, Rina."

"You know who I am," she said dully.

"I do now. I should have guessed it was a sister act. Where is your sister, Rina?"

"Hester's in trouble. She had to leave the country."

"You're sure about that?"

"I'm not sure about anything since I found out Lance is dead."

"How did you find out? You didn't believe me when I told you last night."

"I have to believe you now. I picked up a Los Angeles paper at the hotel, and there was a headline about him—about his murder." Her eyelids lifted heavily. Her dark-blue eyes had changed subtly in thirteen hours: they saw more and liked it less. "Did my sister—did Hester kill him?"

"She may have, but I doubt it. Which way did they say she went—Mexico or Canada or Hawaii?"

"They didn't say. Carl Stern said it would be better if I didn't know."

"What are you supposed to be doing here? Giving her an alibi?"

"I guess so. That was the idea." She looked up again. "Please don't stand over me. I'm willing to tell you what I know, but please don't cross-question me. I've had a terrible night."

Her fingers dabbed at her forehead and came away wet. There was a box of Kleenex on the bedside table. I handed her a leaf of it, which she used to wipe her forehead and blow her nose. She said surprisingly, in a voice as thin as a flute:

"Are you a good man?"

"I like to think so," but her candor stopped me. "No," I said, "I'm not. I keep trying, when I remember to, but it keeps getting tougher every year. Like trying to chin yourself with one hand. You can practice off and on all your life, and never make it."

She tried to smile. The gentle corners of her mouth wouldn't lift. "You talk like a decent man. Why did you come to my sister's house last night? How did you get in?"

"I broke in."

"Why? Have you got something against her?"

"Nothing personal. Her husband asked me to find her. I've been trying to."

"She has no husband. I mean, Hester's husband is dead."

"She told you he was dead, eh?"

"Isn't it true?"

"She doesn't tell the truth when a lie will do."

"I know." She added in an unsentimental tone: "But Hester is my sister and I love her. I've always done what I could for her, I always will."

"And that's why you're here."

"That's why I'm here. Lance and Carl Stern told me that I could save Hester a lot of grief, maybe a penitentiary term. All I had to do was fly here under her name, and register in a hotel, then disappear. I was supposed to take a taxi out to the edge of the desert, past the airport, and Carl Stern was supposed to pick me up. I didn't meet him, though. I came back here instead. I lost my nerve."

"Is that why you tried to phone me?"

"Yes. I got to thinking, when I saw the piece about Lance in the paper. You'd told me the truth about that, perhaps you'd told me the truth about everything. And I remembered something you said last night—the very first thing you said when you saw me in Hester's room. You said—" her voice was careful, like a child's repeating a lesson by rote—"you thought I was Hester, and you said you thought I was dead— that *she* was dead."

"I said that, yes."

"Is it true?"

I hesitated. She got to her feet, swaying a little. Her hand pressed hard on my arm:

"Is Hester dead? Don't be afraid to tell me if she is. I can take it."

"Sorry, I don't know the answer."

"What do you think?"

"I think she is. I think she was killed in the Beverly Hills house yesterday afternoon. And the alibi they're trying to set up isn't for Hester. It's for whoever killed her."

"I'm sorry. I don't follow."

"Say she was killed yesterday. You assumed her identity, flew here, registered, disappeared. They wouldn't be asking questions about her in L.A."

"*I* would."

"If you got back alive."

It took her a second to grasp the idea, another to apply

it to her present situation. She blinked, and the shock wave hit her. Her eyes were like cracked blue Easter eggs.

"What do you think I should do?"

"Fade. Disappear, until I get this thing settled. But first I want your story. You haven't explained why you let them use you for a patsy. Or how much you knew about your sister's activities. Did she tell you what she was doing?"

"She didn't intend to, but I guessed. I'm willing to talk, Mr. Archer. In a way, I'm as guilty as Hester. I feel responsible for the whole thing."

She paused, and looked around the yellow plaster walls. She seemed to be dismayed by the ugliness of the room. Her gaze stopped at the door behind me, and hardened. The door sprang open as I turned. Harsh sunlight slapped me across the eyes, and glinted on three guns. Frost held one of them. Lashman and Marfeld flanked him. Behind them Mrs. Busch crawled in the gravel. In the street Charles Meyer's shabby yellow taxi rolled away toward town. He didn't look back.

I saw all this while I reached for my left armpit. I didn't complete the motion. The day and the night and the day again had dulled me, and I wasn't reacting well, but I knew that a gun in my hand was all they needed. I stood with my right hand frozen on my chest.

Frost smiled like a death's-head against the aching blue sky. He had on a multicolored shot-silk shirt, a Panama hat with a matching colored band, and the kind of white flannels worn by tennis pro's. The gun in his hand was a German machine pistol. He pressed its muzzle into my solar plexus and took my gun.

"Hands on your head. This is a real lovely surprise."

I put my hands on my head. "I like it, too."

"Now turn around."

Mrs. Busch had got to her feet. She cried out: "Dirty bullying bastards!" and flung herself on the back of the nearest gunman. This happened to be Marfeld. He pivoted and slapped her face with the barrel of his gun. She fell turning and lay still on her face, her hair splashing out like fire. I said:

"I'm going to kill you, Marfeld."

He turned to me, his eyes joyous, if Marfeld could feel joy. "You and who else, boysie? You won't be doing any pitching. You're the catcher, see?"

He slapped the side of my head with the gun. The sky swayed like a blue balloon on a string.

Frost spoke sharply to Marfeld. "Lay off. And, for God's sakes, lay off the woman." He spoke to me more gently: "Keep your hands on your head and turn around."

148

I did these things, tickled by worms of blood crawling through my hair and down the side of my face. Rina was sitting on the bed against the wall. Her legs were drawn up under her, and she was shivering.

"You disappoint me, doll," Frost said. "You do too, Lew."

"I disappoint myself."

"Yeah, after all the trouble I went to, giving you good advice, and our years of friendly relationship."

"You move me deeply. I haven't been so deeply moved since I heard a hyena howl."

Frost pushed the gun muzzle hard into my right kidney. Marfeld moved around me, swinging his shoulders busily. "That's no way to talk to Mr. Frost."

He swung the edge of his hand toward my throat. I pulled in my chin to protect my larynx and caught the blow on the mouth. I made a noise that sounded like *gar* and reached for him. Lashman locked my right arm and hung his weight on it. Marfeld's right shoulder dropped. At the end of his hooked right arm, his fist swung into my belly. It doubled me over. I straightened, gulping down bitter regurgitated coffee.

"That's enough of that," Frost said. "Hold a gun on him, Lash."

Frost moved past me to the bed. He walked slackly with his shoulders drooping. His voice was dry and tired:

"You ready to go now, baby?"

"Where is my sister?"

"You know she had to leave the country. You want to do what's right for her, don't you?" He leaned toward her in a parody of wheedling charm.

She hissed at him, grinning with all her teeth: "I wouldn't cross the street with you. You smell! I want my sister."

"You're coming if you have to be carried. So, on your horse."

"No. Let me out of here. You killed my sister."

She scrambled off the bed and ran for the door. Marfeld caught her around the waist and wrestled with her, grinning, his belly pressed to her hip. She slashed his cheek with her nails. He caught her by the hand and bent her fingers backward, struck savagely at her head with the flat of his hand. She stood submissive against the ghastly wall.

The gun at my back had lost contact, leaving a cold vacuum. I whirled. Lashman had been watching the girl being hurt with a voyeur's hot, dreamy eyes. I forced his gun down before he fired. I got the gun away from him and swung it at the left front corner of his skull. He crumpled in the doorway.

Marfeld was on my back. He was heavy and strong, with

an innate sense of leverage. His arm looped around my neck and tightened. I swung him against the door frame. He almost pulled my head off, but he fell on top of Lashman, his face upturned. With the butt of the gun, I struck him between the eyes.

I turned toward Frost in the instant that he fired, and flung myself sideways. His slugs whanged into the wall wide of my head. I shot him in the right arm. His gun clanked on the floor. I got my free hand on it and stood up and backed to the wall and surveyed the room.

The air-conditoner thumped and whirred like a wounded bird in the wall behind my head. The girl leaned white-faced and still on the opposite wall. Frost sat on the floor between us, holding his right arm with his left hand. Blood laced his fingers. He looked from them to me. The fear of death which never left his eyes had taken over the rest of his face. In the doorway, Marfeld lay with his head on Lash-man's chest. His veined eyeballs were turned up and in toward the deep blue dent in his forehead. Except for his hoarse breathing and the noise of the air-conditioner, the room was very tranquil.

Mrs. Busch appeared in the doorway, weaving slightly. One of her eyes was swollen and black, and her smiling mouth was bloody. She held a .45 automatic in both hands. Frost looked into its roving eye and tried to crawl under the bed. It was too low to receive him. He lay beside it, whimpering:

"Please. I'm a sick man. Don't shoot."

The redheaded woman laughed. "Look at him crawl. Listen to him whine."

"Don't kill him," I said. "Strange as it may seem, I have a use for him."

xxxxxxxxxx *chapter* 28

Rina drove Frost's Cadillac. I rode in the back seat with Frost. She had made a pressure bandage and a sling for his arm out of several Dewdrop Inn bath towels. He sat and nursed his arm, refusing to talk, except to give directions.

Beyond the airport, we turned right toward mountains which lay naked and wrinkled under the sun. The road climbed toward the sun, and as it climbed it dwindled, changing to gravel._We came over the first low hump and overlooked a white-floored valley where nothing grew.

Near the crest of the inner slope, a concrete building with a rounded roof was set into the side of the hill. Squat and windowless, it resembled a military strongpoint. It was actually a disused ammunition dump.

Frost said: "She's in there."

Rina looked over her shoulder. Her nervous foot on the power brakes jolted the car to a stop. We slipped out under the brilliant sky. A jet track crossed it like a long white scar. I told Rina to stay in the car.

"You can put your gun away," Frost said. "There's nobody in there but her."

I made him climb ahead of me, up the slope to the single door of the building. Sheathed with rusting steel, the door swung half open. A broken padlock hung from its hasp. I pulled the door wide, holding my gun on Frost. A puff of warm air came from the interior. It smelled like an oven where meat had been scorched.

Frost hung back. I forced him to enter ahead of me. We stood on a narrow platform, peering down into dimness. The concrete floor of the dump was about six feet below the level of the entrance. Framed in light, our shadows fell across it. I pushed Frost out of the rectangle of light, and saw what lay on the floor: a wizened thing like a mummy, blackened and consumed by fire instead of by time.

"You did this to her?"

Frost said without conviction: "Hell, no, it was her husband. You should be talking to him. He followed her here from L.A., did you know that? Knocked her off and set fire to the body."

"You'll have to do better than that, Frost. I've been talking to the husband. You flew him here in Stern's plane to frame him for the killing. You probably brought the body on the same flight. The frame didn't take, though, and it's not going to. None of your dirty little plans is working out."

He was silent for a period of time which was divided into shorter periods by the tic twitching at his eyelid. "It wasn't my idea, it was Stern's. And the gasoline was his idea. He said to put her to the torch, so that when they found the body they couldn't establish when she died. The girl was dead already, see, all we did was cremate her."

He looked down at the body. It was the image of the thing he feared, and it imposed silence on him. He reached out suddenly with his good arm, clawed at my shoulder and caught hold. "Can't we get out of here, Lew? I'm a sick man, I can't stand it in here."

I shook him off. "When you've told me who killed the girl."

There was another breathing silence. "Isobel Graff killed her," he said finally.

"How do you know?"

"Marfeld saw her. Marfeld saw her come tearing out of the house with the fantods. He went in, and there was Hester in the living-room. She had her head beaten in with a poker. The poker was lying across her. We couldn't leave her there. The cops would trace the Graff connection in no time—"

"What was Hester's connection with Graff?"

"Isobel thought they were shacked up, let's leave it at that. Anyway, it was up to me to do something with the body. I wanted to chuck it in the ocean, but Graff said no— he has a house on the ocean at Malibu. Then Lance Leonard got this other idea."

"How did Leonard get into the act?"

"He was a friend of Hester's. She borrowed his car, he came by to pick it up. Leonard had a key to her house, and he walked in on Marfeld and the body. He had his own reasons for wanting to cover it up, so he suggested getting her sister to help. The two sisters are look-alikes, almost like twins, and Leonard knew both of them. He talked the sister into flying here."

"What was going to happen to her?"

"That was Carl Stern's problem. But it looks as though Stern ran out on the whole deal. I don't see how he can afford to do that."

"You're kind of out of touch," I said. "You used to be an operator. When did you start letting goons and gunsills do your thinking for you?"

Frost grimaced and hung his head. "I'm not myself. I been full of demerol for the last three months."

"You're on a demerol kick?"

"I'm a dying man, Lew. My insides are being eaten away. I'm in terrible pain right at this moment. I shouldn't be walking around."

"You won't be walking around. You'll be sitting in a cell."

"You're a hard man, Lew."

"You keep calling me Lew. Don't do it. I ought to leave you here to find your own way back."

"You wouldn't do that to me?" He caught at me again,

152

chattering. "Listen to me, Lew—Mr. Archer. About that Italy deal. I can get you five hundred a week for twenty-six weeks. No duties, nothing to do. A free holiday—"

"Save it. I wouldn't touch a nickel of yours with rubber gloves on."

"But you wouldn't leave me here?"

"Why not? You left her."

"You don't understand. I only did what I had to. We were caught. The girl fixed it herself so that we were caught. She had something on the Man and his wife, evidence against them, and she turned it over to Carl Stern. He forced the deal on us, in a way. I would have handled it differently."

"So everything you did was Stern's fault."

"I don't say that, but he was calling the signals. We had to co-operate with him. We've had to now for months. Stern even forced the Man to lend his name to his big new operation."

"What evidence does Stern hold against the Graffs?"

"Would I be likely to tell you?"

"You're going to tell me. Now. I'm getting sick of you, Frost."

He backed away from me against the doorpost. The light fell on one side of his face and made his profile look as pale and thin as paper. As if corruption had eaten him away till he was only a surface laid on darkness.

"A gun," he said. "A target pistol belonging to Mr. Graff. Isobel used it to kill a girl with, a couple of years ago."

"Where does Stern keep the gun?"

"In a safe-deposit box. I found out that much, but I couldn't get to it. He was carrying it with him last night, though, in the car. He showed it to me." His dull eyes brightened yellowly. "You know, Lew, I'm authorized to pay a hundred grand for that little gun. You're a strong, smart boy. Can you get it away from Stern?"

"Somebody already has. Stern got his throat cut in the course of the night. Or maybe you know that, Frost."

"No. I didn't know it. If it's true, it changes things."

"Not for you."

We went outside. Below, the valley floor shimmered in its own white heat. The jet trail which slashed the sky was blurring out. In this anti-human place, the Cadillac on the road looked as irrelevant as a space-ship stalled on the mountains of the moon. Rina stood at the foot of the slope, her face upturned and blank. It was heavy news I carried down to her.

MUCH later, on the sunset plane, we were able to talk about it. Leroy Frost, denying and protesting and calling for lawyers and doctors, had been deposited with Marfeld and Lashman in the security ward of the hospital. The remains of Hester Campbell were in the basement of the same building, awaiting autopsy. I told the sheriff and the district attorney enough to have Frost and his men held for possible extradition on suspicion of murder. I didn't expect it to stick. The final moves in the case would have to be made in California.

The DC-6 left the runway and climbed the blue ramp of air. There were only a dozen other passengers, and Rina and I had the front end of the plane to ourselves. When the NO SMOKING sign went out, she crossed her legs and lit a cigarette. Without looking at me directly, she said in a brittle voice:

"I suppose I owe you my life, as they say in books. I don't know what I can do to repay you. No doubt I should offer to go to bed with you. Would you like that?"

"Don't," I said. "You've had a rough time and made a mistake, and I've been involved in it. But you don't have to take it out on me."

"I didn't mean to be snide," she said, a little snidely. "I was making a serious offer of my body. Having nothing better to offer."

"Rina, come off it."

"I'm not attractive enough, is that what you mean?"

"You're talking nonsense. I don't blame you. You've had a bad scare."

She sulked for a while, looking down at the Chinese Wall of mountains we were crossing. Finally she said in a chastened tone:

"You're perfectly right. I was scared, really scared, for the first time in my life. It does funny things to a girl. It made me feel—well, almost like a whore—as though I wasn't worth anything to myself."

"That's the way the jerks want you to feel. If everybody felt like a zombie, we'd all be on the same level. And the jerks could get away with the things jerks want to get away with. They're not, though. Jerkiness isn't as respectable as it used to be, not even in L.A. Which is why they had to build Vegas."

She didn't smile. "Is it such a terrible place?"

"It depends on who you pick for your playmates. You picked the worst ones you could find."

"I didn't pick them, and they're not my playmates. They never were. I despise them. I warned Hester years ago that Lance was poison for her. And I told Carl Stern what I thought of him to his face."

"When was this? Last night?"

"Several weeks ago. I went out on a double date with Lance and Hester. Perhaps it was a foolish thing to do, but I wanted to find out what was going on. Hester brought Carl Stern for me, can you imagine? He's supposed to be a millionaire, and Hester always believed that money was the important thing. She couldn't see, even at that late date, why I wouldn't play up to Stern.

"Not that it would have done me any good," she added wryly. "He was no more interested in me than I was in him. He spent the evening in various nightclubs playing footsie with Lance under the table. Hester didn't notice, or maybe she didn't care. She could be very dense about certain things. I cared, though, for her sake. Finally I told them off and walked out on the three of them."

"What did you say to them?"

"Just the plain, unvarnished truth. That Carl Stern was a pederast and probably much worse, and Hester was crazy to fool around with him and his pretty-boy."

"Did you mention blackmail?"

"Yes. I told them I suspected it."

"That was a dangerous thing to do. It gave Stern a reason to want you dead. I'm pretty sure he meant to kill you last night. Lucky for you he died first."

"Really? I can't believe—" But she believed it. Her dry throat refused to function. She sat swallowing. "Just because I—because I suspected something?"

"Suspected him of blackmail, and called him a fag. Killing always came easy to Stern. I went over his rap sheet this afternoon—the Nevada authorities have a full file on him. No wonder he couldn't get a gambling license in his own name.

Back in the thirties he was one of Anastasia's boys, suspected of implication in over thirty killings."

"Why wasn't he arrested?"

"He was, but they couldn't convict him. Don't ask me why. Ask the politicians that ran the cops in New York and Jersey and Cleveland and the other places. Ask the people that voted for the politicians. Stern ended up in Vegas, but he belonged to the whole country. He worked for Lepke, for Game Boy Miller in Cleveland, for Lefty Clark in Detroit, for the Trans America gang in L.A. He finished his apprenticeship under Siegel, and after Siegel got it he went into business for himself."

"What sort of business?"

"Wire service for bookies, narcotics, prostitution, anything with a fast and dirty buck in it. He was a millionaire, all right, several times over. He sank a million in the Casbah alone."

"I don't understand why he would go in for blackmail. He didn't need the money."

"He was Syndicate-trained, and blackmail's been one of their main sources of power ever since Maffia days. No, it wasn't money he needed. It was status. Simon Graff's name gave him his chance to go legit, to really build himself into the countryside."

"And I helped him." The bones had come out in her face so that it was almost ugly. "I made it possible. I could bite my tongue out."

"Before you do, I wish you'd explain what you mean."

She drew in her breath sharply. "Well, in the first place, I'm a psychiatric nurse."

She fell silent. It was hard for her to get started.

"So your mother told me," I said.

She gave me a sidelong glance. "When did you run into Mother?"

"Yesterday."

"What did you think of her?"

"I liked her."

"Really?"

"I like women in general, and I'm not hypercritical."

"I am," Rina said. "I've always been suspicious of Mother and her little airs and graces and her big ideas. And it was mutual. Hester was her favorite, her little pal. Or she was Hester's little pal. She spoiled my sister rotten, at the same time made terrible demands on her: all she wanted was for Hester to be great.

"I sat on the side lines for fifteen years and watched the two girls play emotional ping-pong. Or pong-ping. I was the not-so-innocent bystander, the third one that made the crowd, the one that wasn't simpatico." It sounded like a speech she'd rehearsed to herself many times, There was bitterness in her voice, tempered with resignation. "I broke it up as soon as Mother would let me, as soon as I finished high school. I went into nurse's training in Santa Barbara, and took my P.G. work at Camarillo."

Talking about her profession, or talking out her feelings about her family, had given her back some of her self-assurance. She held her shoulders straighter, and her breasts were bold.

"Mother thought I was crazy. We had a knockdown-dragout quarrel the first year, and I haven't seen much of Mother since. It just happens I like doing things for sick people, especially working with disturbed people. Need to be needed, I guess. My main interest now is occupational therapy. It's mainly what I'm doing with Dr. Frey."

"This is the Dr. Frey who runs the sanitarium in Santa Monica?"

She nodded. "I've worked there for over two years."

"So you know Isobel Graff."

"Do I ever. She was admitted to the san not long after I started there. She'd been in before, more than once. The doctor said she was worse than usual. She's schizophrenic, you know, has been for twenty years, and when it's acute she develops paranoid delusions. The doctor said they used to be directed against her father when he was alive. This time they were directed against Mr. Graff. She believed that he was plotting against her, and she was going to get him first.

"Dr. Frey thought Mr. Graff should have her locked up for his own protection. Every now and then a paranoid delusion erupts into action. I've seen it happen. Dr. Frey gave her a series of metrazol treatments, and she gradually came out of the acute phase and quieted down. But she was still quite remote when this thing happened. I still wouldn't turn my back on her. But Dr. Frey said she wasn't dangerous, and he knew her better than I did and, after all, he was the doctor.

"In the middle of March, he gave her the run of the grounds. I shouldn't second guess a doctor, but that's where he made his mistake. She wasn't ready for freedom. The first little thing that happened set her off."

"What did happen?"

"I don't know exactly. Perhaps someone made a thought-less remark, or simply looked at her in the wrong tone of voice. Paranoid people are like that, almost like radio receivers. They pick a tiny signal out of the air and build it

157

up with their own power until they can't hear anything else. Whatever happened, Isobel took off, and she was gone all night.

"When she came back, she was *really* in a bad way. With that terrible glazed look on her face, like a fish with a hook in its mouth. She was right back where she started in January —worse."

"What night was she gone?"

"March 21, the first day of spring. I'm not likely to forget the date. A girl I used to know in Malibu, a girl named Gabrielle Torres, was killed that same night. I didn't connect the two events at the time."

"But you do now?"

She inclined her head somberly. "Hester made the connection for me. You see, she knew something I hadn't known, that Simon Graff and Gabrielle were—lovers."

"When did this come out?"

"One day last summer when we had lunch together. Hester was practically on her uppers then, I used to buy her lunch whenever I could. We were gossiping about this and that, and she brought up the case. It seemed to be on her mind: she was back at the Channel Club at the time, giving diving lessons. She told me about the love affair; apparently Gabrielle had confided in her. Without thinking what I was doing, I told her Isobel Graff had escaped that night. Hester reacted like a Geiger counter, and started asking me questions. I thought her only interest was in tracking down the person who killed her friend. I let down my back hair and told her all I knew, about Isobel and her runout and her mental condition when she came back.

"I had the early-morning duty that day, and I was the one who looked after her until Dr. Frey got there. Isobel dragged herself in some time around dawn. She was in bad shape, and not just mentally. She was physically exhausted. I think now she must have walked and run and crawled along the shore all the way from Malibu. The surf must have caught her, too, because her clothes were wet and matted with sand. I gave her a hot bath first thing."

"Did she tell you where she'd been?"

"No, she didn't say a thing. Actually, she didn't speak for days. Dr. Frey was worried for a while that she might be going into catatonia. Even when she did come out of it and started to talk again, she never mentioned that night—at least, not in words. I saw her in the crafts room, though, later in the spring. I saw some of the objects she made out of clay. I shouldn't have been shocked after what I've seen

158

in mental wards, but I was shocked by some of those objects." She closed her eyes as if to shut out the sight of them, and went on in a hushed voice:

"She used to make these girl dolls and pinch their heads off and destroy them part by part, like some sort of jungle witch. And horrible little men dolls with huge—organs. Animals with human faces, coupling. Guns and—parts of the human body, all mixed up."

"Not nice," I said, "but it wouldn't necessarily mean anything, would it? Did she ever discuss these things with you?"

"Not with me, no. Dr. Frey doesn't encourage the nurses to practice psychiatry."

She turned in the seat and her knee nudged mine, withdrawing quickly. Her dark-blue gaze came up to my face. It was strange that a girl who had seen so much should have such innocent eyes.

"Will you be seeing Dr. Frey?" she said.

"Probably I will."

"Please don't tell him about me, will you?"

"There's no reason why I should."

"It's a terrible breach of ethics, you know, for a nurse to talk about her patients. I've worried myself sick these last few months since I spilled out everything to Hester. I was such a fool. I believed that she was sincere for once in her life, that all she wanted was the truth about Gabrielle's death. I should never have trusted her with dangerous information. It's obvious what she wanted it for. She wanted to use it to blackmail Mrs. Graff."

"How long have you known that, Rina?"

Her voice, or her candor, failed her for a time. I waited for her to go on. Her eyes were almost black with thought. She said:

"It's hard to say. You can know a thing and not know it. When you love a person, it takes so long to face the facts about them. I've really suspected the whole thing practically from the beginning. Ever since Hester left the Club and started living without any visible income. It came to a head on that horrible double date I told you about. Carl Stern got tight and started to boast about his new place in Vegas, and how he had Simon Graff under his thumb. And Hester sat there drinking it in, with stars in her eyes. I got a queer idea that she wanted me there to see how well she was doing. What a success she'd made of her life, after all. That was when I blew my top."

"What was their reaction?"

"I didn't wait for any reaction. I walked out of the place

—we were in the Bar of Dixie—and went home in a taxi by myself. I never saw Hester again. I didn't see any of them again, until yesterday when Lance called me."

"To ask you to fly to Vegas under her name?"

She nodded.

"Why did you agree to do it?"

"You know why. I was supposed to be giving her an alibi."

"It doesn't explain why you wanted to."

"Do I have to explain? I simply wanted to." She added after a time: "I felt I owed it to Hester. In a way I'm as guilty as she is. This awful business would never have started if it hadn't been for me. I'd got her into it, I felt it was up to me to get her out. But Hester was dead already, wasn't she?"

A fit of shivering took hold of her, shaking her so that her teeth knocked together. I put my arm around her until the spasm passed. "Don't blame yourself too much."

"I have to. Don't you see, if Isobel Graff killed Hester, I'm to blame?"

"I don't see it. People are responsible for what they do themselves. Anyway, there's some doubt in my mind that Isobel killed your sister. I'm not even certain that she shot Gabrielle Torres. I won't be until I get hold of firm evidence; a confession, or an eyewitness, or the gun she used."

"You're just saying that."

"No, I'm not just saying it. I jumped to certain conclusions too early in this case."

She didn't ask me what I meant, and that was just as well. I still had no final answers.

"Listen to me, Rina. You're a girl with a lot of conscience, and you've taken some hard blows. You have a tendency to blame yourself for things. You were probably brought up to blame yourself for everything."

She sat stiff in the circle of my arm. "It's true. Hester was young and always getting into trouble, and Mother blamed me. Only, how did you know that? You have a great deal of insight."

"Too bad it mostly takes the form of hindsight. Anyway, there's one thing I'm sure of. You're not responsible for what happened to Hester, and you didn't do anything very wrong."

"Do you really believe that?" She sounded astonished.

"Naturally I believe it."

She was a good girl, as Mrs. Busch had said. She was also a very tired girl, and a sad and nervous girl. We sat in uneasy silence for a while. The hum of the engines had changed. The plane had passed the zenith of its flight and begun the long descent toward Los Angeles and the red sun. Before the plane touched earth, Rina had cried a little on my shoulder. Then she slept a little.

My car was in the parking-lot at International Airport. Rina asked me to drop her off at her mother's house in Santa Monica. I did so, without going in myself, and drove up Wilshire and out San Vicente to Dr. Frey's sanitarium. It occupied walled grounds which had once belonged to a large private estate in the open country between Sawtelle and Brentwood. A male attendant in a business suit opened the automatic gate and told me that Dr. Frey was probably at dinner.

The central building was a white Edwardian mansion, with more recent additions, which stood on a terraced hillside. Dr. Frey lived in a guesthouse to one side of it. People who looked like anybody else were promenading on the terraces. Like anybody else, except that there was a wall around their lives. From Dr. Frey's veranda, I could see over the wall, as far as the ocean. Fog and darkness were gathering on its convex surface. Below the horizon the lost sun smoldered like a great plane that had crashed and burned.

I talked to a costumed maid, to a gray-haired housekeeper, finally to Dr. Frey himself. He was a stoop-shouldered old man in dinner clothes, with a highball glass in his hand. Intelligence and doubt had deeply lined his face. The lines deepened when I told him that I suspected Isobel Graff of murder. He set his glass on the mantelpiece and stood in front of it, rather belligerently, as though I had threatened the center of his house.

"Am I to understand that you are a policeman?"

"A private detective. Later I'll be taking this to the police. I came to you first."

"I hardly feel favored," he said. "You can't seriously expect me to discuss such a matter, such an accusation, with a stranger. I know nothing about you."

"You know quite a bit about Isobel Graff."

161

He spread his long gray hands. "I know that I am a doctor and that she is my patient. What do you expect me to say?"

"You could tell me there's nothing in it."

"Very well, I do so. There is nothing in it. Now if you'll excuse me, I have guests for dinner."

"Is Mrs. Graff here now?"

He countered with a question of his own: "May I ask, what is your purpose in making these inquiries?"

"Four people have been killed, three of them in the last two days."

He showed no surprise. "These people were friends of yours?"

"Hardly. Members of the human race, though."

He said with the bitter irony of age: "So you are an altruist, are you? A Hollywood culture-hero in a sports coat? You propose to cleanse the Augean stables single-handed?"

"I'm not that ambitious. And I'm not your problem, doctor. Isobel Graff is. If she killed four people, or one, she ought to be put away where she can't kill any more. Don't you agree?"

He didn't answer me for a minute. Then he said: "I signed voluntary commitment papers for her this morning."

"Does that mean she's on her way to the state hospital?"

"It should, but I'm afraid it doesn't." It was the third time in three minutes that he'd been afraid. "Before the papers could be—ah—implemented, Mrs. Graff escaped. She was very determined, much more so than we bargained for. I confess error. I should have had her placed in maximum security. As it was, she broke a reinforced window with a chair and made good her escape in the back of a laundry truck."

"When was this?"

"This morning, shortly before the lunch hour. She hasn't been found as yet."

"How hard is she being looked for?"

"You'll have to ask her husband. His private police are searching. He forbade—" Dr. Frey compressed his lips and reached for his drink. When he had sipped it: "I'm afraid I can't submit to further interrogation. If you were an official—" He shrugged, and the ice tinkled in his glass.

"You want me to call the police in?"

"If you have evidence."

"I'm asking you for evidence. Did Mrs. Graff kill Gabrielle Torres?"

"I have no way of knowing."

"What about the others?"

"I can't say."

"You've seen her and talked to her?"

"Of course. Many times. Most recently this morning."

"Was her mental condition consistent with homicide?"

He smiled wearily. "This is not a courtroom, sir. Next you'll be framing a hypothetical question. Which I would refuse to answer."

"The question isn't hypothetical. Did she shoot Gabrielle Torres on the night of March 21 last year?"

"It may not be hypothetical, but the question is certainly academic. Mrs. Graff is mentally ill now, and she was ill on March 21 of last year. She couldn't possibly be convicted of murder, or any other crime. So you are wasting both our times, don't you think?"

"It's only time, and I seem to be getting somewhere. You've practically admitted that she did that shooting."

"Have I? I don't think so. You are a very pertinacious young man, and you are making a nuisance of yourself."

"I'm used to that."

"I am not." He moved to the door and opened it. Male laughter came from the other side of the house. "Now if you will transport your rather shopworn charm to another location, it will save me the trouble of having you thrown out."

"One more question, doctor. Why did she pick that day in March to run away? Did she have a visitor that day, or the day before?"

"Visitor?" I had succeeded in surprising him. "I know nothing of any visitors."

"I understand Clarence Bassett visited her regularly here."

He looked at me, eyes veiled like an old bird's. "Do you have a paid spy among my employees?"

"It's simpler than that. I've talked to Bassett. As a matter of fact, he brought me into this case."

"Why didn't you say so? I know Bassett very well." He closed the door and took a step toward me. "He hired you to investigate these deaths?"

"It started out as a missing-girl case and turned into a murder case before I found her. The girl's name was Hester Campbell."

"Why, I know Hester Campbell. I've known her for years at the Club. I gave her sister a job." He paused, and the slight excitement ran through him and drained away. The only trace it left was a tremor in the hand that held his glass. He sipped from the glass to conceal its clinking. "Is Hester Campbell one of the victims?"

"She was beaten to death with a poker yesterday afternoon."

"And you have reason to believe that Mrs. Graff killed her?"

163

"Isobel Graff is involved, I don't know how deeply. She was at the scene of the crime, apparently. Her husband seems to accept her guilt. But that's not conclusive. Isobel may have been framed. Another possibility is this, that she has been used as a cat's-paw in these killings. I mean that she committed them, physically, but was incited to do it by somebody else. Would she be open to that kind of suggestion?"

"The more I know of the human mind, the less I know." He tried to smile, and failed miserably. "I predicted that you would be asking hypothetical questions."

"I keep trying not to, doctor. You seem to attract them. And you haven't answered my question about Bassett's visits here."

"Why, there was nothing unusual in them. He visited Mrs. Graff every week, I believe, sometimes more frequently when she asked for him. They were very close—indeed, they'd been engaged to be married at one time, many years ago, before her present marriage. I sometimes think she should have married Clarence instead of the man she did marry. He has an almost feminine quality of understanding, which she was badly in need of. Neither of them is adequate to stand alone. Together, if marriage had been possible for them, they might have made a functioning unit." His tone was elegiac.

"What do you mean when you say that neither of them is adequate?"

"It should be obvious in the case of Mrs. Graff. She has been subject to schizophrenic episodes since her middle teens. She has remained, in a sense, a teen-aged girl inside of a middle-aged body—unable to cope with the demands of adult life." He added with a trace of bitterness: "She has received little help from Simon Graff."

"Do you know what caused her illness?"

"The etiology of this disease is still mysterious, but I think I know something of this particular case. She lost her mother young, and Peter Heliopoulos was not a wise father. He pushed her towards maturity, at the same time deprived her of true human contact. She became in a social sense his second wife before she even reached puberty. Great demands were made on her as his little hostess, as the spearhead of his social ambition. The very vulnerable spearhead. These demands were too great for one who was perhaps predisposed from birth to schizophrenia."

"What about Clarence Bassett? Is he mentally ill?"

"I have no reason to think so. He is the manager of my club, not my patient."

"You said he was inadequate."

164

"I meant in the social and sexual sense. Clarence is the perennial bachelor, the giver of other people's parties, the man who is content to dwell on the sidelines of life. His interest in women is limited to young girls, and to flawed women like Isobel who have failed to outlive their childhood. All this is typical, and part of his adjustment."

"His adjustment to what?"

"To his own nature. His weakness requires him to avoid the storm centers of life. Unfortunately, his adjustment was badly shaken, several years ago, by his mother's death. Since then he has been drinking heavily. I would hazard the guess that his alcoholism is essentially a suicidal gesture. He is literally drowning his sorrows. I suspect he would be glad to join his beloved mother in the grave."

"You don't regard him as potentially dangerous?"

The doctor answered after a thinking pause: "Perhaps he could be. The death-wish is powerfully ambivalent. It can be turned against the self or against others. Inadequate men have been known to try to complete themselves in violence. A Jack the Ripper, for instance, is probably a man with a strong female component who is trying to annul it in himself by destroying actual females."

The abstract words fluttered and swerved like bats in the twilit room. "Are you suggesting that Clarence Bassett could be a mass murderer?"

"By no means. I have been speaking most generally."

"Why go to all the trouble?"

He gave me a complex look. There was sympathy in it, and tragic knowledge, and weariness. He had worn himself out in the Augean stables, and despaired of human action.

"I am an old man," he said. "I lie awake in the night watches and speculate on human possibility. Are you familiar with the newer interpersonal theories of psychiatry? With the concept of *folie à deux?*"

I said I wasn't.

"Madness for two, it might be translated. A madness, a violence, may arise out of a relationship even though the parties to the relationship may be individually harmless. My nocturnal speculations have included Clarence Bassett and Isobel. Twenty years ago their relationship might have made a marriage. Such a relationship may also sour and deteriorate and make something infinitely worse. I am not saying that this is so. But it is a possibility worth considering, a possibility which arises when two persons have the same unconscious and forbidden desire. The same death-wish."

"Did Bassett visit Mrs. Graff before her escape in March last year?"

"I believe he did. I would have to check the records."

"Don't bother, I'll ask him personally. Tell me this, Dr. Frey: do you have anything more to go on than speculation?"

"Perhaps I have. If I had, I would not and could not tell you." He raised his hand before his face in a faltering gesture of defense. "You deluge me with questions, sir, and there is no end to them. I am an old man, as I said. This is, or was, my dinner hour."

He opened the door a second time. I thanked him and went out. He slammed the heavy front door behind me. The people on the twilit terraces turned pale, startled, purgatorial faces toward the source of the noise.

IT was full night when I got to Malibu. A single car stood in the Channel Club parking-lot, a beat-up prewar Dodge with Tony's name on the steering-post. Inside the club, around the pool, there was nobody in sight. I knocked on the door of Clarence Bassett's office and got no answer.

I walked along the gallery and down the steps to the poolside. The water shivered under a slow, cold offshore wind. The place seemed very desolate. I was the last man at the party for sure.

I took advantage of this circumstance by breaking into Simon Graff's *cabaña*. The door had a Yale-type lock which was easy to jimmy. I stepped in and turned on the light, half expecting to find someone in the room. But it was empty, its furnishings undisturbed, its pictures bright and still on the walls, caught out of time.

Time was running through me, harsh on my nerve-ends, hot in my arteries, impalpable as breath in my mouth. I had the sleepless feeling you sometimes get in the final hours of a bad case, that you can see around corners, if you want to, and down into the darkness in human beings.

I opened the twin doors of the dressing-rooms. Each had

a back door opening into a corridor which led to the showers. The one on the right contained a gray steel locker and an assortment of men's beach clothes: robes and swimming trunks, Bermuda shorts and sport shirts and tennis shoes. The one on the left, which must have been Mrs. Graff's, was completely bare except for a wooden bench and an empty locker.

I switched on the light in the ceiling, uncertain what I was looking for. It was something vague yet specific: a sure sense of what had happened on that spring night when Isobel Graff had been running loose and the first young girl had died. *For a second,* Isobel had said, *I was in there, watching us through the door, and listening to myself. Please pour me a drink.*

I closed the door of her dressing-room. The louvers were set high in it, fairly wide apart, and loose, so that the windowless cubicle could air itself. By getting up on my toes, I could look down between the crosspieces into the outer room. Isobel Graff would have had to stand on the bench.

I dragged the bench over to the door and stood on it. Six inches below by eye-level, in the edge of one of the louvers, there was a series of indentations which looked like toothmarks, around them a faint red lipstick crescent, dark with age. I examined the underside of the soft wooden strip and found similar markings. Pain jerked through my mind like a knotted string, pulling an image after it. It was pain for the woman who had stood on this bench in the dark, watching the outer room through the cracks between the louvers and biting down on the wood in agony.

I turned out the light and crossed the outer room and stood in front of Matisse's Blue Coast lithograph. I had a fierce nostalgia for that brilliant, orderly world which had never quite existed. A world where nobody lived or died, held in the eye of a never-sinking sun.

Behind me someone cleared his throat delicately. I turned and saw Tony in the doorway, squinting against the light. His hand was on his gun butt.

"Mr. Archer, you broke the door?"

"I broke it."

He shook his head at me in a monitory way, and stooped to look at the damage I had done. A bright scratch crossed the setting of the lock, and the edge of the wood was slightly dented. Tony's blunt brown forefinger traced the scratch and the dent.

"Mr. Graff won't like this, he is crazy about his *cabaña,* he furnished it all himself, not like the others."

"When did he do that?"

"Last year, before the start of the summer season. He brought in his own decorators and cleaned it out like a whistle and put in all new stuff." His gaze was serious, black, unwavering. He removed his peaked cap and scratched his gray-flecked head. "You the one that bust the lock on the fence gate, too?"

"I'm the one. I seem to be in a destructive mood today. Is it important?"

"Cops thought so. Captain Spero was asking me back and forth who bust the gate. They found another dead one on the beach, you know that, Mr. Archer?"

"Carl Stern."

"Yah, Carl Stern. He was my nephew's manager, one time. Captain Spero said it was one of these gang killings, but I dunno. What do you think?"

"I doubt it."

Tony squatted on his heels just inside the open door. It seemed to make him nervous to be inside the Graffs' *cabaña*. He scratched his head again, and ran thumb and finger down the grooves that bracketed his mouth. "Mr. Archer. What happened to my nephew Manuel?"

"He was shot and killed last night."

"I know that. Captain Spero told me he was dead, shot in the eye." Tony touched the lid of his left eye with his right forefinger. His upturned face resembled a cracked clay death mask.

"What else did Spero say?"

"I dunno. Said it was maybe another gang killing, but I dunno. He asked me, did Manuel have enemies? I told him, yah, he had one big enemy, name of Manuel Torres. What did I know about his life, his friends? He bust up from me long ago and went on his own road, straight down to hell in a low-top car." Through the stoic Indian mask, his eyes shown with black, living grief. "I dunno, I coulden tear that boy loose from my heart. He was like my own son to me, one time."

His bowed shoulders moved with his breathing. He said: "I'm gonna get out of this place, it's bad luck for me and my family. I still got friends in Fresno. I ought to stayed in Fresno, never left it. I made the same mistake that Manuel made, thought I could come and take what I wanted. They wooden let me take it. They leave me with nothing, no wife, no daughter, no Manuel."

He balled his fist and struck himself on the cheekbone and looked around the room in confused awe, as though it was the lair of gods which he had offended. The room reminded him of his duty to it:

168

"What you doing in here, Mr. Archer? You got no right in here?"

"I'm looking for Mrs. Graff."

"Why didden you say so? You didden have to break the door down. Mrs. Graff was here a few minutes ago. She wanted Mr. Bassett, only he ain't here."

"Where is Mrs. Graff now?"

"She went down on the beach. I tried to stop her, she ain't in very good shape. She wooden come with me, though. You think I ought to telephone Mr. Graff?"

"If you can get in touch with him. Where's Bassett?"

"I dunno, he was packing his stuff before. He's going away on his vacation, maybe. He always goes to Mexico for a month in the off-season. Used to show me colored pictures—"

I left him talking to the empty room and went to the end of the pool. The gate in the fence was open. Twenty feet below it, the beach sloped away to the water, delimited by the wavering line of white foam. The sight of the ocean gave me a queasy feeling: it reminded me of Carl Stern doing the dead man's float.

Waves rose like apparitions at the surf-line and fell like masonry. Beyond them a padded wall of fog was sliding shoreward. I went down the concrete steps, met by a snatch of sound which blew up to me between the thumpings of the surf. It was Isobel Graff talking to the ocean in a voice like a gull's screek. She dared it to come and get her. She sat hunched over her knees, just beyond its reach, and shook her fist at the muttering water.

"Dirty old cesspool, I'm not afraid of you."

Her profile was thrust forward, gleaming white with a gleaming dark eye in it. She heard me moving toward her and cowered away, one arm thrown over her face.

"Leave me alone. I won't go back. I'll die first."

"Where have you been all day?"

Her wet black eyes peered up from under her arm. "It's none of your business. Go away."

"I think I'll stay with you."

I sat beside her on the impacted sand, so close that our shoulders touched. She drew away from the contact, but made no other move. Her dark and unkempt bird's-head twisted toward me suddenly. She said in her own voice:

"Hello."

"Hello, Isobel. Where have you been all day?"

"On the beach, mostly. I felt like a nice long walk. A little girl gave me an ice-cream cone, she cried when I took it away from her, I am an old horror. But it was all I had to eat all day. I promised to send her a check, only I'm afraid to go home. That dirty old man might be there."

"What dirty old man?"

"The one that made a pass at me when I took the sleeping-pills. I saw him when I passed out. He had a rotten breath like Father's when he died. And he had worms that were his eyes." Her voice was singsong.

"Who had?"

"Old Father Deathmas with the long white dirty beard." Her mood was ugly and ambiguous. She wasn't too far gone to know what she was saying, just far enough gone to say it. "He made a pass at me, only I was too tired, and there I was in the morning back at the old stand with the same hot and cold running people. What am I going to do? I'm afraid of the water. I can't stand the thought of the violent ways, and sleeping-pills don't work. They simply pump you out and walk you up and down and feed you coffee and there you are back at the old stand."

"When did you try sleeping-pills?"

"Oh, a long time ago, when Father made me marry Simon. I was in love with another man."

"Clarence?"

"He was the only one I ever. Clare was so sweet to me."

The wall of fog had crossed the foam-line and was almost on top of us. The surf pounded behind it like a despondent visitor. I didn't know whether to laugh or cry. I looked down at her face, which slanted up close to mine: a pale ghost of a face with two dark eye-holes and a mouth-hole in it. She was tainted by disease and far from young, but in the foggy night she looked more like a child than a woman. A disordered child who had lost her way and met death on the detour.

Her head leaned on my shoulder. "I'm caught," she said. "I've been trying all day to get up the nerve to walk into the water. What am I going to do? I can't endure forever in a room."

"In the church you were brought up in, suicide is a sin."

"I've committed worse."

I waited. The fog was all around us now, an element composed of air and water and a fishy chill. It made a kind of limbo, out of this world, where anything could be said. Isobel Graff said:

"I committed the worst sin of all. They were together in the light and I was alone in the darkness. Then the light was like broken glass in my eyes, but I could see to shoot. I shot her in the groin and she died."

"This happened in your *cabaña?*"

She nodded faintly. I felt the movement rather than saw it. "I caught her there with Simon. She crawled out here and died on the beach. The waves came up and took her. I wish that they would take me."

"What happened to Simon that night?"

"Nothing. He ran away. To do it again another day and do it and do it and do it. He was terrified when I came out of the back room with the gun in my hand. He was the one I really intended to kill, but he scuttled out the door."

"Where did you get the gun?"

"It was Simon's target pistol. He kept it in his locker. He taught me to fire it himself, on this very beach." She stirred in the crook of my arm. "What do you think of me now?"

I didn't have to answer her. There was a moving voice in the fog above our heads. It was calling her name, Isobel.

"Who is it? Don't let them take me." She turned on her knees and clutched my hand. Hers was fish-cold.

Footsteps and light were descending the concrete steps. I got up and went to meet them. The beam of light wavered toward me. Graff's dim and nimbused figure was behind it. The long, thin nose of a target pistol protruded from his other hand. My gun was already in mine.

"You're covered, Graff. Drop it directly in front of you."

His pistol thudded softly in the sand. I stooped and picked it up. It was an early-model German Walther, .22 caliber, with a custom-made walnut grip too small to fit my hand. The gun was loaded. Distrusting its hair-trigger action, I set the safety and shoved it down under my belt.

"I'll take the light, too."

He handed me his flashlight. I turned its beam upward on his face and saw it naked for an instant. His mouth was soft and twisted, his eyes were frightened.

"I heard my wife. Where is she?"

I swung the flash-beam along the beach. Its cone of brilliance filled with swirling fog. Isobel Graff ran away from it. Black and huge on the gray air, her shadow ran ahead of her. She seemed to be driving off a fury which dwarfed her and tormented her and mimicked all her movements.

Graff called her name again and ran after her. I followed along behind and saw her fall and get up and fall again. Graff helped her to her feet. They walked back toward me, slowly and clumsily. She dragged her feet and hung her head, turning her face away from the light. Graff's arm around her waist propelled her forward.

I took the target pistol out of my belt and showed it to her. "Is this the gun you used to shoot Gabrielle Torres?"

She glanced at it and nodded mutely.

"No," Graff said. "Admit nothing, Isobel."

"She's already confessed," I said.

"My wife is mentally incompetent. Her confession is not valid evidence."

"The gun is. The sheriff's ballistics department will have the matching slugs. The gun and the slugs together will be unshakable evidence. Where did you get the gun, Graff?"

"Carl Walther made it for me, in Germany, many years ago."

"I'm talking about the last twenty-four hours. Where did you get it this time?"

He answered carefully: "I have had it in my possession continuously for over twenty years."

"The hell you have. Stern had it last night before he was killed. Did you kill him for it?"

"That is ridiculous."

"Did you have him killed?"

"I did not."

"Somebody knocked off Stern to get hold of this gun. You must know who it was, and you might as well tell me. Everything's going to come out now. Not even your kind of money can stop it."

"Is money what you want from me? You can have money." His voice dragged with contempt—for me, and perhaps for himself.

"I'm not for sale like Marfeld," I said. "Your boss thug tried to buy me. He's in the Vegas clink with a body to explain."

"I know that," Graff said. "But I am talking about a very great deal of money. A hundred thousand dollars in cash. Now. Tonight."

"Where would you get that much in cash tonight?"

"From Clarence Bassett. He has it in his office safe. I paid it to him this evening. It was the price he set on the pistol. Take it away from him, and you can have it."

THERE was light in Bassett's office. I knocked so hard that I bruised my knuckles. He came to the door in shirt sleeves. His face was putty-colored, with blue hollows under the eyes. His eyes had a Lazarus look, and hardly seemed to recognize me.

"Archer? What's the trouble, man?"

"You're the trouble, Clarence."

"Oh, I *hope* not." He noticed the couple behind me, and did a big take. "You've found her, Mr. Graff. I'm so glad."

"Are you?" Graff said glumly. "Isobel has confessed everything to this man. I want my money back."

Bassett's face underwent a process of change. The end product of the process was a bright, nervous grin which resembled the rictus of a dead horse.

"Am I to understand this? I return the money, and we drop the whole matter? Nothing more will be said?"

"Plenty more will be said. Give him his money, Clarence."

He stood tense in the doorway, blocking my way. Visions of possible action flitted behind his pale-blue eyes and died. "It's not here."

"Open the safe and we'll see for ourselves."

"You have no warrant."

"I don't need one. You're willing to co-operate. Aren't you?"

He reached up and plucked at his neck above the open collar of his button-down shirt, stretching the loose skin and letting it pull itself back into place. "This has been a bit of a shock. As a matter of fact, I am willing to co-operate. I have nothing to hide."

He turned abruptly, crossed the room, and took down the photograph of the three divers. A cylindrical safe was set in the wall behind it. I covered him with the target pistol as he spun the bright chrome dials. The gun he had used on Leonard was probably at the bottom of the sea, but there could be another gun in the safe. All the safe contained was

173

money, though—bundles of money done up in brown bank paper.

"Take it," Graff said. "It is yours."

"It would only make a bum out of me. Besides, I couldn't afford to pay the tax on it."

"You are joking. You must want money. You work for money, don't you?"

"I want it very badly," I said. "But I can't take this money. It wouldn't belong to me, I would belong to it. It would expect me to do things, and I would have to do them. Sit on the lid of this mess of yours, the way Marfeld did, until dry rot set in."

"It would be easy to cover up," Graff said.

He turned a basilisk eye on Clarence Bassett. Bassett flattened himself against the wall. The fear of death invaded his face and galvanized his body. He swatted the gun out of my hand, went down on his hands and knees, and got a grip on the butt. I snaked it away from him before he could consolidate his grip, lifted him by the collar, and set him in the chair at the end of his desk.

Isobel Graff had collapsed in the chair behind the desk. Her head was thrown back, and her undone hair poured like black oil over the back of the chair. Bassett avoided looking at her. He sat hunched far over to one side away from her, trembling and breathing hard.

"I've done nothing that I'm ashamed of. I shielded an old friend from the consequences of her actions. Her husband saw fit to reward me."

"That's the gentlest description of blackmail I ever heard. Not that blackmail covers what you've done. Are you going to tell me you knocked off Leonard and Stern to protect Isobel Graff?"

"I have no idea what you're talking about."

"When you tried to frame Isobel for the murder of Hester Campbell, was that part of your protection service?"

"I did nothing of the sort."

The woman echoed him: "Clare did nothing of the sort."

I turned to her. "You went to her house in Beverly Hills yesterday afternoon?"

She nodded.

"Why did you go there?"

"Clare told me she was Simon's latest chippie. He's the only one who tells me things, the only one who cares what happens to me. Clare said if I caught them together, I could force Simon to give me a divorce. Only she was already dead. I walked into the house, and she was already dead." She spoke resentfully, as though Hester Campbell had deliberately stood her up.

"How did you know where she lived?"

"Clare told me." She smiled at him in bright acknowledgment. "Yesterday morning when Simon was having his dip."

"All this is utter nonsense," Bassett said. "Mrs. Graff is imagining it. I didn't even *know* where she lived, you can bear witness to that."

"You wanted me to believe you didn't but you knew, all right. You'd had her traced, and you'd been threatening her. You couldn't afford to let George Wall get to her while she was still alive. But you wanted him to get to her eventually. Which is where I came in. You needed someone to lead him to her and help pin the frame on him. Just in case it didn't take, you sent Mrs. Graff to the house to give you double insurance. The second frame was the one that worked—at least, it worked for Graff and his brilliant cohorts. They gave you a lot of free assistance in covering up that killing."

"I had nothing to do with it," Graff said behind me. "I'm not responsible for Frost's and Marfeld's stupidity. They acted without consulting me." He was standing by himself, just inside the door, as if to avoid any part in the proceedings.

"They were your agents," I told him, "and you're responsible for what they did. They're accessory after the fact of murder. You should be handcuffed to them."

Bassett was encouraged by our split. "You're simply fishing," he said. "I was fond of Hester Campbell, as you know. I had nothing against the girl. I had no reason to harm her."

"I don't doubt you were fond of her, in some peculiar way of your own. You were probably in love with her. She wasn't in love with you, though. She was out to take you if she could. She ran out on you in September, and took along your most valuable possession."

"I'm a poor man. I have no valuable possessions."

"I mean this gun." I held the Walther pistol out of his reach. "I don't know exactly how you got it the first time. I think I know how you got it the second time. It's been passed around quite a bit in the last four months, since Hester Campbell stole it from your safe. She turned it over to her friend Lance Leonard. He wasn't up to handling the shakedown himself, so he co-opted Stern, who had experience in these matters. Stern also had connections which put him beyond the reach of Graff's strong-arm boys. But not beyond your reach.

"I'll give you credit for one thing, Clarence. It took guts to tackle Stern, even if I did soften him up for you. More guts than Graff and his private army had."

"I didn't kill him," Bassett said. "You know I didn't kill him. You saw him leave."

"You followed him out, though, didn't you? And you didn't come back for a while. You had time to slug him in the parking-lot, bundle him into his car, and drive it up the bluff where you could slit his throat and push him into the sea. That was quite an effort for a man your age. You must have wanted this gun back very badly. Were you so hungry for a hundred grand?"

Bassett looked up past me at the open safe. "Money had nothing to do with it." It was his first real admission. "I didn't know he had that gun in his car until he tried to pull it on me. I hit him with a tire-iron and knocked him out. It was kill or be killed. I killed him in self-defense."

"You didn't cut his throat in self-defense."

"He was an evil man, a criminal, meddling in matters he didn't understand. I destroyed him as you would destroy a dangerous animal." He was proud of killing Stern. The pride shone in his face. It made him foolish. "A gangster and drug-peddler—is he more important than I? I'm a civilized man, I come from a good family."

"So you cut Stern's throat. You shot Lance Leonard's eye out. You beat in Hester Campbell's skull with a poker. There are better ways to prove you're civilized."

"They deserved it."

"You admit you killed them?"

"I admit nothing. You have no right to bullyrag me. You can't prove a thing against me."

"The police will be able to. They'll trace your movements, turn up witnesses to pin you down, find the gun you used on Leonard."

"Will they really?" He had enough style left to be sardonic.

"Sure they will. You'll show them where you ditched it. You've started to tattle on yourself already. You're no hard-faced pro, Clarence, and you shouldn't try to act like one. Last night when it was over and the three of them were dead, you had to knock yourself out with a bottle. You couldn't face the thought of what you had done. How long do you think you can hold out sitting in a cell without a bottle?"

"You hate me," Bassett said. "You hate me and despise me, don't you?"

"I don't think I'll answer that question. Answer one of

mine. You're the only one who can. What sort of man would use a sick woman as his cat's-paw? What sort of man would cut a young girl like Gabrielle off from the light so he could collect a bounty on her death?"

Bassett made an abrupt squirming gesture of denial. The movement involved the entire upper half of his body, and resembled a convulsion. He said through rigid jaws:

"You've got it all wrong."

"Then straighten me out."

"What's the use? You would never understand."

"I understand more than you think. I understand that you spied on Graff when his wife was in the sanitarium. You saw him using his *cabaña* for meetings with Gabrielle. You undoubtedly knew about the gun in his locker. Everything you knew or learned, you passed on to Isobel Graff. Probably you helped her to run away from the sanitarium, and provided her with the necessary pass-keys. It all adds up to remote-control murder. That much I understand. I don't understand what you had against Gabrielle. Did you try for her yourself and lose her to Graff? Or was it just that she was young and you were getting old, and you couldn't stand to see her living in the world?"

He stammered: "I had nothing to do with her death." But he turned in his chair as if a powerful hand had him by the nape of the neck. He looked at Isobel Graff for the first time, quickly and guiltily.

She was sitting upright now, as still as a statue. A statue of a blind and schizophrenic Justice, stonily returning Bassett's look:

"You did so, Clarence."

"No, I mean I didn't plan it that way. I had no idea of blackmail. I didn't want to see her killed."

"Who did you want to see killed?"

"Simon," Isobel Graff said. "Simon was to be the one. But I spoiled everything, didn't I, Clare? It was my fault it all went wrong."

"Be quiet, Belle." It was the first time that Bassett had spoken to her directly. "Don't say anything more."

"You intended to shoot your husband, Mrs. Graff?"

"Yes. Clare and I were going to be married."

Graff let out a snort, half angry and half derisive. She turned on him:

"Don't you dare laugh at me. You locked me up and stole my property. You treated me like a chattel-beast." Her voice rose. "I'm *sorry* I didn't kill you."

"So you and your moth-eaten fortune-hunter could live happily ever after?"

"We could have been happy," she said. "Couldn't we, Clare? You love me, don't you, Clare? You've loved me all these years."

"All these years," he said. But his voice was empty of feeling, his eyes were dead. "Now if you love me, you'll be quiet, Belle." His tone, brusque and unfriendly, denied his words.

He had rebuffed her, and she had a deep, erratic intuition. Her mood swung violently. "I know you," she said in a hoarse monotone. "You want to blame me for everything. You want them to put me in the forever room and throw the key away. But you're to blame, too. You said I could never be convicted of any crime. You said if I killed Simon *in fragrante—in flagrante*—the most they could do was lock me up for a while. Didn't you say that, Clare? Didn't you?"

He wouldn't answer her or look at her. Hatred blurred his features like a tight rubber mask. She turned to me:

"So you see, it was Simon I meant to kill. His chippie was just an animal he used—a little fork-legged animal. I wouldn't kill a pretty little animal."

She paused, and said in queer surprise: "But I did kill her. I shot her and smashed the connections. It came to me in the dark behind the door. It came to me like a picture of sin that she was the source of the evil. And she was the one the dirty old man was making passes at. So I smashed the connections. Clare was angry with me. He didn't see the wicked things she did."

"Wasn't he with you?"

"Afterwards he was. I was trying to wipe up the blood— she bled on my nice clean floor. I was trying to wipe up the blood when Clare came in. He must have been waiting outside, and seen the chippie crawling out the door. She crawled away like a little white dog and died. And Clare was angry with me. He bawled me out."

"How many times did you shoot her, Isobel?"

"Just once."

"In what part of the body?"

She hung her head in ghastly modesty. "I don't like to say, in public. I told you before."

"Gabrielle Torres was shot twice, first in the upper thigh, then in the back. The first wound wasn't fatal, it wasn't even serious. The second wound pierced her heart. It was the second shot that killed her."

"I only shot her once."

"Didn't you follow her down to the beach and shoot her again in the back?"

178

"No." She looked at Bassett. "Tell him, Clare. You know I couldn't have done that."

Bassett glared at her without speaking. His eyes bulged like tiny pale balloons inflated by a pressure inside his skull.

"How would he know, Mrs. Graff?"

"Because he took the gun. I dropped it on the *cabaña* floor. He picked it up and went out after her."

The pressure forced words from Bassett's mouth. "Don't listen to her. She's crazy—hallucinating. I wasn't within ten miles—"

"You were so, Clare," she said quietly.

At the same time, she leaned across the desk and struck him a savage blow on the mouth. He took it stoically. It was the woman who began to cry. She said through tears:

"You had the gun when you went out after her. Then you came back and told me she was dead, that I had killed her. But you would keep my secret because you loved me."

Bassett looked from her to me. A line of blood lengthened from one corner of his mouth like a red crack in his livid mask. The blind worm of his tongue came out and nuzzled at the blood.

"I could use a drink, old man. I'll talk, if you'll only let me have a drink first."

"In a minute. Did you shoot her, Clarence?"

"I had to." He had lowered his voice to a barely audible whisper, as though a recording angel had bugged the room.

Isobel Graff said: "Liar, pretending to be my friend! You let me live in hell."

"I kept you out of worse hell, Belle. She was on her way to her father's house. She would have blabbed out everything."

"So you did it all for me, you filthy liar! Young Lochinvar did it for Honeydew Heliopoulos, the girl of the golden west!" Her feelings had caught up with her. She wasn't crying now. Her voice was savage.

"For himself," I said. "He missed the jackpot when you failed to kill your husband. He saw his chance for a consolation prize if he could convince your husband that you murdered Gabrielle. It was a perfect set-up for a frame, so perfect that he even convinced you."

The convulsion of denial went through Bassett again, leaving his mouth wrenched to one side. "It wasn't that way at all. I never thought of money."

"What's that we found in your safe?"

"It was the only money I got, or asked for. I needed it to go away, I planned to go to Mexico and live. I never thought of blackmail until Hester stole the gun and betrayed me to those criminals. They forced me to kill them, don't you see, with their greed and their indiscretion. Sooner or later the case would be reopened and the whole truth would come out."

I looked to Graff for confirmation, but he had left the room. The empty doorway opened on darkness. I said to Bassett:

"Nobody forced you to kill Gabrielle. Why couldn't you let her go?"

"I simply couldn't," he said. "She was crawling home along the beach. I'd started the whole affair, I had to finish it. I could never bear to see an animal hurt, not even a little insect or a spider."

"So you're a mercy killer?"

"No, I can't seem to make you understand. There we were, just the two of us in the dark. The surf was pounding in, and she was moaning and dragging her body along in the sand. Naked and bleeding, a girl I'd known for years, when she was an innocent child. The situation was so dreadfully horrible. Don't you see, I had to put an end to it somehow. I had to make her stop crawling."

"And you had to kill Hester Campbell yesterday?"

"She was another one. She pretended to be innocent and wormed her way into my good graces. She called me Uncle Clarence, she pretended to like me, when all she wanted was the gun in my safe. I gave her money, I treated her like a daughter, and she betrayed me. It's a tragic thing when the young girls grow up and become gross and deceitful and lascivious."

"So you see that they don't grow up, is that it?"

"They're better dead."

I looked down into his face. It wasn't an unusual face. It was quite ordinary, homely and aging, given a touch of caricature by the long teeth and bulging eyes. Not the kind of face that people think of as evil. Yet it was the face of evil, drawn by a vague and passionate yearning toward the deed of darkness it abhorred.

Bassett looked up at me as if I were a long way off, communicating with him by thought-transference. He looked down at his clasped hands. The hands pulled apart from each other, and stretched and curled on his narrow thighs. The hands seemed remote from him, too, cut off by some unreported disaster from his intentions and desires.

I picked up the telephone on the desk and called the county police. They had routines for handling this sort of thing. I wanted it out of my hands.

Bassett leaned forward as I laid the receiver down. "Look here, old fellow," he said civilly, "you promised me a drink. I could use a drink in the worst way."

I went to the portable bar at the other end of the desk and got a bottle out. But Bassett received a more powerful sedative. Tony Torres came in through the open door. He slouched and shuffled forward, carrying his heavy Colt revolver. His eyes were dusty black. The flame from his gun was pale and brief, but its roar was very loud. Bassett's head was jerked to one side. It remained in that position, resting on his shoulder.

Isobel Graff looked at him in dull surprise. She rose and hooked her fingers in the neck of her denim blouse. Tore the blouse apart and offered her breast to the gun. "Kill me. Kill me, too."

Tony shook his head solemnly. "Mr. Graff said Mr. Bassett was the one."

He thrust the revolver into its holster. Graff entered behind him, diffidently. Stepping softly like an undertaker, Graff crossed the room to the desk where Bassett sat. His hand reached out and touched the dead man's shoulder. The body toppled, letting out a sound as it struck the floor. It was a mewling sound, like the faint and distant cry of a child for its mother.

Graff jumped back in alarm, as if his electric touch had knocked the life out of Bassett. In a sense, it had.

"Why drag Tony into this?" I said.

"It seemed the best way. The results are the same in the long run. I was doing Bassett a favor."

"You weren't doing Tony one."

"Don't worry about me," Tony said. "Two years now, two years in March, this is all I been living for, to get the guy that done it to her. I don't care if I never get back to Fresno or not." He wiped his wet forehead with the back of his hand, and shook the sweat off his hand. He said politely: "Is it okay with you gentlemen I step outside? It's hot in here. I'll stick around."

"It's all right with me," I told him.

Graff watched him go out, and turned to me with renewed assurance: "I noticed that you didn't try to stop him. You had a gun, you could have prevented that shooting."

"Could I?"

"At least we can keep the worst of it out of the papers now."

"You mean the fact that you seduced a teen-aged girl and ran out on her in the clutch?"

He shushed me and looked around nervously, but Tony was out of hearing.

"I'm not thinking of myself only."

He glanced significantly toward his wife. She was sitting on the floor in the darkest corner of the room. Her knees were drawn up to her chin. Her eyes were shut, and she was as still and silent as Bassett was.

"It's a little late to be thinking about Isobel."

"No, you are wrong. She has great recuperative powers. I have seen her in worse condition than this. But you could not force her to face a public courtroom, you are not so inhuman."

"She won't have to. Psychiatric Court can be held in a private hospital room. You're the one who has to face the public rap."

"Why? Why should I have to suffer more? I have been victimized by an Iago. You don't know what I have endured in this marriage. I am a creative personality, I needed a little sweetness and gentleness in my life. I made love to a young woman, that is my only crime."

"You lit the match that set the whole thing off. Lighting a match can be a crime if it sets fire to a building."

"But I did nothing wrong, nothing out of the ordinary. A few tumbles in the hay, what do they amount to? You wouldn't ruin me for such a little thing? Is it fair to make me a public scapegoat, wreck my career? Is it just?"

His earnest eloquence lacked conviction. Graff had lived too long among actors. He was a citizen of the unreal city, a false front leaning on scantlings.

"Don't talk to me about justice, Graff. You've been covering up murder for nearly two years."

"I have suffered terribly for those two years. I have suffered enough, and paid enough. It has cost me tremendous sums."

"I wonder. You used your name to pay off Stern. You used your corporation to pay off Leonard and the Campbell girl. It's a nice trick if you can work it, letting Internal Revenue help you pay your blackmail."

My guess must have been accurate. Graff wouldn't try to argue with it. He looked down at the valuable gun in my hand. It was the single piece of physical evidence that would force his name into the case. He said urgently:

"Give me my gun."

"So you can put me down with it?"

Somewhere on the highway, above the rooftop, a siren whooped.

"Hurry up," he said. "The police are coming. Remove

the shells and give me the gun. Take the money in the safe."

"Sorry, Graff, I have a use for the gun. It's Tony's justifiable-homicide plea."

He looked at me as if I was a fool. I don't know how I looked at Graff, but it made him drop his eyes and turn away. I closed the safe and spun the dials and rehung the photograph of the three young divers. Caught in unchanging flight, the two girls and the boy soared between the sea and the sky's bright desolation.

The siren's whoop was nearer and louder, like an animal on the roof. Before the sheriff's men walked in, I laid the Walther pistol on the floor near Bassett's outflung hand. Their ballistics experts would do the rest.

ABOUT THE AUTHOR

Ross Macdonald was born near San Francisco in 1915. He was educated in Canadian schools, traveled widely in Europe, and acquired advanced degrees and a Phi Beta Kappa key at the University of Michigan. In 1938 he married a Canadian girl who is now well known as the novelist Margaret Millar. Mr. Macdonald (Kenneth Millar in private life) taught school and later college, and served as communications officer aboard an escort carrier in the Pacific. For over twenty years he lived in Santa Barbara and wrote mystery novels about the fascinating and changing society of his native state. Among his leading interests are conservation and politics. He is a past president of the Mystery Writers of America. In 1964 his novel *The Chill* was given a Silver Dagger award by the Crime Writers' Association of Great Britain. Mr. Macdonald's *The Far Side of the Dollar* was named the best crime novel of 1965 by the same organization. Recently, he was presented with the Mystery Writers of America's Grand Master Award. *The Moving Target* was made into the highly successful movie *Harper* in 1966. *The Goodbye Look* (1969), *The Underground Man* (1971), *Sleeping Beauty* (1973) and *The Blue Hammer* (1976) were all national bestsellers. Ross Macdonald died in 1983.

THE THRILLING AND MASTERFUL NOVELS OF ROSS MACDONALD

Winner of the Mystery Writers of America Grand Master Award, Ross Macdonald is acknowledged around the world as one of the greatest mystery writers of our time. *The New York Times* has called his books featuring private investigator Lew Archer "the finest series of detective novels ever written by an American."

Now, Bantam Books is reissuing Macdonald's finest work in handsome new paperback editions. Look for these books (a new title will be published every month) wherever paperbacks are sold or use the handy coupon below for ordering:

NERO WOLFE

He's not much to look at and he'll never win the hundred yard dash but for sheer genius at unraveling the tangled skeins of crime he has no peer. His outlandish adventures make for some of the best mystery reading in paperback. He's the hero of these superb suspense stories.

BY REX STOUT